NORTHERN
FORESTS

PANTHEERA

NICOBAR

GYRE

OENTELLUS

TANAGUA

MANASLANGUA

The
GREAT/GIANT
LAKE

Enchantica

MYSTERY WOOD

M000288736

The Glory of the Golden Dragon

by

Andrew Bill

Acknowledgements
All characters designed by Andrew Bill.
All characters sculpted by Andrew Bill, Ken Fallon,
Andrew Hull and Jenny Oliver.
Colour illustrations by Steve Simmons.

ISBN 0 948511 11 7

Author's Note

I'm not going to say that wrestling with plot and prose for the third time was unpleasant or even unenjoyable, but in trying to describe the ordeal entailed, the phrase 'swimming through treacle' springs to mind.

This latest offering is brimful with new adventures and faces, and opens the doors to many more exciting story lines.

This book also launches 'Dragongorge', our fabulous new range of dragons, which embraces dragons of all kinds and descriptions (see genealogy chart within).

I have to thank everyone who has contributed in whichever way to the creation of this new novel.

Steve Simmons, Robert Simpson and John Woodward are responsible for the illustrations.

A big thank you to Phil Holland for granting extra time. Another big thank you to my grandmother, Mrs Marjorie Wood, who once again bore the brunt of my battles with the beast that was to become Book 3. Also, Mom and Dad and Theresa!

Sculptor Ken Fallon and colourist Paula Skelson need to be mentioned for their superb work on the new Enchantica figurines, and of course the remainder of the highly talented population of 156, King Street for their efforts in producing the Holland Studio Craft ranges.

To Alex, Neil and Geddy, thanks for a brilliant concert NEC, '92.

To those who have helped me – you deserve a medal.

To those who have suffered me – you deserve peace and quiet.

To those who have enjoyed me (if you will pardon the expression!) you deserve another helping – and here it is!

A.B.

Do you know Enchantica?
You have been there . . .
In your dreams,
Your nightmares.
Do you know Enchantica?
Close your eyes,
Open your mind,
Escape the chains of disbelief.
Do you know Enchantica?
Then take the hand
of the child within you
And let the adventure begin . . .

Do you know Enchantica?
You are already there.

Contents

The White Ring

Jonquil the winged banf and the six windsprites could only stare in horror as the deadly jaws of the hungry gracklin bore down upon them.

Two rows of blood-stained daggers reached for the cowering group; the ugly, powerful head which contained them stretched into a terrifying smile. Denied flight by the injured, the able bodied fliers simply threw themselves across the bodies of their stricken fellows; Judruff diving forward to shield the helpless, prone form of his son, Comet. The monstrous teeth closed on one of Judruff's wings and he was hoisted effortlessly into the air. Comet screamed at the sight of his father dangling from the gracklin's mouth, rising to his doom. All those who watched knew what was to follow, the great beast would lift the falcon king to a convenient height and then simply toss him into its vast gape and devour him.

Suddenly Comet's screams of grief and desperation were overtaken by a roar of defiance from Jonquil. With a blur of frantic wings the banf launched himself from the defeated windsprites and flew like an arrow into the monster's face. Too late the giant lizard tried to evade Jonquil's attack and before it could flinch the banf smacked the gracklin hard in the eye with his fist. A piercing scream racked with pain and rage erupted from the belly of the beast forcing wide its powerful jaws and allowing Judruff to fall to freedom. A savage lunge at Jonquil swiftly followed, the beast continuing to snap furiously at the agile banf as he spiralled and zigzagged overhead, but all that the monster could claim was a mouthful of the air that Jonquil had inhabited a moment before.

The flying banf hovered tantalisingly close to the gracklin's head daring it to attack. He even boldly met the wingless dragon's snout with the soles of his feet on some of its furious strikes allowing himself to be hurled into a backwards dive by the force. He would flippantly dance tip-toe on the monster's thorny crown, cursing and taunting it for its sluggishness, only leaping to safety a fraction of an instant before its rushing valley of cruel teeth came for him.

The terrible beast matched every winged exertion Jonquil made through the air, with an hypnotic swaying of its great head; slanted scaly brows giving its hungry eyes, already bloated with enmity, an accentuated expression of evil fury. Those eyes, black holes enraged with a ring of white, were indeed the mirrors of its malevolent soul, and their murderous stare, coupled with the array of death-dealing spikes they were set above, could drain the courage of even the greatest warrior if they should dare to look upon them. Jonquil chose not to. To return the gracklin's deadly stare would mean his downfall, so the banf concentrated on staying alive, aloft, and one flutter out of the monster's reach.

It was a dangerous ploy, and Jonquil only prayed that he had strength enough in his wings to give his friends sufficient time to escape. Judruff and the others were not slow to respond to the banf's brave sacrifice and quickly gathered themselves up to move out of harm's reach. Meanwhile Jonquil slowly began to lead the gracklin away from the grove of evergreens and his fellows, diving and swooping within a hair's breadth of death in his efforts to monopolise the giant's lust for blood.

The gracklin's stout rear legs thundered into the thick carpet of snow, which was broken here and there by heavily frosted rashes of bush and bracken, its fearsome snorting head leading the charge at Jonquil. Its scaly hide was camouflaged with the mottled shades of the forest; broad dark bands shrinking and eventually failing at the tip of its long, muscular tail; a tail which now thrashed violently at the loose snow and vegetation as the great lizard began to boil with frustration. The awesome creature's much smaller forelimbs, armed with the most vicious hooked claws, pawed impatiently at the air, eager to get to grips with the vulnerable body of its winged prey.

Jonquil continued to tease the powerful beast further and further away from his companions, flitting to and fro between the trees like a suicidal butterfly dancing above two terrible snapping jaws. The banf's tortured flight muscles which had hitherto only mildly complained about his antics were now screaming for respite and Jonquil knew that they would not keep him from death for much longer; he had to rest.

The banf conceded to his weariness and swooped away from the gracklin. He rose swiftly to the high boughs of a nearby green oak, perched near to the trunk of the tree and fell breathlessly against its stout bole. The giant lizard bellowed its seething rage up to the inaccessible Jonquil, its rear claws tearing deep trenches into the leafy ground and its tail whacking the tough flanks of the towering tree. The gracklin was incensed by the banf's situation and for a while paced determinedly around the green oak, stamping and roaring and occasionally punctuating its complaints with a petulant slamming of its great head against the mossy bark; and despite the indomitable stature of the mature tree, Jonquil was a little alarmed to feel it shake with the force of the angry monster's attacks.

After a final, frustrated head butt the fearsome creature gazed up malevolently at the loftily perched banf and then grudgingly turned its attention elsewhere. There was only a bare scattering of dark figures fleeing through the surrounding forest now and although the ravenous beast carefully followed the movements of the frantic individuals with its wild eyes, unfortunately it was not tempted to pursue any of them. Perhaps the gracklin was tired of a diet of bitter goblin flesh and had promised itself some sweeter meat.

Eventually, just as the banf had feared, the great lizard sniffed at the ground, found the trail which led back to the evergreens and remembered the other winged banfs that it had discovered along with Jonquil. With a triumphant blast from its mighty lungs, thrusting two billowing jets of steam into the freezing air, the gracklin pounded back along the trail to seek out its helpless quarry.

As exhausted as he was Jonquil knew he had to try and save his friends, they were probably out in the open by now, struggling through the thick ground cover, vulnerable and exposed. He had to act. Diving from his perch, the banf threw open his wings and swept down from the tree, in a long graceful arc, to chase the giant lizard.

The evergreen copse loomed ahead and Jonquil bent all his might on beating the gracklin to it. His plan was to overtake the charging monster, swerve across its path, skimming its blunt snout, and in so doing draw its attention away elsewhere. However, unbeknown to Jonquil, gracklins have excellent rear-view vision, and just as Jonquil was about to surge past the sprinting gracklin, the monster skidded to an abrupt stop, threw its head across Jonquil's flight path and caught the speeding banf with a bone-jarring blow. Jonquil was hurled a considerable distance by the slamming jaws of the gracklin, tumbling through the air in a crumpled daze to land limply amongst the heaps of snow and dry vegetation.

The grinning beast slowly turned towards the banf's groaning body, it had no need for haste. Its powerful claws casually crunched through the rashes of crisp bracken to where Jonquil was lying, its maniacal eyes gleaming with pleasure, its slavering jaws anticipating the sweet taste of banf flesh.

The forest fell deathly silent, as if every living creature was holding its breath with dread. All Jonquil could hear through his buzzing semi-consciousness, was the slow, heavy pounding of the gracklin's footfalls, and the steady rumble of its growling breaths getting louder with every giant step nearer. Jonquil lifted his head and his eyes nearly burst with terror when they finally focused on the terrible, hypnotic stare of the gracklin. Its hungry eyes shone out from a dark, ferocious head which hung down from its hunched shoulders and swayed with the powerful tread of its muscular legs; its dripping gates of death stealthily lowering towards him. The banf felt his whole body suddenly ache with doom.

Just as the fang-laden bite of the monster was about to snatch Jonquil to his death, a blurry cloud of white screamed through the air above the banf's head and thudded into the hard crown of the lizard's skull. The gracklin leapt backwards into the air as if stung by a swarm of mighty bees and as it did so another lethal flight sang overhead and buried themselves deeply into the monster's throat. The force of this airborne attack was so strong that the gracklin was thrown back on to one leg and hopped precariously backwards before finally crashing onto the snowy undergrowth, dead.

Jonquil gingerly rose to his feet to survey the collapsed form of the gracklin, his amazed curiosity quickly overriding his aches and bruises. He staggered forward to discover what it was that had saved him from the jaws of death.

Protruding from the head and neck of the felled beast was an ugly peppering of white arrows, their half-buried shafts standing in a steaming network of oozing, ruby rivulets. As Jonquil stood before the monstrous lizard, which was now sprawled lifelessly beneath the trees, he marvelled at how a flight of such slender darts could bring down so mighty a beast. Of course, unbeknown to Jonquil, these were fairy arrows; formidable weapons whose barbed heads had been steeped in enchanted potions. Once aimed and fired, doom to even the greatest quarry.

The banf turned away from the dead gracklin to search the forest with his eyes, and as he did so, his eyes focused on an emerging wall of inconspicuous warriors, silently approaching from the shady backdrop of the naked trees. At their head strode a proud fairy queen, grey eyes blazing from a fierce but finely shaped countenance. She carried an ornate longbow at her shoulder and a half empty quiver at her hip. It was only when she stood at close quarters to the banf that he noticed the shimmering, iridescent rise of her graceful wings; delicately framing her slender, warlike figure against the gloom of the forest. She bore a simple circlet of gleaming fairy silver on her head, beneath which her exquisite, silky hair fell in a glistening shower upon her shoulders and back. Her body was clothed in a full, majestic coat of plate-mail, the like of which the banf had never seen. The individual plates were leaf shaped and carved from a shining, translucent stone, which caught the pale light thrown up from the snow in glittering waves of red and purple.

It was Trinia, Queen of the Falls fairies, and her expression was one of barely suppressed excitement.

"I am Trinia," she said to him. "And I greet you, Jonquil the Wanderer, in the name of the secret folk who live behind the Dancing Waters."

The queen's voice was like a quiet song as it floated on the air towards him.

"And there is someone else," she continued. "Who has a most urgent desire to greet you too."

The fairy monarch turned and gestured towards the attending line of her similarly clad archers, who then parted to reveal a hitherto unseen figure, waiting somewhat impatiently for his time to come forward.

Jonquil's eyes almost burst with joy when his gaze fell upon the shadowy shape standing with the tall bowmales and bowmaidens. His slightly hunched stance, his long pointed ears, his sparkling amber orbs were unmistakable.

"Rattajack!" Jonquil cried, and despite his aching head and bruised limbs, the banf ran towards the terragon flinging wide his arms in welcome. Rattajack sprang forward to meet the banf, and half way between the slain form of the gracklin and the curved line of fairy archers, the two long separated friends came together in a tight embrace. A cry of sheer delight exploded from Jonquil's throat as his arms closed around Rattajack's neck, the terragon piped rapturously, both their eyes glassy with tears.

The fairy band gathered around the two companions in a wide circle and cheered appreciatively at the sight of these two strange winged beings locked in each others arms.

Of course as soon as Rattajack noticed Jonquil's wings he let out a cry of such

excitement that for a moment Jonquil had thought the gracklin must have sprung back to life behind him; but then he remembered, when last he had seen his faithful friend the banf had needed a carrier-dragon to fly, he had not been equipped with the means to do it himself. Rattajack stared with incredulous wonder at the feathery additions to his dearest friend, and spread out his own green wings as if to indicate the source of his amazement. As he did so, Jonquil unfolded his wings until the long, white primary feathers just touched the outstretched bony points at the tips of the terragon's leathery span. The two companions glanced from side to side at their touching wing tips and then back to each other. Almost immediately the two friends saw the funny side of their mutual display and dissolved into uncontrollable laughter, hugging each other once more with renewed affection.

Finally, Queen Trinia approached them and placed a gentle hand on both their shoulders.

"This is a happy meeting," she said, "Our hearts rejoice with the sight of such happiness."

"Thank you . . . er . . . your majesty" Jonquil began, "and . . . er . . . thank you for killing the wingless dragon, I could almost feel its breath on my flesh."

"It was an evil beast," Trinia told him. "Spawn of Mezereon's black arts. We have killed many in the forest this day, and yet I fear many more have escaped us to haunt these wooded vales for years to come."

Jonquil followed the queen's fearful gaze into the distant shadows of the trees, a rash of goose flesh rising at the base of his neck at the thought of further encounters with the giant striding lizards. Trinia's soft tones drew him back from fear.

"At least the Dark Sorcerer's master no longer lives to cast a shadow upon our worlds," she said.

"You know that the Ice Lord is dead?" Jonquil asked with wide eyed wonder.

"We do," the queen answered him. "And of the part you played in his downfall. We, the free peoples of Enchantica, owe you a great debt, Jonquil the Wanderer. You have brought us great hope and joy."

The banf just smiled in return, for once, lost for words.

"But tell me, were you alone in the forest, my friend?" The fairy asked him.

Suddenly Jonquil remembered his fellow fliers still in peril, and his cheeks flooded with shameful colour for not thinking of them sooner.

"No, no!" He cried. "There are others, others like me. Somewhere in that direction over there." The banf pointed vaguely towards the grove of evergreens. "They may be in danger, I must go to them."

"No, my friend," the queen commanded him. "Let us find your fellows. We have far sight and can walk unseen in the forest's shadows. None can hide from our eyes. If your friends are still with the living, we shall find them. And with our enchanted bows protect them from all dangers." The fairy queen gave Jonquil's shoulder a reassuring squeeze. "Fear not, they shall be returned to you."

At this, Trinia strode over to one of her archers in the circle, and gave instructions in her own lyrical tongue. The command soon spread around the circle and then all but a few of the surrounding band of archers sprinted away in the direction Jonquil had indicated, and melted into the trees.

Trinia, accompanied by her much smaller entourage, returned to Jonquil and Rattajack. Whilst they waited for the search party to return with the windsprites, the fairy queen spoke to Jonquil about the Three Wizards, who were waiting to greet Jonquil and Rattajack in the Banf Kingdom, and that in a short while, the banf and the terragon would be able to join in all of the celebrations.

Suddenly Jonquil's eyes lifted into space as if in a dream and he gently drew Rattajack close to him. It was almost as if Trinia had spoken of something fearful.

"Home . . . ," he murmured, " . . . Home."

The one thing that had kept the banf battling on through all his great trials and adventures, apart from his desire to find Rattajack again, had been the thought of walking beneath the eaves of the White Ring and stepping into his homeland once more. It had been the sustenance of his spirit since that first day when he and Rattajack had been snatched by the Swamp Demon. And yet now, now that all the fighting and the suffering was over and he was finally free to go where he pleased, it had been the one thing that had completely slipped his mind.

"Home . . . "

Jonquil had grown too used to disappointment. He had been on his way home for so long that he had somehow convinced himself that he was never going to get there. At every attempt, someone or something had connived a diversion; jumping unexpectedly from the bushes or swooping down from the skies.

The banf had never asked to be swept up into the titanic struggle for control of the world, even though, by accident, he had ended up a major player. Jonquil had only ever wanted small adventures, of the troll-baiting, treasure finding, simple exploring kind. He felt decidedly uncomfortable with the role of hero, which for some inexplicable reason the banf had been cast.

"Home . . . "

The word seemed so strange, so remote. Was it possible? Would he really make it there this time?

Jonquil looked deeply into Rattajack's reassuring eyes and a beaming smile slowly blossomed on his face. Home! To Peeli, Peart, Yargle, Chuckwalla, Snappa and of course . . . Meadolarne. She who loved him, and the only being in the world he could ever invite to share his life with Rattajack.

They were all waiting for him, safe behind the benevolent glare of the tall, white mushrooms. Waiting for Jonquil the Wanderer to cease his wandering, and return for good to his people, and a life of peaceful domesticity within the boundaries of the Banf Kingdom; never to wander again. The vision of this new life filled the banf with a warm glow. Rest, relaxation, and the ordinary company of good friends. What more could an adventure-sore forest dweller desire?

"Come on," he finally whispered to Rattajack. "Let's go home."

Accompanied by Queen Trinia and her attendants, Jonquil and Rattajack set off along the trail which led to the White Ring. They had only journeyed a short while when the main group of fairies rejoined them with the six windsprites safely in tow. Judruff and the others rejoiced to see Jonquil safe and well and embraced him warmly. Comet's broken wing had been skilfully bound and poulticed with potent herbs by the fairies, who excelled in the lore of woodland healing, the other injured fliers had been afforded similar care and now seemed much heartier.

Judruff was both amazed and fascinated to meet Rattajack. Jonquil had talked incessantly about him during his time with the windsprites, so Judruff almost felt he knew everything there was to know about the terragon, including the fact that he and Jonquil had been born at exactly the same time. The falcon king was delighted to finally meet Rattajack in the flesh, and see with his own eyes a fine example of a legendary creature. A creature that up until that moment had only been to him a figment of ancient stories.

Rattajack was equally impressed with the similarity between the windsprites and the banfs, especially now that the one banf he cared most about had somehow acquired a similar pair of wings; and so felt sure that these winged strangers were beings he could easily grow to like.

The greetings exchanged and the reunions complete the mixed band of woodlanders set off through the trees to follow the winding trail to Jonquil's home.

Sightings of the enemy were becoming increasingly rare. What remained of the terrible armies that had arrogantly laid siege to the Banf Kingdom had by now either fled northwards or surrendered. The woodland band occasionally encountered a motley crowd of black-clad figures, sprinting towards them or dashing across their trail, their ugly faces contorted with blind panic, but they invariably offered no attack. These few wretched individuals were far more desirous of dark sanctuary than pointless vindictive conflict. There was a power at the creatures' heels filling the latterly gloomy forest with an intense, painful brilliance, and the miserable goblins and trolls that fled from it could entertain no other thought than escape. Nevertheless these sudden meetings prompted a swift response from the ever watchful fairy archers, no sooner was movement spotted amongst the surrounding trees than an arrow was at the string of every keen-eyed woodland bowmale or bowmaiden. They were clearly prepared to take no chances with the unpredictable soldiers of Vrorst.

There was one moment which struck a terrible note of fear in Jonquil when the blood chilling roar of a gracklin was heard deep within the stretch of forest at their flank. In the blinking of an eye all of the fairies had armed their bows and dispersed into the nearby trees preparing to meet the attack. Rattajack,

Jonquil and the windsprites drew close together as all seven fliers were suddenly reminded of their recent nightmarish experience. Surrounded by Trinia's bold warriors, the huddled group cowered on the ground like frightened children, as the awesome sound of the great lizard's crashing progress resounded from just beyond their sight. The gracklin's pounding footfalls were amplified by their fear and Jonquil and the windsprites were sure that the terrible lizard, which sounded every bit as mighty and fearsome as the one which had attacked them, was moving closer to the trail, perhaps already sniffing at their delicious scent. The tension of waiting for the beast to approach was unbearable and it was all Judruff could do to prevent some of the younger windsprites from taking flight and scattering into the upper branches.

However, it soon became clear that the monster was not moving towards them, its next bellowing roar unmistakably further away. The crisis melted and each of the winged banfs breathed a deep, tremulous sigh of relief.

Trinia once more pronounced it safe to proceed and Rattajack and the still shaking fliers wearily rose to their feet to follow the fairy leaders onwards. Not all of the woodland archers returned to the group however, a small number of them set off in pursuit of the unseen monster, to ensure that no other innocent wayfarers would be terrorised by the malignant creature.

As they trudged on, Jonquil could not help a wry smile. It had almost happened again. Another incident to divert him from his homeward path. This second gracklin could so easily have charged through the fairy lines and struck at the petrified fliers. He and Rattajack would have been seized in its terrible jaws and carried off into yet another interminable adventure . . . and yet it did not happen. The giant lizard had not come for the banf and the terragon. It had turned away to look for others to wreak its malice upon.

Jonquil hardly dared hold the thought in his mind but perhaps he really was meant to make it back to his home after all. Perhaps the adventure was finally drawing to its conclusion, and when, in future years, he reached his present position in his fireside tales, he would be able to turn to the enthralled audience of fellow banfs after a long, dramatic pause and simply say . . . "the end!"

They would all cheer and cry out that this was the greatest adventure of all time, and as a tired but happy Jonquil leaned back from the dying fire, bathed in the warm glow both from the gleaming embers and the surrounding adoration, he would let out a satisfied sigh and think, "Yes, that was the greatest adventure of all time, and now it's all over."

The smile that these comforting thoughts inspired stayed on the banf's face almost the entire length of that long day's hike through the snow beneath the bare trees. Then it suddenly developed into a triumphant roar of laughter as Jonquil and the rest of the travellers caught their first sight of the magnificent wall of white mushrooms rising majestically in the distance.

The banf and the terragon cast a brief glance at each other and then launched themselves into a mad dash for home. The two of them sprinted over the snowy trail like the wind, kicking clouds of sparkling leaves into the sharp air behind them, much to the amusement of the rest of the travellers who could not help but share the obvious joy emanating from these two long-absent adventurers.

Jonquil and Rattajack covered the last stretch of ground in only a few moments and it wasn't until the final few paces that the banf remembered his wings. With a giant leap and a laughing roar Jonquil swept upwards and flung himself against the spongy trunk of the nearest mushroom.

The banf slammed into the stout, yielding body, gripping it with a passionate embrace; both arms and legs clamped tightly about its wide girth. The banf screwed up his eyes and pressed his cheek hard against the soft velvet of the giant stalk. It felt warm and wonderful against his wind-blown skin. And soon Jonquil began to feel the mushroom's pulsating enchantment slowly seep into his fatigue-ridden body, every aching bone and sinew gently drowning in its exquisite current.

After a few long luxurious moments, the magical glow finally flooded every fibre of Jonquil's being making him feel strong again, banishing the darkness that had shrouded his heart for so long, assuaging his fears and pain. Now that he was once more bathed in the powerful aura of the White Ring, Jonquil knew that he was safe, secure, nothing could harm him. He had come home.

Rattajack gazed lovingly at his friend who clung like a limpet to the white trunk. Jonquil's face, a portrait of sheer ecstasy; eyes still tightly closed, a dreamy grin of rapture drawn between his cheeks. He looked as if he might remain up there forever.

At last, Jonquil allowed himself to slowly slide down the smooth stalk of the mushroom and fold into a lazy bundle within its broad roots. He smiled fondly at Rattajack, a smile which seemed to sum up all the peace and contentment now flowing through his slumped body. The terragon trotted over to the banf's prone form and tenderly nuzzled his cheek. Jonquil wrapped his arms around Rattajack's neck and allowed his friend to gently lift him to his feet. For a moment the two companions stood motionless, nose to nose, staring deeply into each others eyes. Jonquil's quiet voice broke the spell.

"We're home, Ratters," he said "We're home!"

By the time the windsprites and the fairies arrived at the White Ring and stood in awe beneath its towering eaves, the two companions had already passed through to the protected forest within.

Judruff slowly stepped forward as if in a trance and reverently placed his palm against one of the pale trunks, his eyes ascending its great height until they finally reached the magnificent spread of the mushroom's massive canopy. The falcon king seemed mesmerised by the sheer majesty of the giant mushrooms; and by the look of amazed delight that soon brightened his face it was plain that he could feel their inherent power too.

The other windsprites quickly followed Judruff's lead and instinctively

11

reached out to embrace the glowing stalks. As they did so, the injured were instantly purged of their pain and the weary renewed. The ancient goodness that surged within these mighty fungi crept into the bodies of all that touched them, filling them only with joy and hope. Even the fairies entered the light radiating from the white wall, throwing back their heads and arms to fully receive its penetrating glory.

The mighty White Ring, for years beyond knowledge undefeated guardian of its precious interior, shed its potent light upon the assorted travellers gathered before it. A light which for the good-hearted was a subtle, soothing glow, but for the evil, a searing wall of white fire.

The hounds of Vrorst with their dreadful war machines had tried to conquer the shining wall with missiles and giant spears, and though they had gained a few superficial fractures, the power of the dazzling mushrooms refused to fade, and at the end the brilliant barricade remained as much an obstacle to the Ice Lord's ambition as ever before.

For Judruff, and the rest of the windsprites, who now silently bathed in its soft illumination, the pristine wall of mushrooms which dwarfed them, was a legendary symbol of absolute purity and truth. A fortress of good, rising from the black soil as an impenetrable barrier against the advance of darkness. Judruff marvelled that his ancestors could ever bear to leave behind a homeland that was encompassed by such a beautiful border; and he feared that when the time came, he might not wish to return now that his eyes had feasted upon this wondrous sight.

Trinia and her people also felt humbled by the ancient protector. The fairies knew well the true source of the Ring's potency, and on reflection considered themselves privileged to have been drawn into a conflict which enabled them to experience a wonder of the world, of which otherwise they would have remained sadly ignorant.

The White Ring had for centuries repelled the evil of the forest. However, from this day forward Trinia felt sure that its irresistible power would serve to attract all of the noble forest peoples to witness and pay homage to its benevolent majesty.

A great cheer suddenly rang out from the other side of the mushroom wall, scores of excited voices raised in wild celebration. The fairies and the six falcons quickly filed between the wide trunks and passed beneath the immense domed caps of the white wall to enter the land of the banfs. A most curious sight was waiting to greet them on the other side, a spectacle which left them both breathlessly surprised and deeply amused.

Mushroom Lodgings

When the windsprites and the fairies emerged from beneath the eaves of the White Ring, their eyes fell upon the source of the joyful clamour. Jonquil and Rattajack were being tossed and bounced like corks in an ocean of uproarious banfs and terragons.

In true banf-style they were to be carried to the oaken halls of the king with high ceremony and splendour, even though from the northern curve of the Ring to the great city was at least two days march.

The Three Wizards had asked Merlion to send a happy host of banfs to welcome the returning heroes to their homeland. The wise lords had decided to allow Jonquil and Rattajack a leisurely journey to the Oak Palace, rather than a swift conveyance, because they knew that the banf and the terragon would need time to re-acquaint themselves with their old way of life, and relish the peace and tranquillity that they had both been long denied. Not that there was anything peaceful or tranquil about the merry mob that now overwhelmed the two friends with good wishes and salutations.

Children cheered and clapped. Teenaged, middle aged and old aged banfs sang and danced with each other with an energy they had been forced to restrain for so long. It had been a very long winter so any excuse for a knees-up was more than welcome.

The windsprites and the fairies could not help but be impressed by the outrageous spectacle of the banf and the terragon being carried off into the white forest at the head of such an unruly band of chanting beings. Judruff and his fellow fliers were irresistibly drawn in to the bubbling crowds, whilst Trinia and her fairy followers, in a flash of stars and crystal wings, shrank to the size of bees and flew on ahead like the wind to the Oak City.

After getting over the initial shock of Jonquil's and the windsprites wings, which inspired great curiosity and a good deal of strokes, prods and demands for flying demonstrations, the boisterous band of banfs and terragons, most of whom were completely unknown to the two companions, began to settle somewhat and start the inevitable rounds of chatter. After a great deal of pleading, Jonquil and Rattajack finally succeeded in persuading the reluctant revellers to let them walk; and then the banf felt able to try and find out just exactly what had happened to his homeland during the great conflict.

Much to his frustration, however, in true banf fashion, the group's leaders answered every question of Jonquil's with three or four of their own; and after a while he found himself telling much more of his own story than he was hearing of theirs.

Jonquil couldn't help thinking that some of Vrorst's interrogators at the Throne Citadel could have learned a thing or two from a mob of banfs, once they have got the curiosity bit between their teeth.

With a titanic effort Jonquil eventually succeeded in turning the topic of conversation to the great siege, and at this the banfs became very excited.

Although the White Ring was swiftly regenerating itself, reversing most of the damage that Vrorst's war machines had inflicted upon it, in places it was still possible to see where the wall had been breached. Jonquil was happy to see that the broken stems of giant mushrooms that had been crushed or beheaded, now had healthy crops of a new generation sprouting at their feet.

The litter of boulders, sharpened stakes and spears that lay about the white wall served as an ugly reminder of the furious onslaught launched against it by the enemy. The snow surrounding the Ring was patterned and churned by a great disturbance of prints and tracks, a reminder of the fearsome host that had gathered there to do battle with the enchanted barrier of the banfs. Some of the heavy missiles had flown too high or too far to meet their targets and had crashed into some of the ancient green-oaks that grew just inside the enchanted ring. A few of the 'grand old friends of the forest' had been speared by a variety of vicious weapons, or suffered broken branches from falling rocks. The banfs vowed that they would not rest until every maimed or injured tree had been sought out and its wounds attended to. The green-oaks were part of the fabric of the banfs' world, most beloved of all trees, and the banfs would do everything in their power to help or heal them.

Two of the ring-leaders of the banf reception party, Lobel and Squilp, had been eye witnesses to much of the terrible attack on the White Ring. They told Jonquil all about the siege; the terrifying snow storms, the drumming, the mighty war engines, the scream of the flying projectiles, the assorted ranks of black-clad warriors just waiting for their chance to charge over the buried remnants of the wall and massacre the harmless mushroom dwellers sheltering within. When it began to look as if the White Ring might be defeated, Squilp remembered seeing packs of terrifying wingless dragons being ushered forward as if they were to be the murderous vanguard of Vrorst's assault; giant lizards snapping at their handlers who urged them on with long spears and whips. Jonquil smiled uneasily at this enthusiastic account, the memory of his own horrific encounter with the gracklin too fresh for comfort.

Jonquil listened to the two banfs with acute interest. He didn't wish to be spared the minutest detail of the violent adventure that his fellow mushroom dwellers had been involved in. It was as if by hearing all about what had happened to his home and his people whilst he had been unavoidably detained elsewhere, Jonquil would somehow be compensated for his long months of absence, and for being denied the opportunity to share in the lives and experiences of his loved ones during all that time.

The one fact that really astounded Jonquil was that in order to achieve an effective siege, the Winter army had been forced to completely surround the White Ring. The size of force required to do this was incomprehensible, and more importantly, where was this monstrous army now? If all the collected powers of goblins, trolls, northmen, gracklins, sorcerers and dragonlords that had made up the siege-force of Vrorst had fled into the surrounding forest, it wouldn't be safe for the banfs to venture beyond the protection of the White Ring for years.

Suddenly Jonquil had to remind himself that for him there was to be no more venturing. From now on he was destined to be a home-loving banf, a resident not an adventurer.

The great swarm of chattering banfs, terragons and windsprites encountered a succession of delightful mushroom villages on their slow, rambling journey.

There was Leaflover, Greenbloom, Goldenbark, Rootharvest, and the haunting Waterveil; an exquisite little settlement which nestled between two gargantuan green oaks growing on steep opposing banks. A joyful forest river tumbled between them from on high and twin clusters of tightly grown mushroom houses rose from their twisted roots. As its name suggested, the village was embraced by a gentle cloak of spray that lifted past the glistening roofcaps in graceful diaphanous plumes. In the Summer, when strong shafts of sunlight lanced the forest roof, and one of the golden beams struck the spiralling water cloud, it was shot through with glittering sheets of colour; a mesmeric, fragmented rainbow glancing off the weaving walls of mist and transforming the rows of water droplets hanging from the mushroom eaves into strings of sparkling jewels.

After crossing over the gurgling body of the forest river by means of a simple bridge; an oak bough, thrown down from above by some ancient Winter storm and carved into a sturdy platform; the light-hearted procession met an inquisitive contingent of Waterveil residents waiting for them on the other side, the majority of whom promptly joined the growing crowd in a noisy, embracing wave.

After travelling some distance from the great white boundary Jonquil noticed the depth of snow begin to recede. Vrorst had concentrated the bulk of his icy malice on the wall of white mushrooms in an attempt to smother its radiance, consequently most of the interior of the kingdom had escaped the worst of his destructive attention.

As the festive following progressed, Jonquil feasted his eyes on the heartwarming panorama stretching out before him. His eyes had long been denied the wondrous spectacle of soaring green oak trunks dominating the landscape as far as it could be seen in any direction. Those in the far distance filling the spaces between the giants nearby in an endless procession of pale grey lines. The immense trees and their root pillars rose with supreme authority into the barren roof of mingled branches, their stout arms spreading out into the canopy like the spokes of mighty wheels, as if they had the weight of the sky, the stars and the whole universe to support. The Banf Kingdom truly was the first home of the green oaks. For although the majestic trees were kings wherever they rose in the great forest, in banf soil they grew prouder and mightier than anywhere else, their incredible stature and proliferation an unmistakably unique phenomenon of this enchanted protectorate.

Jonquil tried to forget that it was Winter and recall how the forest looked and felt in Summer, when everything beneath the towering verdant crust was softly bathed in green-stained sunlight.

As his imagination took hold, the crunchy floor was no longer laden with powdery snow that exploded into white showers before his feet, it was smothered beneath an all encompassing blanket of woodland flowers. Gemberry bushes were rising against the oak buttresses in luxuriant thickets. Spearherb and longflax, bluehemp and trumpetvine joined with the triumphant bracken to form dense hedges and scrub. The air throbbed with the noisy wings of insects and birds; always busy, always hungry, visiting the surrounding banks of flowers with an urgency only they could explain. The finely sculpted blooms of the trumpetvines were attended by both; bullying bumble bees competing with the delicate hummers. These tiny birds, clothed in exquisite iridescent plumage, darted to and fro on swiftly drumming wings in a blur of dazzling colours, moving between the flowers like scattered gems.

The air felt warm and soothing, and the scent of the woodland herbs gently fusing with the sweetly spoken cadences of birdsong filtering down from above, created an intoxicating energy that soaked into every pore, which for Jonquil and Rattajack was the very essence of life.

Judruff, Comet, Merle, Hulse, Farlin and Dern, the six winged relatives from the Marble Fortress, felt very privileged to walk alongside Jonquil and Rattajack through this awe-inspiring landscape, and very much at home with all its friendly, welcoming inhabitants.

The falcon king's thoughts inevitably strayed to his own land of trees far away, the Fruit Forests of the West. Judruff had never seen the kingdom of his forefathers, but he had inherited the love that all windsprites bore for their stolen homeland. The falcon king had promised his eldest son Indri, as Judruff's father, Jacama, had promised him, that the throne he ascended to would be the one which now lay empty and neglected in the ancient arboreal halls of Gwiddian, the mother tree. Now he had come to the home of the banfs and seen for himself the wonders of the green oak forest, Judruff was more resolved than ever to fulfil his vow to his son and restore the bountiful forests of the West to their long absent inhabitants.

Eventually the shadows won their battle with the failing light and that long, momentous day died. The banf procession met the darkness on the outskirts of Goldenring, the home village of Lobel and Squilp, who were still Jonquil's and the assorted travellers' self-appointed guides.

Goldenring was a typical banf settlement, a naturally occurring circle of house mushrooms that in the Summer would undoubtedly enjoy the generous attention of a strong sunbeam. Even though the mushroom village was now only illuminated by the soft glow of witches' lanterns, specially cultivated in various nooks and crannies within the furrowed skins of the houses, Jonquil was reminded so much of his own settlement, Oak-Goldeneye. He was sure his home village would look almost exactly the same at that moment in time, were he there to gaze upon it; a sleepy little ring-village like the one before him, fringed by stout oaks, rambling roofcaps huddled untidily within a weaving framework of ancient roots. Jonquil half expected the curious faces that peered out from windows and doorways at the approach of the merry invasion to be the familiar ones of home, his own beloved friends and family, but with a slight twinge of regret he realised that they were just more friendly strangers.

Although Jonquil and Rattajack delighted in the cheerful company of their new friends, they both secretly longed to see the beloved faces of their loved ones from Oak-Goldeneye. That would just make the joyous homecoming complete. Jonquil assumed that they were all waiting with the Wizards and the King at the Oak Palace, for a grand reunion, and he knew that he and Rattajack would be seeing them all very soon; but he wouldn't be a banf if he wasn't being impatient.

As the merry band entered into the heart of the round village, Jonquil was delighted to hear the distant screech of a woodwidger, one of the commonest nocturnal sounds of the forest, echoing profoundly in the distance. The comical, tiny, bat-like dragons, barely as long as a banf's forearm and the only true dragons to dwell within the Ring, like many small creatures were possessed of a disproportionately loud voice, and were never ashamed to use it. Jonquil remembered his cousin, Peeli, once encouraged one as a pet, and then had to try and firmly discourage it because of the horrendous noise it made, usually after everyone had gone to bed.

Widgers of all descriptions were found throughout the forests of Enchantica, in almost every environment. Jonquil and Rattajack had often hunted for the prized eggs of widgers in the marshes and swamps when they were younger, although the taking of the eggs was severely frowned upon. Widger eggs were the most exquisite of objects, their textured, iridescent shells sparkled like precious jewels in the sunlight, and were always a joy to discover, but also always the inspiration for an incessant, peace-shattering bout of widgering, that could go on for hours. Marshwidgers, woodwidgers, waterwidgers, cavewidgers all played a fascinating role in the education of every young adventurous banf, growing up with the mushrooms beneath the sky of green leaves.

The grand procession passed the night as guests of the good inhabitants of Goldenring, and by some miracle every banf who had joined the party, from whichever village, was found some food to eat and a roof to lie under.

Jonquil, Rattajack and the windsprites were led by Squilp to a mansion of a house mushroom that the banf villager was proud to call his own.

"It must have grown from the same soil for a hundred years," Jonquil thought to himself as he gazed up at the multi-layered slopes of roof that hunched and fanned across the great rise of the dwelling, blossoming between the fork of two converging aerial roots. Bulging clusters of points and apexes crept along the twists of the roots, housing numerous bays and towers.

"A hundred and fifty, actually," Squilp told him later. "My own grandfather planted its spores."

Squilp's banfina Ollandia greeted the weary travellers warmly at the traditionally narrow entrance to the mushroom house, their handful of giggling children huddling behind her in the hallway. With a broad welcoming smile Ollandia ushered each and every one of her guests inside.

It was customary for all banf houses to have a relatively narrow front doorway, just wide enough for a single banf to enter. It made no difference how large or small the residence may have been, the entrance was always the same size, one banf's width. It was considered very unlucky indeed for two persons to enter a dwelling side by side, single file was always the rule. Another ritual which was guaranteed to bring good fortune was that if a terragon was present in the company, the noble creature should always enter first, for it was common knowledge amongst the more lore-conscious banfs that terragons carried good luck on the soles of their feet, and if they were allowed to cross the threshold first, that luck would wipe off inside. However, if the terragon was to enter second, or worst last of all, not only would the good luck stay on them but they would innocently pick up any more good luck that happened to be inside and leave with that on their feet too.

Needless to say Rattajack was invited to be first to enter Squilp and Ollandia's home.

In a large central chamber, whose walls had been layered into a tight coil of spiral stairways, and eventually rose to meet a breathtaking sweep of giant gills, a magnificent feast had been laid. The room was illuminated by the ubiquitous witches' lanterns, which for the interior had been specially grown in finely carved oak urns filled with the finest green oak leaf mould. The wooden vessels were held by equally elaborately crafted oak stands, and a ring of these grand illuminators stood sentinel against the wrinkled walls of the room. The light which emanated from the delicate clusters of conical fungi was more insistent than bright, and was reflected with jewel-like clarity in the taught skins of succulent gemberries, mooncherries and other saved Autumnal fruit.

The prized delicacies were piled high upon numerous bowls and platters along with a further extravagant selection of forest harvest, including nuts, green shoots, summers blooms preserved in crystallized honey, and of course a wide choice of delicious mushrooms, all carefully arranged on flaxen cloths. The Winter which currently still ruled over the banfs may have been the longest and hardest ever to descend upon the Great Forest, but the ingenuity of the mushroom dwellers had proved to be stronger. The preserving of a wide variety of forest fare, for years on end if necessary, was a banf speciality, and the store rooms of Ollandia's house were overflowing with oak barrels and boxes, mushroom leather sacks and flagons, sun-baked clay pitchers and jars, all brim full of the finest array of food stuffs that the Green Sky had to offer, and that was fine indeed.

Jonquil was glad to see that pine kernels had also been included in the banquet for he knew that these were a particular favourite with the windsprites, although their eyes seemed to delight in all that they saw laid out before them. Indeed the sight of the feast quickly reminded Jonquil that he and the other six fliers couldn't remember eating a substantial meal since leaving the Marble Fortress; a day which now seemed more than a lifetime ago.

Giant mushroom velvet cushions stuffed with dry leaves had been positioned around the food, but Jonquil was intrigued to note that there were far more seats and place settings in the circle than bodies present in the room. Squilp and Ollandia were clearly expecting more guests.

The air inside the mushroom house bore none of the bitter cold that lingered outside. The enchantment of the house mushrooms created a warm, restful atmosphere that meant there was no need for interior fires or stoves. If the banfs wished to cook, they always did so outside on open flames. The only reason a banf would ever leave his home during the Winter months was if it grew in a particularly exposed position; the flaps of mushroom leather that were used to shutter the windows were no use against the rampaging icy gales of the dark season.

Squilp, who was a banf of middling years, with a satisfied paunch and a round cheerful face, formerly welcomed Jonquil, Rattajack and the windsprites to his home. However, before he invited them to eat, he announced a special surprise for the two companions. At this point carved oak hoods were lowered on to the gleaming crops of witches' lanterns and the large round chamber slowly dimmed into darkness. Jonquil and Rattajack could just about see each other's outline in the heavy gloom, and they both held their breath in wondrous anticipation.

Suddenly the hoods were lifted from the light stands and the chamber illuminated once more.

A crowd of grinning banfs and terragons were now gathered around the gleeful Squilp, and Jonquil's eyes, mouth and arms flew open when he focused on their faces.

"Meadolarne! Yargle! Peeli! Chuckwalla!" he roared, and the two companions charged towards the group to embrace the Oak-Goldeneye contingent.

A tearful reunion followed. Jonquil and Rattajack were hugged and patted and bombarded with questions. Meadolarne, Yargle and the others had been warned about Jonquil's wings, but their wonder and surprise at actually seeing and touching his long feathered additions was painted boldly on their faces.

Meadolarne's party had travelled the long distance from Jonquil's home village in the company of the two friends best loved banfs and terragons, including Opolla, Meadolarne's mother; young Peart, and his terragon, Jotterel; Finf and Jaboa, Targrin and Fanalopa, and many more good friends and family.

They all marvelled at how much Jonquil had changed. Not just the fact that he had grown wings, but that his whole stature had become taller, stronger and sleeker. Jonquil introduced Judruff and the other windsprites to his and Rattajack's loved ones, and the Oak-Goldeneyers were intrigued at the similarities between these winged beings and themselves. They were also fascinated by the flying suits that Jonquil and the other fliers were wearing, and would have pored over these fascinating new discoveries for hours if Ollandia hadn't reminded everyone of how hungry they were.

On receiving the invitation from their hosts, the assorted visitors fell into the softly yielding embrace of the large cushions and began to heartily devour the sumptuous meal. Bowls which had once overflowed with food were steadily levelled. Countless flagons of gemberry juice, spearherb tea, rosebell wine and other fine liquids were enthusiastically drained, refilled and then drained once more. The superb spread which Ollandia and other neighbouring banfs and banfinas had strived so hard to create was done great justice that night; a hoard of empty vessels and platters that Jonquil helped carry into the scullery was the evidence. Jonquil thanked Ollandia on behalf of all and then returned with her into the main chamber to relax with the rest of the company for a while before retiring.

Lobel turned up half way through the feasting with a large tribe of curious Goldenringers; all of them terrified of missing out on an evening of tale swapping, that they knew would be thrilling and unique considering the bizarre nature of the company. The eager banfs tried to squeeze more of Jonquil's amazing adventures out of him, but instead the winged banf told them that the story of the windsprites; of how mushroom dwellers became sky soarers, was an infinitely finer tale and bade Judruff recount the legend of his people.

Judruff, who hadn't been expecting to be the centre of attention, still had his mouth half full of gemberries when the enthusiastic stare of the gathering suddenly turned upon him; and he almost choked when Jonquil invited him to speak. After a moment or two's composure, however, the falcon king swallowed the last of the fruit, cleared his throat, threw a wry glance at Jonquil as if to say, "thanks friend," and embarked on the long saga of the windsprites and the sad tale of the Fruit Forests of the West.

Even though Judruff had been a little reluctant at first to begin such a mournful history in such merry company, the old feelings soon overcame him and with long stares and glassy eyes he slowly unfolded the heart-rending tragedy of the windsprites eviction from their homeland by the evil Destroying Angels.

None of the banfs present in Squilp and Ollandia's house could fail to be moved by the falcon king's words, and the large round chamber grew silent and thoughtful.

However, not wanting to send his hosts and fellow guests to their beds with sombre thoughts to haunt them, after he had finished his sad tale Judruff began to sing a lay, one of the ancient poems of the former tree-banfs, that described the splendour and joy of life in the fruit forests. A life which none of those windsprites present or indeed any living had ever known, but it was a merry song and before long had all of the falcons and most of the banfs singing or humming along with it.

The song was old, composed in an age of joy and peace, in an age when such a people as the tree-banfs still existed, in a kingdom that had now not seen a king for more than a hundred years. Because of the invasion of the terrible Destroying Angels and the timely intervention of the Lord Waxifrade, the tree-banfs had been transformed into the windsprites; a dispossessed, despairing people who clung to the pale vestiges of a life none could remember. True, they now had the gift of flight, an acquisition many would consider to be priceless compensation, and yet there was not a single soul sitting beneath Squilp's mushroom roof, or residing in the wind scarred heights of the Marble Fortress who would not trade every feather, to stand once more beneath the boughs of Gwiddian, the mother tree, wingless citizens of a wondrous kingdom restored.

Finally the company broke up and began to retire to their respective beds. It seemed that Squilp had invited quite a large proportion of the crowd who had invaded the banquet with Lobel to stay at his large house, and they were gradually shepherded off in various directions by Ollandia and other members of the family to empty rooms that could accommodate them.

For the benefit of the excited banf children, most of whom had alternated between bouts of playing and sleeping during the long evening, those windsprites who were able, leapt dramatically into the air and flew up to the doors of their respective bedchambers, situated along the sweep of the spiral stairway, leading off from the high walls. The banf children, despite nearly falling asleep on their feet with tiredness, squealed with delight at this exciting display, and would demand many repeat performances from Jonquil and the other able-bodied fliers before allowing them to leave the village of Goldenring the next day.

Meadolarne and Opolla were given the next room to Jonquil and Rattajack, and when the banf finally flopped down on to his long mushroom velvet mattress, he stared up at the carved ceiling of his room, and let the bright memories and feelings of the long day flood back into his mind. When Jonquil eventually drifted off to sleep, he was bathed in the warm glow of happiness and relief; and although he was excited about the day to come with the Wizards and the King, he could just as easily have slipped back to the comfortable rise of

Oak-Goldeneye, without any fuss, and quietly started his new life with Rattajack and Meadolarne.

The terragon who had curled up contentedly at Jonquil's feet was also satisfied; his beloved friend had returned to him and soon he would have his snug old nest back, in which to dream of their great adventures beyond the White Ring.

The Oak Palace

The following few days were so packed with emotion, exhilaration, stunning colour and pageantry that after a while they all began to blur in Jonquil's mind; so that when, in later times, he tried to recall his pleasant experiences at the Oak City they all became lost in a dizzy kaleidoscopic haze.

Jonquil, Rattajack, the windsprites and the Oak-Goldeneyers were received at the wide foot of the long, meandering stairway that led to Merlion's palace, by the three High Witches of the Seasons; Bruntian of Spring, Vijian of Summer and Quillion of Autumn.

The three gracious ladies were robed in long splendid gowns of their particular colours; Bruntian's long brunette tresses were tied and plaited with bright sprigs of pearly blossom, exquisite clusters of pale petals decorating the verdant drapes of her luxuriant dress; Vijian's flaxen hair flowed over her shoulders in waves of golden silk, her elegant costume of amber, saffron and topaz, sparkled with jewelled borders, and the bright flowers of the cornfield glowed in her braided hair. Quillion as always was breathtaking in her robes of scarlet and purple, her hand extended in friendship and welcome to the merry group, and her serene smile warming their hearts.

The eyes of the assorted travellers could not grow large enough to accommodate the sheer spectacle that filled their sight. Green oaks the size of mountains, rising to infinity. Huge boughs as wide as rivers, reaching out from the vast bodies of the trees like giant muscle-bound arms, each colossal limb snaking out to find the edge of the mighty trees' shadow supported by its own private army of stout, intermingled root pillars.

Over many centuries the four Mother Oaks had, through their own intense industry and toil, created a private inner forest beneath their own vast canopies, with trunks and branches as dense and populous as any other that graced Enchantica's soil; their four, towering, majestic bodies soaring at its heart.

The foothills of the gnarled oak mountains were huge coils of thick, ancient root, weaving and binding to form cavernous refuge from the Winter extremes for the surrounding mushroom dwelling population. Opposing walls of thickly woven aerial roots had been encouraged and engineered to grow down either side of a long, wide stairway. The long, tumbling tongue of steps wriggled past a host of minor entrances leading to various caves and tunnels, great rashes of mushroom towers that thrust into the turmoil of the immense root columns, and eventually spread into the base of the four mighty trunks. This was the stairway that would take Jonquil's group to the Wizards and the King.

The acorn was the official symbol of the banf monarch, and had been used extensively in the elaborately carved friezes that decorated the interior chambers of the palace. Merlion's ancestors had created the ancient domed rooms by growing and knotting a myriad roots and young branches into thick, living walls.

"Welcome, my friends," Merlion said to them when the group finally arrived at the royal chamber. "Your homecoming, Jonquil the Wanderer and Rattajack the Faithful, has been long awaited."

Jonquil couldn't help feeling that there was something very familiar about his King's face. He had seen those refined looks and mannerisms somewhere before. However, such was the excitement of the occasion that the banf gave this queer phenomenon no further thought.

The king was adorned with the finest cuts of mushroom leather and silky hemp. His oak crown, sculpted into the likeness of an acorn, was perched proudly upon his noble head; and although the quality of his clothing paled before the majesty of the Wizards, who flanked the King with the bright, colourful banks of their followers; for a banf he was very grandly attired.

Merlion had just risen from a throne that grew out of the oak floor as a contorted eruption of strangled roots and stems; some of the twisted, gnarled limbs alive and in leaf. The kingly seat stood against a richly decorated wall of woven wood, glorious pictures of trees and leaved garlands magnificently designed and carved into the ancient timber.

Standing proudly at the King's side was a handsome, scaled creature with an attentive intelligent face. His two large orb-like eyes blazed with the red of Autumn sunsets. This rather aristocratic fellow was tawny and orange with a bright cinnamon belly, his collar was beautifully carved from the rare wood of the ruby oak into a wreath of overlapping auburn oak leaves. It was Kinkajou, the royal terragon, and the striking creature's eyes, which were benevolent and reassuring like those of all terragons, lit up at Rattajack's approach.

Jonquil could tell from the sudden twitching of his companion's ears that the two terragons had already embarked on a secret, unspoken discourse.

As soon as Merlion had completed his heartfelt greeting, the Three Wizards stepped forward to give their salutations to the two companions.

"Hail! Jonquil the Hero and Rattajack the Incomparable!" Orolan cried.

"I see you have found your wings at last!" Waxifrade said to the banf with a knowing smile.

"What an adventure you have both had since last we saw you!" Fantazar exclaimed.

The Lords of the Seasons made no secret of their joy at seeing both Jonquil and Rattajack alive and well and safely returned to their home at last.

The gorgeous cloaks and tunics of the three great lords stood out from the dark oak backdrop with a radiance that somehow defied the slight illumination of the King's Chamber.

The three fabulous power crystals, set into the hearts of solid gold Sea Stars that the Wizards wore about their necks, burned with renewed triumphant energy. Tiny fragments of coloured fire played over Jonquil and Rattajack's entranced faces as they stared transfixed at the brilliant, glittering gems. The three mighty stones had the glory of the seasons harnessed within them, and the shards of burning colour that flashed and sparkled across their jewelled forms carried the promise of a new, brighter dawn.

Merlion's throne room was a circular, domed chamber of quite modest proportions compared to the grand vaults the Three Wizards and their illustrious followers would have been used to.

Shallow clefts and hollows, originally designed to house neat crops of bright light fungi, had been artfully crafted into the breathtaking decorations which covered the surface of the walls. Every last stem and strand of the woven limbs had been worked by the artists' chisels, creating a mesmerising mingle of interlocking fretwork; animals, mushrooms and symbols of the forest carried on sweeping, weaving lines, that spiralled and tangled in seemingly impossible, endless, intricate patterns.

Over the years the living lanterns had taken delight in the deep relief of the carvings, and burst from their original wells to creep all over the indented surface of the curved walls and ceiling. They had multiplied in such profusion that almost every nook and ridge had been populated by the glowing conical caps, burning with a constant light against the dark oak. The effect for the King and his guests was exquisite; a glistening, scattered starscape; clusters and constellations every bit as delicate and varied as the real thing which blazed above the treetops in the midnight sky.

There was a good deal of excitement caused when Judruff was presented to the banf king. For when the two came face to face, all in the company saw at once that the King of the Windsprites and the King of the Banfs were almost identical in features and stature. Apart from a small difference in years, a little grey at Merlion's temples, a tuft of a beard on Judruff's chin, the two of them might have been long lost twins. Indeed, for a few long moments, the two kings could do nothing but stare in disbelief at each other, neither able to find words to express their wonder.

It was then that Jonquil realised why Merlion had seemed so familiar to him. It was obvious when the two kings were together, but in the excitement of the occasion, Jonquil's whirling senses just hadn't been able to make the connection.

After all of the guests had been presented and received, which included Trinia and her fairy band, Merlion's consort and daughter, Queen Abalarne and Princess Falarine, entered the royal chamber. They greeted the company politely and then took their places beside the King. The High Gathering then settled down to listen to the story of the great adventure.

The simple mushroom dwellers of Oak-Goldeneye, who hadn't expected for a moment to be invited to join the company in Merlion's throne room, were overjoyed when the Three Wizards advised the King that after all the waiting and worry they had endured for the sake of Jonquil and Rattajack, it was only fair they should be included.

When the time came for the two companions to unburden themselves of their long story, they rose to their feet and the whole company waited with bated breath for Jonquil to speak.

Rattajack's not insubstantial part in the overthrow of the enemy, after his separation from the banf, was told by Trinia, when Jonquil had finished the last part of his epic saga. To Jonquil's utter amazement and delight, the fairy queen made it known that she and her people had the gift to hear and understand the terragon's silent tongue. The banf was both astonished and envious.

The fairy queen's archers had captured the terragon as he had trespassed across their domain. Ensnaring him in their enchanted webs. Judruff suddenly became very interested in Trinia's description of the fairy webs and at a later time asked the fairy queen if such potent traps might be used against the windsprites' sworn enemies, the Destroying Angels. Much to the falcon king's surprise, Trinia and her people knew of Mezereon's pale demons, for they were the corrupted forms of northern fairies and elves. The fairy queen promised to aid Judruff in his quest to rid the Fruit Forests of their deadly scourge; their two great nations would ally to defeat the unnatural enemy.

The part of Jonquil's tale that inspired the most attention from the great lords was of course the final part; Vrorst's last battle on the footslopes of the snowy forest mountain. Jonquil and the windsprites relived every terror-filled moment as they had stood vulnerable and alone against the might of the Ice Sorcerer and the great dragon, Grawlfang.

As always the Wizards seemed to glean much more information from the banf and the fliers' honest account than any of them were conscious of providing; and when the banf told them that the great white dragon had seized the Winter Orb in its jaws and flown with it to Mezereon as Vrorst had commanded with his dying breath, the company fancied they saw the slightest note of disquiet darken the Wizards' otherwise calm, stoical demeanour.

The Three Wizards had clearly not known of this final act, although they were probably not greatly surprised that the mighty Winter Orb had passed on to another. The real surprise would come if the cowardly Mezereon ever found the courage to use it.

At the end of the grand audience Jonquil felt quite exhausted and was glad when the Three Wizards finally drew the evening to its close, so that he and

Rattajack could withdraw with their brethren to their Oak Palace lodgings and pass a content and peaceful night.

The banfs of Oak-Goldeneye and the six windsprites spent a blissful next few days at the Oak City. The presence of the Wizards of Light in the heart of the Banf Kingdom transformed the Protected Forest once again, only this time there were no icy reprisals hurled down from the Winter skies to spoil the beneficial effects of the warmer climate.

The buds which dared to burst out of their sticky envelopes could now enjoy the warmth of an unseasonal sun; and when necessary a shower of cool rain rather than a cruel blizzard of sap-freezing snow.

When the last vestiges of the Winter chill was finally banished from the air, the inhabitants of the Oak City felt confident enough to leave the dark caves of the Oak foothills and return to their abandoned Summer homes that proliferated amongst the giant tangle of roots and trunks. The intimate collections of mushroom dwellings had remained empty for so long that when the exiled communities finally re-established themselves, great celebrations were organised and well hidden Winter stores plundered to provide feasts for a long succession of home-returning parties. Jonquil and his friends spent the next few days and nights attending a good many of these hearty jubilations, never tiring from the endless good cheer and merriment that greeted them at every neighbouring mushroom settlement.

Jonquil didn't idle away all of his free time, however, he spent some of it in worthy employment, and when he had finished, sat back to admire the object which was attached to a looped strip of mushroom leather.

It was a gift for Meadolarne, and a most splendid one at that. A whistle, carved by the banf's own fair hands from a slipper nut; the fruit of the Iron Beech tree. Its note was the loudest, truest sound Jonquil had ever heard from a crafted instrument, and later when he presented it to Meadolarne he told her that no matter how far away he was, if she blew the whistle he would hear her.

This was a heartfelt attempt to allay Meadolarne's fears that she was about to lose him again, for despite his constant assurances, the banf knew that she was not totally convinced that he was home to stay; indeed Meadolarne had secretly resigned herself to the fact that it was only a matter of time before his wanderer's feet carried Jonquil away again.

Nevertheless, the beautiful banfina was delighted with her gift and after sounding a good few blasts upon it to test its worth, carried it proudly about her neck from that day forward.

The windsprites had been overwhelmed by the welcome they had received from their flightless cousins. The fact that the banfs' very own world hero, Jonquil, also had wings endeared the falcons to them even more, and before long countless banf children were asking their parents if they too would have wings when they grew up.

Judruff and the other fliers felt very much at home with the banfs, but they each knew that as soon as all six windsprites were fit for the long flight northwards, they must depart the forest paradise they had grown to love so much, to join their brothers and sisters in the fight against Mezereon at Dragonskeep.

Abalarne, Merlion's beautiful consort, was steeped in the lore of medicinal herbs, and renowned as a great healer. It was to the queen that the fairies had turned to solicit healing potions for the injured limbs of the windsprites; and it was to Falarine, daughter of Merlion and Abalarne, that Comet, youngest son of Judruff, had lost his heart whilst being tenderly nursed for a broken wing by the beautiful banf princess.

Since the dramatic discovery at the grand audience of Judruff and Merlion's shared resemblance, the King of the Falcons and the King of the Banfs had spent long hours together discussing the ancient histories of their respective peoples.

The two Kings slowly unravelled their long and distinguished ancestries, and the list of names that testified to each others pedigree took hours to complete.

The tree-banfs, the predecessors to the windsprites, had migrated from the Banf Kingdom, northwards to the great fruit forests, hundreds of years before. By painstakingly counting back through the ranks of their forefathers, Merlion and Judruff arrived at two ancient kings; Mirrabal and Olban. These two monarchs seemed to correspond in time and beyond whom the Falcon King could delve no further.

Finally, Merlion took his windsprite double down to the Halls of Carvings; the sacred oak tunnels upon whose walls the whole history of the banf race was depicted. There amongst the time-weathered, dust-laden friezes of ancient history, the two kings broke through the seal of prehistoric cobwebs and located the faded images of the two ancestral kings.

To the great surprise and delight of Merlion and Judruff, it was discovered that Mirrabal of the mushroom dwellers and Olban of the tree-banfs had been no less than twin brothers; first born sons of Pelgrin the Great.

Why the twins had separated and halved their banf subjects between them was not clear, but perhaps they had decided that if one of them founded a new throne elsewhere, they could both rule as kings, which as twins, was their right.

Jonquil pointed out that even the oak portrait of Pelgrin bore a resemblance to the two living kings; and it was clear to all that despite the passing of hundreds of years and the long separation of the races, the twin royal blood lines had remained strong and true. The spirit of Pelgrin was undoubtedly alive in both Merlion and Judruff.

Several days after Jonquil and Rattajack's jubilant arrival at the Oak City, the Lords of the Seasons called a High Council.

The two companions had been so engrossed with their friends, both old and new, that they had failed to notice the startling metamorphosis that had gradually risen through the towering heights of the four giant trees.

Former naked, storm ravaged branches, that had withstood a Winter so fierce that it threatened to kill every tree in the forest, were now newly clothed with bright green rosettes of young leaves. The densely layered canopy that had once swept over the vast embrace of the massive Mother Oaks as a colossal viridescent dome, was now almost fully restored. The secret of this enchanted transformation had been the placing of Fantazar's Fire Orb upon a special plinth in the deepest chamber of the Oak Palace. The power of the Spring globe had warmed the toes of the four mighty trees like an irresistible green fire, awakening the long dormant sap and forcing the huge old bodies back to life.

Jonquil did not appreciate the full glory of the Spring Wizard's work until he landed on the open platform of the High Cradle, Merlion's traditional Summer court. As its name suggested, the High Cradle was a wide, shallow bowl formed from a plaited weave of hefty branches, suspended from the tangle of intertwining limbs that filled the dense interior of the four great boles.

Although a lengthy succession of reticulating stairways formed the conventional route to the Wizards' council in the lofty hammock, and was the path most of the invited participants were forced to take, Jonquil just couldn't resist exercising his wings and flying to the high meeting. The banf managed to persuade Judruff and Hulse to join him in this rather showy display, and to the great delight of the assorted banfs and injured windsprites who gradually made their way along the winding stairway, Jonquil and the two falcons performed an exquisite aerial ballet, weaving through the criss-crossed cage of rugged, serpentine limbs in graceful sweeping curves.

When all of the banfs and the fliers eventually appeared at the high framework, they found the Wizards, the King and Queen and the fairies already installed, their brilliant costumes enjoying the full attention of radiant sunlight. A wide ring of entwined branches lying proud of the knotted wood floor provided seating for all.

Alongside Trinia was seated a distinguished array of her fellow fairy royalty; including King Trillil of the Hidden Caves, Queen Fristal and King Rivilan of the Sapphire Vale, and the four sons of King Jolandil, Lord of the Seven Silver Streams.

The fairy monarchs and princes were resplendent in ceremonial versions of the traditional mail tunics they wore for battle.

The long, dazzling coats were made of delsidian, a beautifully marbled, lustrous stone highly prized by the fairies; not only for its beauty and colour, which could be any shade of the rainbow, but for its great strength and remarkable light weight. This unusual combination made delsidian an ideal material for battle armour. The individual pieces of colourful stone had been crafted into overlayed patterns of leaves or feathers, each of the precious components finished off with a fine frame of silver or gold filigree. There were few things made from the treasures of the Green Sky Forest more handsome or extravagant than a full coat of delsidian mail; and the fairy royalty assembled at the court of King Merlion wore theirs with great pride.

On their heads, each high fairy wore a fabulous circlet of gold filigree enriched with elegant arrangements of freshwater pearls and polished waterstones – the fairy equivalent of diamonds and rubies; and considered even more precious by Commonlanders, for the river gems, like delsidian, were found only within the secret kingdoms of the enchanted folk. Suspended from the bases of their delicate crowns were long, ornamented strands of gold chain, some of which had been woven into long plaits with their silky hair, others left to drip down their pale foreheads or hang as sparkling frames to their pear-shaped faces.

The open platform of Merlion's Summer court was contained within a luxurious wreath of thick foliage, which screened an extensive array of arboreal dwellings. Elegant spikes of oak flowers conjured forth by the enchantment of the Spring Orb and the affectionate caress of the strengthened sun, rose like extravagant candles from the bowers of polished leaves.

Sweet throated birds encouraged by the blossom, cast their songs to the tamed breeze and performed brightly coloured dances in the sun-filled space above the gathering's heads. The nectar-rich blooms had also attracted a chorus of bees and honeybottles, the high and low voiced insects droning an hypnotic harmony as they indulged themselves amongst the cones of pale pink stars. Jonquil's heart was made happy when amongst the clouds of blossom-busy creatures he spotted the dazzling flight of his favourite birds; the hummers. The banf delighted to see the tiny creatures, hardly bigger than the bustling bees they accompanied, tracing iridescent lines of reflected sunlight between the opposing walls of blossom; and then hovering with perfect rigidity like living diamante, their glorious plumage sparkling to rival any jewel.

Where all of these wonderful birds and insects had come from nobody cared to ask, it was simply enough that they were there, adding colour and music to the upper branches.

When all had settled, the High Council was begun.

Following Vrorst's demise, the Great Lords had discussed and deliberated with each other for many days and had finally decided on how to take the first step towards achieving a lasting peace for the Commonlands – there was to be a Great Council!

"We will find a wide open space," Fantazar told the gathering. "And drive back the snow with the power of the Fire Orbs to create an oasis of warmth and peace. Just as we have here in the Banf Kingdom."

"There we will raise a city," Waxifrade continued. "Large enough to accommodate emissaries and contingents from all the kingdoms of the Commonlands, who we shall invite to come and sit with us and present their opinions."

ROOT OF THE WO[R]

THE
FRUIT FORESTS
of the WEST

ANCONEUS

GLOSTOMORG

VRORST'S
KINGDOM

DOOMSLANG

GATES of
FROZEN
KINGDOM

DRAGONGORGE

DRAGONGORGE

THE FOREST RIVER

DRAGONSKEEP

THE SUMMER

NORTHERN
FORESTS

OLD
FROZEN
PALACE

MOUNTAINS of
MENACE
(DARK MOUNTAINS)
#2

FFORI

NICOBAR

PANTHEERA

OENTELLUS

GYRE

TANAGUA

MANASLANGUA

The
GREAT/GIANT
LAKE

THRONE
CITADEL

GAOL WATER

THE CANVAS
CITY

MYSTERY WOOD

Enchantica

© ROB SIMPSON '94

An intrigued silence gripped the company, each individual trying to visualise a place where all the races of the world could come together and sit one with another in the quest for peace. Jonquil found it a most thrilling prospect and hoped that he would be amongst those from the Banf Kingdom invited to attend.

"If they will come and sit with us in the true spirit of peace and reconciliation," Orolan announced. "All the races of Enchantica will be welcome to attend!"

"Peace and reconciliation!" Trinia exclaimed. "What do the followers of Vrorst know of such things?"

The golden crowns of the fairy monarchs sparkled in the spears of sunlight stabbing through the breeze-kissed canopy as they conferred indignantly with one another.

"My friends," the Summer Wizard replied "Vrorst may be dead but his power over Enchantica is yet to be broken. He leaves behind a legacy of powerful armies. Kings and chieftains who, as long as they believe we seek only their destruction, will never attempt the path of peace. We must talk to our enemies and convince them that we genuinely desire an end to hostility, whoever they are! We must offer them an alternative to eternal enmity. We must abandon old hatred, for it serves only as rich food for evil minds. Only by forging new alliances and friendships can we protect Enchantica from the coming of a new Vrorst!"

"All the peoples of Enchantica who have the ability to choose between good and evil, must be given the opportunity to do so," Waxifrade added calmly. "The Great Council is that opportunity."

"Of one thing we may be certain," Fantazar continued "If our former enemies can find the courage to come to the City of Peace, we will know why they have come, and would be fools not to talk to them."

The Three Wizards continued to describe their ambitious plans to the gathering, some elements of the company still unconvinced that such a grand scheme could ever succeed; but all willing to travel to the appointed place and join with the Wizards in their great quest for peace.

After a while Queen Abalarne asked how long the building of this fabulous City of Peace would take; the company clearly expecting the Wizards to talk in terms of many months if not years.

Fantazar triumphantly gave their answer.

"Within thirty days of us arriving at our chosen site, you will all receive your invitations to attend the Great Council."

"Impossible!" laughed King Rivilan. "Thirty days to build a city. Even with the aid of great sorcery such a feat could not be achieved?"

"Then come to us in thirty days, my friend," Orolan smiled. "And you will see a city raised from nothing. And I promise you no sorcery of any kind will play a part in its construction."

The Wizards had succeeded in stunning the whole gathering into silence.

Eventually Judruff asked if they intended to return to the Throne Citadel when the Great Council had been concluded.

Suddenly a cloud crept across the sun and a slight chill entered the air. This subject was clearly a cause of great sadness to the Three Wizards and when Orolan spoke his voice was low and subdued.

"Our first intentions had been to return to the Throne Citadel and reclaim our historic seat of power," he began. "The City of the Crystals housed the Sacred Vessels for centuries, and we could have wished for no better power anvil from which to conduct the symphonies of our respective colours.

But the Sacred Vessels are no more and even the great citadel itself has suffered grievous hurt during its long months of occupation by the Ice Sorcerer. Can it be restored to its former magnificence? Should it be restored? For when the great test came, it failed to withstand the grand treachery of the Lord of Ice.

Of one thing we three are now certain. Never again must the power that drives the cycle of the seasons be vulnerable to the threats or ambitions of those that might seek to subdue it. It must be placed beyond the reach of evil forever.

Where can such an impregnable site be found ? Does such a place exist ? Here, perhaps, in the Banf Kingdom? For the powerful White Ring prevented Vrorst from reaching us, even though he had an army thousands strong to aid him. Should we perhaps build a new Citadel here? Cradled within the arms of these four mighty trees, in the heart of the Third Well of Hope?"

Merlion and Abalarne could not help looking a little alarmed at this suggestion, the banf king shifting uneasily in his seat. Merlion wasn't a selfish being but he liked the Oak Palace just the way it was; and like most forest dwellers disliked all change except the change of the seasons.

"It is for us three to put right the harm that our once brother, Vrorst, has inflicted upon this noble world," Fantazar continued. "The eternal wheel of Spring, Summer, Autumn and a Winter without fear or evil . . . . this we three vow to restore!"

Waxifrade added his voice.

"Eventually we shall find a new home for the sacred power," he said. "A secret place, hidden from the eyes of the envious; safe from all thieves!"

Orolan concluded.

"The answers to all the great questions shall be found at the Great Council!"

A wave of relief washed over the assembly at the Wizards' words. The seasons were the cradle of life itself, without them the world they all knew and loved would simply cease to exist. Vrorst had succeeded in upsetting the ageless balance and nearly destroyed Enchantica with his lust for victory. The company gathered in the High Cradle took comfort from what they had heard, and all vowed to do what they could to aid the grand restoration of the Commonlands.

Now that the serious business of the High Council had been concluded, the

Wizards announced their intention to depart, but before they did so they summoned Jonquil and Rattajack before them.

"We have a most pleasant duty to perform before we begin our journey to the appointed place." Orolan told the two companions. "We have been asked to preside over the presentation of gifts, in recognition of your brave deeds."

Jonquil and Rattajack suddenly felt very self conscious and a little embarrassed.

"Do not feel uncomfortable, my friends," the Summer Wizard told them, as if he could read their thoughts. "There is not one being gathered here in this high place that would deny your right to these rewards. We all salute and thank you."

This sentiment was echoed by the whole company who were now gathered around the two companions and the Wizards to witness the splendid ceremony.

King Merlion told Jonquil and Rattajack that even as he spoke the royal wood chisellers were hard at work crafting the story of their, now famous, adventure in the Halls of Carvings. Jonquil the Hero and Rattajack the Incomparable were about to be immortalised as part of banf history.

Merlion turned aside from the two companions and a banf courtier stepped forward proffering a mushroom velvet cushion which held an exquisite collar of oak leaves with an acorn, carved from the golden iridescent wood of the saffron oak; one of the rarest and most precious of banf materials. Compared to silver and gold the gift may have appeared poor, but any inhabitant of the Protected Forest would have valued an item made from saffron wood far higher.

As the king lifted the extravagant collar from the cushion, Orolan surreptitiously raised his eyes to the sky and a rapier of sunlight pierced the canopy high above and struck the polished faces of the leaves setting Merlion's hands ablaze with golden fire.

Rattajack's old, weatherworn treevine collar was gently eased over his ears by Jonquil and replaced with the precious oak leaves by Merlion. Kinkajou piped and trilled loudly in appreciation of the handsome investment, his sentiments echoed by the rest of the gathering, especially Trinia and the fairies who had grown very fond of the remarkable terragon in the relatively short time they had known him.

The golden wood shone emphatically in the bright sunshine, the gleaming acorn lying proudly on Rattajack's chest. The terragon turned to Jonquil, who could only stare opened mouthed in return; they were both stunned by the priceless gift.

A second mushroom velvet cushion was offered to the king and this time Merlion raised a thin braid of strong mushroom cord from which hung a large, golden wood acorn about the size of a bush pheasant's egg. The gift of a sculpted acorn, of any material, was a high honour and the King's privilege; only those personally honoured by their monarch were given leave to wear an acorn about their person.

Although a number of Merlion's subjects had been awarded acorns during his reign, none had ever received a prize of such value.

However, the acorn had even greater riches to reveal apart from the wealth of its fabric; for when Merlion presented it to Jonquil, he showed the banf a tiny clasp on the acorn's side which when pressed caused its body to spring open, exposing a tear-shaped pine diamond set into one half. Sealed within the crystal clear drop of sculpted tree resin was a tiny blue fire lantern; one of the rarest and most precious mushrooms known to the banfs.

Jonquil was speechless; it was the most beautiful and fascinating object he had ever seen; and he simply couldn't believe that it was being offered to him as a gift. The banf was too afraid to take the fabulous object in his hands and yet at the same time his eyes couldn't leave it.

"The blue fire lantern," Merlion told the banf, "was given to my father many years ago by a brave, young, banf explorer like yourself. Therefore I think it is only fitting that I should now give it to you. The tree resin for the lens came from one of the four great Mother Oaks. The acorn case is made from precious saffron wood, and is a gift from the people."

Jonquil was so moved by Merlion's words that he was unable to thank the King with his voice, so he tried to do so with his eyes and Merlion understood. The banf king lifted the cord over Jonquil's head saying; "Let this be a true light against dark shadows!"

As the acorn came to rest about Jonquil's neck a hearty cheer rose up from the company. The banf turned with emotional eyes to Meadolarne and the banfina was cheering and clapping with all her might, proud tears streaming from her glassy eyes.

Home beckoned to Jonquil and Rattajack; that beloved, sun-speared mushroom ring secreted within a rambling wreath of writhing roots that was Oak-Goldeneye.

Home also beckoned to the windsprites, and after an emotional farewell, especially between Comet and Falarine, the falcons took to the air and swept back into the north.

The Wizards' departure from the Banf Kingdom was a fabulous spectacle. A river of bright standards and flags burst forth from the boundary of white mushrooms and surged into the forest.

The three great lords rode in highly decorated carriages with their respective High Witches, flanked by exuberant banner-waving attendants in seasonal livery. The mood was high; there was laughing and dancing, and the silent trees were serenaded with a sparkling repertoire of joyful songs.

Their destination lay in one of the vast expanses of flat country that dominated the southern half of the Commonlands. An area known well to the three lords situated between the two great rivers known as Power Water and Gaol Water. There, in a shallow, stream-served basin they planned to raise their City of Peace. On a map of Enchantica the place would have appeared just below the site of the Throne Citadel but in truth was more than a hundred leagues south of the ice-encrusted tower.

To keep them safe upon their long journey the Wizards had created an enchanted cloud across the opening in the White Ring from which the grand procession was to issue. As the colourful parade poured through, each individual acquired a shimmering aura of protection, then collectively they wound their way between the stark, snow-laden giants as a ghostly, glittering snake.

As they marched, the brightly attired retinue broadcast showers of seeds and enchanted flower petals about them; a precious mixture harvested from the beloved blooms of the Forgotten Island; so that ever after the route the Wizards' incandescent train took through the forest was marked by a glorious carpet of exotic flowers.

Seated beside a campfire on the homeward trail, Jonquil was re-examining Merlion's precious gift, when his eyes fell upon the wooden acorn Old Yargle proudly wore fastened to the cord of his shouldercloak. Mindful of the fact that one could only wear an acorn by royal favour, Jonquil asked the old banf how he had come to earn such a rare privilege.

Old Yargle then enthralled the whole, happy home-returning group with the tale of his quest for the fire lanterns; and how he and Chuckwalla had accidentally stumbled across a cluster of rare blue fire lanterns in the process; despite the fact that they were being hunted by Grogoda, one of the fiercest great she-trolls in the whole of the Green Sky Forest, at the time.

When they had finally returned to the safety of the Banf Kingdom, Yargle had made a gift of the one rare light-fungi, he had taken, to his King; who in those days was King Himbrel, Merlion's father. In gratitude and in recognition of his brave deed, the then young Yargle was presented with his acorn; carved from a cutting of the royal throne itself.

"So it was you Merlion spoke of?" Jonquil exclaimed.

"Well, it's possible," Yargle responded with a smile.

Jonquil pressed the tiny clasp on the golden acorn and suddenly a dazzling beam of intense blue-white light burst from his hand, slicing a broad swathe through the heavy darkness of the leafy forest. The brilliant band soared right up to the high ceiling of the mighty trees and illuminated the underside of the newly burst leaves brighter than day. The light emanating from the pine diamond lens was too powerful to regard and Jonquil had to shield his eyes to save them from the worst of the blinding glare.

"And yet by the light of day," Old Yargle mused. "They look nothing at all. Yes, my dear Jonquil, that could well be the same blue fire lantern I gave to the King's father all those years ago; a rare and inestimable gift indeed!"

The Golden Alliance of the Sun

An ocean of snow sweeping out to dominate every horizon greeted the Three Wizards, as they walked alone into the centre of a wide plateau lying within a ring of shallow hills. Fantazar, Orolan and their brother Waxifrade stood back to back facing out into the white desert, their three Fire Orbs, poised on fingertips, burning with impatient power.

Rashes of multicoloured stars sparked across the glistening bodies of the three globes, and gradually a ring of power began to grow until it encapsulated the Wizards themselves; a diaphanous belt of glittering lights, glowing with every shade of the rainbow and trembling like a heat haze.

In the face of the Orbs combined sorcery, the snow rapidly capitulated and a solitary pool of green began to grow, the vibrant colour of the returning grassland claiming the ground about the Wizards like a stain of emerald ink upon a shimmering silk sheet.

An oasis of green, forty leagues in diameter, was eventually liberated from the cloak of Winter Vrorst had lain over the flat landscape. The whole of the plateau which lay inside the rolling white banks was freed, the snow pushed back until it stood as a dripping wall, guarding the borders of the vast verdant depression.

No sooner had the Fire Orbs finished their work than the first signs of the city that was to come began to appear.

Beginning at the centre, great pools of brightly decorated fabric were laid out over the grass, loud splashes of colour that stained the ground a myriad hues. A lake of gold was stretched out beneath the unhindered sun at the very heart of the work, consecutive rings of smaller, assorted coverings arranged around it, reaching out across the flat carpet of turf creating a 'mille-fleurs' sea of colour.

An army of workers busied themselves across the mighty multicoloured rosette, hammering pegs around the fringes of the cloths, attaching cords or carrying and connecting poles.

Suddenly a shout rang out and all eyes turned towards the centre of the plateau. Then, heralded by a tumultuous cheer from the assembly, a crown of canvas began to rise from the ground, its central peak climbing like a steeple into the bright blue sky. Gradually rings of lesser dwellings began to grow from the flat pools of colour, the idle folds of flamboyant material hauled into life aloft a forest of stout poles.

The central residence continued to rise until it towered over the rest of the settlement with ornate, glistering peaks. A cathedral of extravagant drapes, it was made from a richly embellished satin-like, golden canvas, which harnessed the full glory of the sun and shone like a beacon across the leagues of empty wind-waved grass.

The great 'Canvas City', as the huge tented settlement was later to be popularly known, had been standing only a short time before the first of the invited parties began to arrive.

Those who had answered the call for peace journeyed to the city of many colours, more and more standards rising over the white mounds surrounding the green plain, heralding the arrival of a seemingly endless succession of attending monarchs and emissaries; and gradually the city of canvas was occupied.

As expected, among the first to stand on the brow of one of the low hills and gaze down in wonder upon the gaudy spectacle of the tented city, were the visitors from the southern fairy kingdoms.

Trinia, Trillil, Rivilan, Fristal and several more brother and sister monarchs . . . all wearing their finest coats of delsidian, which blazed like clustered jewels in the radiant attention of the sun . . . could only marvel at the sea of brilliant tents before them, embellished with a forest of bright flags and banners that wriggled and glittered in the soft breeze of the plains. The Wizards had indeed been true to their words and raised a city in the short time they had promised; and even though it was not quite what the fairy monarchs had anticipated, the vast spread of the multicoloured encampment was breathtakingly bold and splendid. The Three Wizards might have chosen to incarcerate themselves in a great fortress or imposing palace for the purpose of meeting with the princes of Enchantica, but instead they had raised an open settlement of insubstantial canvas, innocuous and undefended, glowing with the warmth of its welcome.

The fairy monarchs were given a hearty greeting by the Wizards and housed in a number of the luxurious canvas dwellings close to the golden palace.

Slowly, the great gathering that the Wizards had foreseen began to take form; and those who had doubted the Great Council were delighted to see that representatives of almost all of Enchantica's free peoples were either already installed or soon expected at the Canvas City.

The Kings and Queens of the fairy realms from all the forests and tree-lined valleys of Enchantica were present. Many elven monarchs had also made the journey; from the green woods in the deep south to the freezing pine forests of the far north. Representatives of the nomad tribes, who had once been free to roam over the great emerald plains, before the curse of Winter had been cast upon the ground, were also dwelling in the vast settlement. Dwarflords from the South Points and various other mountainous kingdoms throughout Enchantica, had marched to take their part in the grand dialogue.

They were joined by the chieftains of the Lake People, who were attired in magnificent ceremonial dress; shaped plates of stained reed, woven and knotted into intricate patterns, and worn in elegant layers like elaborate armour. Their extravagant headdresses were adorned with mountainous plumes of flowering reed grass; dyed gold, orange or purple, they rose and cascaded like the softest feathers.

Every other monarch and high representative that assembled in the domed council chamber of the Silk Palace, was also careful to be seen in their finest and most impressive costumes.

Even the attendance of the mer-kings and queens of Enchantica had been catered for. The shallow basin which contained the tented city was served by several meandering rivers. These waterways, formerly frozen, had been liberated by the Wizards Fire Orbs. Further trenches had been worked into the surface of the plateau, and in places deep ponds and lakes excavated. Even the interior of the great silk palace itself was furnished with water channels, so the invited monarchs of the undersea, the mer-rulers of the deep rivers, and those whose lake realms were currently sealed beneath a thick frozen lid, could also join the Grand Discourse.

Some of the powers gathered in the Canvas City were old friends and allies, some up until entering the peaceful spread of the Wizards' City had been sworn enemies.

Some of these were kings who had once sided with Vrorst, either through choice or otherwise. The allied monarchs of the West; master galleon builders, who were responsible in no small part for the Ice Lord's mastery over the seas, had braved the wrath of their former adversaries and travelled to the Wizards' Council.

Many of the northern monarchs, traditionally Winter's staunchest supporters were also represented, some of whose kingdoms actually lay within the icy embrace of Vrorst's former frozen realm. The Wizards were greatly heartened that these ferocious kings and chieftains had decided to put aside their enmity and join the Forces of Light. It soon became clear that even those peoples who dwelled in the far north were tired of the season of white and longed to see the land stained green once more.

It took a number of years for all of the invited races to manage the long journey to the green plain, which for some of the distant populations involved traversing almost half of the known world, across a difficult terrain that for the most part was still firmly gripped by the jaws of Winter. The Three Wizards could follow the progress of these marching columns with the power of the Fire Orbs, and so could tell at a glance how successful their call for peace was going to be.

The five kings of the eastern brotherhood, whose fortified cities had suffered greatly under the fierce bombardment of ice and snow hurled at them by Vrorst, were eager and determined to join their fellow Enchantica monarchs at the Great Council.

However, in the aftermath of Vrorst's demise, they had been left with the huge task of digging themselves free of the great snow barricades that had been piled against their gates; and the slow rebuilding and strengthening of their weakened defences. The welfare of their long besieged people was also a priority; many were homeless and injured; the ravaged communities weary from the incessant hammering of Vrorst's aerial assaults.

However, once the sick, injured and displaced had been attended to, the work could start on forcing open the great gates; and then a mighty, glorious host would put to the trail to march the many hundreds of leagues through the mountains and the snow plains which lay between the rise of the eastern peaks and the City of the Wizards.

Almost a year after the first golden peak of the Silk Palace had been raised from the grass, the combined standards of Gyre, Entellus, Pantheera, Nicobar and Fforl; the five great kingdoms of the east; were sighted climbing the white ridge above the sun-soaked plateau.

The hand picked armies that accompanied the Eastern Kings, spread out along the brows of the snowy hills, their highly polished shields and breastplates dazzling in the sun like an approaching wall of fire.

The Three Wizards rejoiced to see the five kings at the Council and a great feast was held in their honour to celebrate a renewal of the old alliance between the two powerful brotherhoods.

Such an auspicious, glittering array of monarchs and chieftains had never before been seen gathered together in one place; and it was into this unique and auspicious gathering that Jonquil and Rattajack, accompanying King Merlion and Queen Abalarne, were welcomed.

At the first of the High Councils, the vast assembly was seated on a wide ring of satin cushions, within a high, domed chamber in the very heart of the Silk Palace of the Wizards.

The three great lords appeared before the majestic company in the fabulous victory robes that Yim had been working so hard to complete in his cramped workshop.

Flanked by Bruntian, Vijian, Quillion and a host of colourful supporters, the eyes of the collected monarchs feasted upon a brilliant sea of flowing costume.

Their rich lengths of saffron, carmine and malachite shimmered with a mesmeric light that seemed almost to be generated by the material itself. Scores of delightful motifs including dragonflies, butterflies, leaf sprays and exotic jewelled birds had been painstakingly embroidered on to the iridescent surface of the bright cloth, each robe dripping with glittering ornaments fashioned from the colour of their season.

The first thing the Wizards asked of the illustrious throng was to swear allegiance to a new alliance.

The great ring of sovereigns and leaders was suddenly bathed in a flood of golden light radiating from a burning sphere, which magically materialised and hovered just above the floor in the centre of the wide circle. Into this blazing globe a golden dragon appeared, its great wings swept out like dazzling sheets of flame as it soared within the gleaming, diaphanous orb.

An awestruck silence gripped the gathering, the ring of eyes sparkling with reflected golden stars. Then the distinguished figures all raised their right hands until their palms were painted with the brilliant yellow light. The magnificent, ethereal dragon threw back its noble head and roared, with a giant, reverberating voice. A mighty jet of flame burst from its jaws and surged upwards towards the ceiling, then it fell in an all encompassing fountain of glittering fire that instantly engulfed the ring of monarchs.

For a few long moments, the Wizards and circle of illustrious beings were sealed inside a dancing wall of golden flame. Suddenly with a crack of enchantment, the fiery illusion disappeared, and a vast rolled tapestry dropped dramatically from the ceiling to fall just above the great lords' heads. The colossal sheet of woven silks almost filled the entire width of the great domed chamber, and emblazoned across its surface for all to see, was a breathtaking representation of the glorious image that had just appeared in the centre of the ring; a golden dragon, wings held aloft, rising proudly against the rays of the rising sun – the emblem of the new Golden Alliance.

A jubilant cheer erupted throughout the company, and all of those present saluted the golden banner, the standard that was to represent the dawning of a new world.

The dragon was the age-old symbol of justice, and the sun, seen as the antithesis of Winter, and the eventual bringer of the Great Thaw. There wasn't one king, queen, chieftain or elder, sitting beneath the sweeping folds of the giant council chamber, who didn't long to see the green spears of Spring stabbing through the snow and the buds of the long silent trees bursting with new life. Even those who had formerly raised arms against the Wizards of Light now offered themselves to the Golden Alliance, and prayed for an end to the season of fear. The golden sun was the symbol of hope; warmth against cold, light against darkness, good against evil. The great gathering of distinguished leaders embraced it without reservation, and so the Golden Alliance of the Sun was born.

One of the first matters to be settled by the High Council was the issue of Mezereon; Grand Corrupter and heir apparent to the power of Winter.

There was urgent business to be conducted at Dragonskeep that couldn't wait any longer. Okra and Gremba, joint leaders of the combined goblin hordes, had led a huge army of fierce warriors through the secret mountain valleys, to support Mezereon against the rising of the dwarfs, windsprites and carrier-dragons at the ancient castle. With the arrival of the goblin armies, the task of overthrowing the Dark Sorcerer and liberating the thousands of prisoners languishing in his dungeons had begun to look hopeless for the struggling bands of rebels.

Just as they had vowed, in the interests of peace, the Three Wizards extended the hand of friendship, both to Mezereon and his forces garrisoned at

Dragonskeep, and to the black legions commanded by the goblin king and queen bivouacked on the narrow cliff tops beside it. They invited all to disarm and join the rest of Enchantica in the great quest for peace on the green plateau.

Sadly, as expected, the answer was arrogant and negative. The forces of Mezereon considered themselves far superior to any armies that the Three Wizards could muster. The Winter commanders believed the huge fortress to be impregnable to attack, and indeed, perched on the lip of Dragongorge, and surrounded by a steep, impassable shield of high mountains, Dragonskeep never could fall to a conventional army.

With great reluctance the Wizards turned their attentions away from Dragonskeep, and focused on the snow-bound mountains of the East. With the aid of the Fire Orbs and the seeing crystal possessed by the city of Fforl, the Wizards summoned forth Halmarand; famous battle-seasoned veteran and Commander-in-Chief of the allied armies of the Eastern Kings.

General Halmarand commanded a flight of over a hundred varrazaugas, or 'lion dragons'. Powerful bipeds, mighty of limb and claw, and possessed of an indomitable spirit.

These ferocious battle-steeds were amongst the most feared of all warrior dragons, for with total disregard for danger they threw themselves bodily into the thick of battle, hurling their broad, muscular bulk against the pikes and spears of the enemy without flinching. As non-fire-breathers, these vicious creatures had to scrap face to face with their foe; slashing claws and granite jaws, whacking tail and thrashing wings more than making up for their lack of flame.

Seated upon their backs were noble battle knights sheathed in elaborate golden armour; the elite dragonriders of the eastern realms. Poised in their arms were mighty war lances, their long lengths decorated with engravings and finished with lethal armour-piercing tips.

To help protect the 'lions' from the fences of cruel, iron-tipped spears during their insane charges, the dragons were also furnished with embellished body armour; almost all of it shielding the underside of the fierce beasts as that was invariably the aspect presented to the enemy as they stooped maniacally into the fray.

When Halmarand's flight was in the air, the dragons and riders burned with the reflected fire of the sun, the extravagant plumes and cloaks of the golden riders sailing like flags in the upper draughts.

Now that the violent snowstorms had subsided, the dragon flight of Fforl was able to give an immediate response to the Wizards' plea, rising like a terrible avenging serpent from the lofty battlements of the northernmost of the five kingdoms, to strike at the very heart of the dark power at Dragonskeep.

With Halmarand at their head, the 'lion flight' followed the slow climb of the eastern sun as it hauled itself above the foothills of the Marble Fortress, the great snaking skein invisible within the blinding beams of the naked morning.

Beneath them, encamped along the cliffs above Dragongorge, the dark legions sprawled over the bare rock like an ugly black stain, but before one goblin warrior had the chance to cry out or fix an arrow to his bow, the first chain of screaming dragons fell upon them out of the burning sky, their knights leaning out from their saddles, lances poised, searching for their first victims.

A line of fearsome shadows suddenly dropped on to the cliff ledge, rippling and leaping as they raced along the rocky contours, each winged shape swallowing more ground as the dragons swiftly bore down upon the black bivouacs of the enemy.

The sky was darkened by a plummeting wall of wings, stretched spans of skin clawing great volumes of air in a plunging embrace. Large horned heads, encased in gold, were thrust forward on broad, sinewy necks, their powerful bodies folded to strike; thick belts of muscle rising like twisted rope beneath their scaly skin, every fibre taught with the force of the dive. A sweeping scythe of dagger teeth and bared claws cut deep into the fray, cleaving the rising forest of dark spears asunder; the hurtling bodies of the dragons smashing into the hastily assembled goblin ranks like boulders into rotten wood.

As the ferocious dragons crashed into the walls of dark armour, their sabre-like talons ploughing into the the clusters of bodies and spraying the cliff top with an explosion of clattering iron-clad warriors, the swiftly borne lances of the golden knights drove hard into the bunched columns of goblins and trolls, skewering their prey with a violent crunch of metal through metal.

As Halmarand had planned, his surprise attack caught the dark hordes completely unaware, the first wave of his formidable dragons wreaking havoc and confusion amongst the exposed armies on the cliff-tops.

The Winter commanders had foolishly discounted Halmarand and his flight of lion dragons, wrongly believing Fforl and the other eastern realms to be still besieged by rampaging icestorms, which denied the use of dragons; but unbeknown to Mezereon and his generals, with Vrorst's downfall the murderous tempests had abruptly ceased, and the strong arm of the East was free to flex its considerable muscle once more.

This horrifying revelation had struck the Dark Sorcerer like a hammer blow. Now that the East was free he didn't feel quite so confident, or quite so arrogant.

After the first devastating attack, Gremba tried desperately to rally some sort of answer from his troops; herding large numbers into dense, spear-bristling mobs, to present a deadly reception for a plummeting dragon. This tactic might have worked with any other dragon onslaught, but Halmarand's 'lions' were impervious to fear, and insensible of danger; therefore the huddled groups of fierce warriors brandishing their stout pikes and halberds, rather than proving an effective deterrent against their swooping attackers, simply provided the dragons with easier targets.

At Okra's urgent behest, an eruption of dark-clad goblins and trolls spewed forth from the many exits of the massive castle to aid their hard beset brothers on the cliffs, surging down the steep bank which led away from the outer walls like a violent black flood.

Without consulting the commanders responsible for defending the great garrison, the goblin queen ordered the huge iron gates that sealed the main entrance of the eastern wall to be hauled open, to allow more of her screaming soldiers to rush out into the battle.

Too late the arrogant generals, scornfully watching the efforts of the black hordes from their lofty perches amongst the upper battlements, realised what Okra had done, and that in her impatience and folly she had exposed the very heart of their defences to attack.

This was exactly as Halmarand had hoped; a second and third wave of 'lions' dropped in two converging lines to engage the mass outpouring of bodies, swooping through each others flight path to allow the succession of golden knights to rake the angry sea of creatures with their thrusting lances. This was one of Halmarand's favourite engagement patterns, which he called 'crossed swords'; it left the ranks of the enemy totally bewildered, not knowing which way to turn to defend themselves; and after the lancers had taken their toll, the dragonsteeds eagerly returned to plough their own furrows into the writhing black field.

The general himself was no slouch when it came to battle, not for Halmarand the comfort and safety of a battlement view, he was a soldier first and foremost. With him at their head, the fourth and final wave of the 'lion flight' tilted into the wind and flew like a glittering spear at the yawning gates of the outer wall.

The crowds of black warriors still vacating the great castle suddenly checked their advance when they saw Halmarand's approach, and tried to push back against the flow of bodies to re-enter the protection of the mighty stone walls. At the same time, soldiers of the garrison were wrestling with the heavy iron doors trying to heave them shut, but the confusion in the giant mouth of the gateway and the sheer volume of bodies filling the space, made it impossible. Before the castle defenders had closed even a third of the gate, Halmarand burst in upon them, the bared talons of Agamanthra, the general's mighty steed, reaching for the heart of the dark mob.

The plunging dragon tore into the wall of warriors crammed into the gateway, showering the tall faces of the inner bastions with a black wave of bodies. The cannoning dive carried Halmarand far inside the castle walls, the first half of his attacking column following his devastating progress through the jaws of the main gate. The remainder of the fourth wave aimed higher in the castle, assaulting the banks of archers rapidly taking up position on the battlements above the outer level.

Once inside the main body of the fortress, Halmarand and his fellow knights dismounted from their horned chargers, drew their swords, and alongside the ferocious dragons, fought hand to hand with the enemy. Level by level, wall by wall the Fforlian dragonriders and their steeds drove the enemy before them. The ranks of archers above were too busy fending off the attack from the air to offer any aid to their besieged brothers below and it soon began to look as if the whole of the eastern wing of Dragonskeep might fall to the dragonknights.

Mezereon and his commanders were in a state of great alarm, and although they still had many thousands of warriors stationed throughout the remainder of the garrison to call upon, Halmarand's formidable reputation and his astonishing success so far against them, filled the Winter leaders minds only with thoughts of capitulation and flight.

The matter was finally settled by the return of the rebels. A renewed offensive, inspired by the glorious spectacle of the 'lion flight' in action against the goblin hordes, was launched by the combined forces of the windsprites, carrier-dragons and free-dwarfs.

The carrier-dragons had not wasted the time intervening since their last assault, Charlock, with a few of his fellows, had flown hundreds of leagues along the great trench of dragongorge to the cliffs of the crested dragons and enlisted their help in the struggle against Mezereon. The prince of the carriers now returned with a vast flock of sacrospines; hawk dragons, jewel dragons, white dragons, kirrocks, swifts, sky-dancers, all flocking together into a thick bristling swarm, hungry for revenge against the evil Mezereon.

This was their opportunity to force the Dark Sorcerer to answer for the thousands of young dragons he had stolen from them with his snowdragon raiding parties. Charlock had rallied fighting dragons from every species that dwelled within striking distance of the great castle. The noise of their combined anger shattered the air like splitting rock, and when the first of the Winter warriors laid eyes on the great pall of winged beasts rising like the shadow of death from the depths of the gorge, the last remnants of courage abandoned them and they threw down their weapons and wept.

The dwarfs made their triumphant return into battle by creeping through the secret tunnels which wormed their way into the thick armour of the fortress. This serious breach of Dragonskeep defences did little to improve the already flagging morale of its defenders. The short, grim fighters decided to work their way downwards rather than up, to try and reach the expansive dungeons, wherein languished hundreds of their kind, and thousands of other prisoners; all potential weapon bearers who the dwarfs knew would be only too eager to join the uprising.

The windsprites, now charged with renewed vigour since the triumphant return of Judruff, fell upon the north face of the great garrison, each flier armed with a bow and a swift arm, peppering the towering ramparts that rose before them with a constant hail of arrows. Flying in small harrying flocks, that darted skilfully about the towers and turrets, they were too fleet for the responding bursts of black arrows that arced angrily after them. With the King once more at their head, the falcon warriors returned with a spirited offensive, the air about the black defenders sheltering behind the walls screaming with the song of their arrows.

Gradually the enemy was driven higher and higher into the castle on all sides, until the only resistance that remained was a hardcore of elite warriors concentrated inside the impregnable confines of the High Keep. Halmarand was surprised that as yet they had seen nothing of the fierce, ice-breathing snowdarts that Dragonskeep had long boasted of, although he had an intuitive feeling he knew why they had been saved.

When the fighting outside the High Keep was finally brought to an end, a great host of dragonknights, dragonsteeds, gorge dragons, dwarfs, fliers and assorted rebels and prisoners massed about its grim walls, to launch the last assault of the momentous battle against the Captains of Winter.

Suddenly, an eruption of white wings burst from the roof of the keep, a surging plume of snowdragons, punching into the air like a rising white fountain. The allied forces immediately tensed themselves for a vicious last pitched-battle, but when the towering column of white beasts eventually shattered into an exploding star of dispersing bodies, it became startlingly clear that this was not an attack, but a mass escape.

As Halmarand had secretly feared, the swift white dragons had been held back as vehicles of flight for the Winter commanders, Mezereon and his captains unwilling to send their last means of escape into battle. The general's knights gave spirited pursuit but he knew that his 'lions' and the dragons from the gorge were no match in speed for the sleek snowdarts who could outpace the wind.

Even though he had just led the liberation of Dragonskeep, the last great stronghold of the Winter armies, it was with a heavy heart that the old veteran stood upon its highest ramparts and watched the disappearing streaks of white melting into the darkening skyscape of the evening; the remaining arch-captains of Winter making good their escape.

As a succession of High Councils followed that first momentous gathering, the glorious assembly raised and discussed many important issues concerning the plight of the Commonlands.

The Wizards spoke of the yet to be defeated power of Winter, for until Vrorst's great Fire Orb was recovered, his threat to peace in Enchantica could not be lifted. They urged the former allies of Vrorst who were present at the Grand Discourse to persuade their brother monarchs still at war, to end the bloody struggle and join with the Golden Alliance. The Three Lords also appealed for the north kings to hand over the evil architects of Vrorst's former empire, who they might be tempted to protect. Such dangerous individuals would now only scheme to prolong the season of white, and attempt whatever desperate feats they could to sabotage the coming of the Great Thaw.

Just as the Wizards had hoped and predicted, the Great Council was deemed a glorious success by all who visited the draped halls of the Silk Palace. The cause of peace and reconciliation was genuinely furthered and strengthened, in the presence, and under the benevolent yet irresistible authority, of the three Lords of the Seasons.

One morning, there was a great uproar and commotion when three huge beings stole everyone's attention by arriving unannounced and swooping low over the blazing Silk Palace, their vast wings parting the warm air with a thrilling roar. The magnificent dragons circled the immense field of patterned peaks, their huge wheeling forms of gold, green and red whipping up a whirlwind of excitement, and when they finally alighted on the three open spaces that had been specially set aside for the purpose of receiving airborne visitors; Carobus, Hoolock and Perslane were discovered as their passengers.

Jonquil and Rattajack wasted no time in renewing their fond acquaintances with the three Guardians, and for their part the great beasts were overjoyed to see both companions alive and well after all of their mind-boggling adventures. The grievous injuries received by the dragons during their valiant defence of the Sacred Vessels, especially those sustained by Snarlgard, had been fully healed by Carobus and his brother High Wizards. They had worked tirelessly on the dragons' wounds since their arrival at the island on the black galleons, and now they were all three as strong and majestic as ever.

A touching scene was played out when the Lords of the Seasons strode forth from their luxurious shelter to greet their powerful creations. The immense dragons bowed their great heads to lay their chins gently upon the Wizards' outstretched hands, and in the softest tones that only the dragons could hear, the three lords bestowed their welcome.

The Three Guardians had been summoned for a purpose, a great task awaited the Forces of Light; the reopening of the crystal mines. For until the three lords could once again draw upon the enchantment of the Treeflame, Sunfire and Bloodstar crystals hidden within the deep seams of rock in the secret tunnels, Enchantica could not be delivered from the curse of Winter. Not only had Vrorst's minions sealed the entrances with great rockslides and no doubt caused large amounts of damage within, they had set a mighty sentinel at the mouth of the main cave in the Crystal Valley; a devastating mountain of a creature that squirmed with seven, terrifying heads . . . .the awesome dragon, Massazauga.

Jonquil was amazed to hear Orolan's description of the ferocious beast that the enemy had installed at the entrance to the mines. The immense creature was like seven Guardians of the Vessels in one dragon, able to breathe fire through each of its terrible heads at once. No mortal army could ever face the wrath of Massazauga, for the great beast could attack its foes with sheets of flame in all directions, and the heat of its fire was as the bowels of a volcano.

Arangast suddenly lifted his great head to the sky and belched forth a searing tower of white flame that boiled the air into a frenzy. Then he cast an eye to the banf and the terragon and muttered with a sparkle, "That for Massazauga!"

That same evening, as the sun melted on to the western horizon as a glorious inferno, broad searching beams sweeping out across the plain and piercing the carmine sky with a volley of radiant spears, the air above the city was suddenly filled with a whirlwind of fire. Golden armour, caught by the sun, blazed in mesmeric circles, a stunning wheel of winged silhouettes slowly dropping from the burning skyscape in a great unwinding spiral, flowing to the ground as a glittering golden stream.

Halmarand and the knights of his victorious 'lion flight' had arrived from Dragonskeep, and they fell upon the landing grounds within the sprawl of patterned tents with a storm of wafting wingbeats; the revered general leaping spryly from his magnificent mount and striding purposefully towards the rise of the Wizards' shimmering mansion, accompanied by an entourage of lieutenants.

For many days, Halmarand was locked in close conference with the Three Wizards, for at the first High Council to follow his arrival, the veteran warrior-general had been unanimously voted Supreme Commander of the Golden Alliance forces. There were many pressing issues to discuss, many of which could bring great influence to bear on the future of Enchantica.

The restoration of the crystal mines was one of the most urgent, and it was decided that as soon as the Orb of Winter had been recovered and made safe by the Wizards, the former Guardians of the Crystal Vessels; Arangast, Gorgoyle and Snarlgard, should be despatched to the Crystal Valley to do battle with the seven headed monster.

Once the three dragon princes learned of their quest, they shook the air with their roars of approval, eager to undo the hurt that Winter had inflicted upon their masters when the Sacred Vessels had been stolen and then destroyed.

The Wizards conveyed to Halmarand their deep concern over the whereabouts of Vrorst's Fire Orb; especially now that Mezereon had fled from Dragonskeep and was known to have been the intended recipient of the mighty power globe.

One of the general's first acts in his new lofty position was to instigate a massive hunt for Mezereon and the remaining high captains still at liberty. A vast net was to be thrown over Enchantica, linked by power crystals and fast dragonflights, to ensnare the fugitives.

The fairies and the elves were to scour the forests, the nomads the wide expanses of the plains, the dwarfs and eastern men the mountainous regions, the merfolk the seas; and those places inaccessible to pedestrian scouts, the dragonlords would cover on their soaring mounts.

During their stay at the Canvas City, Jonquil and Rattajack had been greatly intrigued and inspired by all the talk of battle and daring exploits afoot; and a part of Jonquil longed to ask Halmarand to find room for Rattajack and himself amongst his dragonflight; but then a nagging voice at the back of the banf's mind kept reminding him of the assurance he had given to Meadolarne . . . to cease his wandering.

Both Jonquil and Rattajack had taken an instant liking to Halmarand, and Rattajack had struck up quite a friendship with the general's fearsome dragonsteed, Agamanthra. The two scaleskins swapped tales in their inimitable silent tongue for hours at a time; in fact the terragon became quite a celebrity with most of the 'lions' in Halmarand's flight; listening intently to their battle sagas and tales of Dragongorge . . . a subject to tug at the hearts of all dragons. Then, for his part, Rattajack would speak to them of banfs, wizards, mushrooms, forests and anything else that came to mind, all of which for some reason the terragon couldn't fathom, the host of ferocious battle-chargers seemed to find intensely interesting.

Although the general could be grim and officious at times, burdened as he was with his important new role and responsibilities, when the day was done, and the old warrior relaxed with his pipe in the warm evening air, he displayed a most attractive quality to the two companions . . . he was a great storyteller.

A few restful hours spent with Halmarand, and Jonquil soon felt that his and Rattajack's adventures in the world had been both tame and inconsequential compared to a warrior-general's lifetime of bold escapades. Rattajack smiled to himself when he heard the general duplicate stories that his dragon had already spoken of, although the two versions almost always compared word for word. Such was the enormity of the great hazards and trials that Halmarand and Agamanthra regularly faced together, that exaggeration would have been superfluous. The general and the dragon's long tales of heroism and derring-do lit up the evenings for the two companions and the more time they spent with them the more their respect and affection grew for the veteran warlord, and Rattajack's for his valiant battlesteed.

It was whilst in Halmarand's company, late one night, that Jonquil and Rattajack paid a visit to a very solemn place in the Canvas City, that neither of them had known existed.

The Silk Palace was not only divided by width but also by height; constructed around a vast central pavilion . . . the imposing space used for the High Councils, a raised honeycomb of chambers and corridors had been crafted from various wooden platforms and draped screens. Situated within one of the high canvas towers towards the summit of the great golden canopy, was a chamber adorned with the most surprising choice of colours. Whereas the majority of the Wizards' dwelling was decorated with exquisite tapestries and embroideries naturally combining materials of gold, green and red, this lofty vault was hung with towering pleated lengths of blue, white and silver . . . the shades of Winter.

It was one of those austere, peaceful places that demands whispers, and after the dazzling gaiety of the Seasons of Light, the cool silence of the Winter drapery caused an icy shiver to scamper along Jonquil's spine.

Halmarand stepped slowly into the large chamber, his mouth drawn into a tight line, his eyes, fixed rigidly ahead. Jonquil glanced at Rattajack and found the terragon in a similarly transfixed state of solemnity. They were both staring at a pale, diaphanous veil draped across their view, halving the tall chamber. For a few moments, Jonquil's eyes refused to see beyond this thin, pearlescent sheet, which shimmered softly as it rippled in a secret draught; but then a shaft of moonlight suddenly pierced the gloom behind the transparent barrier, stealing in through an open vent in the vaulted roof, and as it did so two icy fingers gripped the banf's throat.

Standing atop a short flight of steps rising in the centre of the high room, now bathed in a single beam of pale light, was a long oblong dais. A rich mantle of deep blue velvet fell in neat lines from its stark geometric shape, to lie in perfect creases upon a descending white star of delicate, silver-threaded tapestry, which partly covered the rise of polished stairs. Suspended from high above, an extravagant canopy, edged in silver fringe and braid, its luxuriant folds of glistening fabric tied and gathered into embellished arcs of pristine pleats; its snaking drapes, falling in long sweeping curves to frame the angles of the low base.

The four corners of the summit of the stepped platform were marked with tall candles, each of the long wax stems held by elaborate silver stands fashioned into the likenesses of obeisant dragons; the steady flames of the candles burning with an icy blue light.

Reclining upon the imposing catafalque, dressed in majestic robes of white and silver that spilled over the low walls of the base in glittering slopes, was a kingly figure. His bearded head, encapsulated by a wizard's peak, resting upon a cushion of silver silk, and his arms clothed in ruched sheaths of white lying neatly at his sides.

If Jonquil had not known otherwise he might have thought the resplendent lord only sleeping, such was the air of peace and contentment he exuded; but despite the tranquillity of the exquisitely draped resting place, the presence of the once mighty wizard still raised a rash of goose flesh on the banf's skin.

"Do you wish to see closer?" Halmarand's reverent tones asked Jonquil.

The banf nodded, and the general parted the delicate screen for the two companions to enter the silken mausoleum. Although the body of Vrorst still commanded a certain power, when Jonquil and Rattajack gazed upon his reclining form they saw that the malevolence and darkness that once ruled the great sorcerer had departed from his bones. Enveloped in the glowing haze radiating from the moonstruck brilliance of his white garments, Vrorst looked more like a fallen king than a defeated villain; his features noble, not cruel. Attached to a chain of glittering snowflakes draped across the sorcerer's chest, was a large Enchantica Rose, fashioned from solid silver. Set into its heart, was a dazzling Snowstar; the power crystal Vrorst had first adopted to create his season before he was seduced by the awesome malevolence of the Blackhearts. Vrorst was robed as he must have been in the very early days of Enchantica, when the Brotherhood of the Wizards numbered four not three.

The Wizards had chosen to honour their once brother and grieve the death that they had not wished for. Vrorst and his blackened soul had been parted, and his body, now free of its evil fire, had been reverently presented to the world as a memorial to the once great and worthy Lord of Winter.

Jonquil and Rattajack forged new friendships and rekindled many old ones during their time at the Great Council. The banf and the terragon had spent endless fireside nights listening to Judruff, Charlock and Tarbet's tales of the battle for Dragonskeep; the heroes of the great battle having followed after Halmarand to attend the Grand Discourse; the dwarflord and his brothers having travelled as the carrier-dragons' nervous but determined passengers. Jonquil and Rattajack loved every day that they spent at the Canvas City, in the company of the great and the wise, but inevitably the time came for the two companions to leave. Meadolarne, their family and friends were at home, patiently waiting for their return, and Jonquil and Rattajack decided that they had kept their loved ones waiting long enough.

When the day finally arrived for them to leave, the banf and the terragon took with them a lavish hoard of fabulous gifts and good wishes; including a stunning delsidian coat, crafted especially for Jonquil in the workshops of the secret forest kingdom behind the falls, presented to the banf by Queen Trinia on behalf of the fairy realms. Jonquil was overjoyed with this princely gift and was told by the Three Wizards that it was indeed the most wondrous and precious of things.

"A delsidian coat," Trinia added, "is made from enchanted stone. Its unique and extraordinary qualities will reveal themselves at unexpected moments."

Then a great mystery was solved for Jonquil when the Summer Wizard presented him with a small gift of his own.

It was a diminutive crystal globe and Jonquil recognised it immediately as the one formerly belonging to Hexerne.

"It is only fitting, my friend," Orolan told the banf. "That you should keep the spy!"

Jonquil stared at the Wizard with surprise.

"The spy?" He asked.

"The eye at Vrorst's shoulder!" Orolan exclaimed. "You had been wondering about it, had you not?"

Jonquil stared incredulously at the diminutive crystal globe in his palm, glinting with all innocence in the bright morning light.

"This was the spy? But I thought it was a person!" The banf gasped.

"Aha! So did Vrorst," Orolan explained. "The Orb of Winter tried to reveal the small crystal to the Ice Sorcerer, but because he was expecting to see a face revealed to him, and was so arrogantly confident that he was right, he blinded himself to the truth. It was through our agents that the orb found its way to Vrorst, and subsequently to Hexerne and then to you. We had no idea of the important part this simple crystal was to play in the fate of the Ice Sorcerer. We had intended it simply as a spy, a listening orb, to eavesdrop on Vrorst's councils. We instilled it with no more power than a toy. It was through your

steadfast courage, Jonquil, that it became Vrorst's downfall and our salvation."

The banf stared at his bewildered reflection in the polished skin of the orb, then Rattajack's face appeared next to his own, and they both gazed in renewed wonder at the little thing that had caused the Ice Lord so much anguish and disruption; 'the eye at Vrorst's shoulder'. For Jonquil and Rattajack, the simplicity of the device only served to illustrate the great wisdom and power of the Three Wizards; subtle and ingenious were their methods, patient and effective; much like the glory of the seasons themselves.

"The orb's days of espionage and secrecy are over." Orolan continued. " I have transformed it into a seeing globe, so that you may never lose sight of your friends here at the Canvas City when you are at home in the forest. Or lose sight of your loved ones in the forest, if ever you should find yourself away from home!"

Jonquil looked up at the Summer Wizard, and there was a distinct twinkle in Orolan's eye.

And so, with many fond farewells and an assurance from the Three Wizards that they would all meet again before too long, Jonquil and Rattajack returned to the dark eaves of their vast forest home and retraced their steps once more along the path of flowers that led to the Banf Kingdom.

The great lords were to be surprised themselves one bright morning when a great excitement of mer-folk surged along the rivers leading towards the Silk Palace. Olm and Sylphen led a great host of their people through the crystal water towing a succession of floating barges in their wake. Much to the Three Wizards astonishment and delight displayed on the richly adorned floating rafts were the three Sacred Vessels made anew. The mer-folk had forced their way in to the Bay of Voices and scoured every last stretch of the submerged basin to find the precious fragments of the power chests. Then with a degree of skill and ingenuity that was unmatched in Enchantica, the loyal swimmers had painstakingly repaired the ancient vessels and made them whole again.

The Three Wizards were deeply moved by this deed and the strong affection they already bore for the people of the undersea, soared to new heights.

The great gathering of wizards and monarchs was to remain on the verdant plateau for seven, long, productive years before the three Lords of the Seasons decided it was time to seek for a permanent home for their power.

During that time, Halmarand pressed on with his search for Mezereon and moved his centre of operations to the ancient fortress of Dragonskeep, and Jonquil and Rattajack set about enjoying their self proclaimed retirement. Enjoying the good life in the Banf Kingdom, and looking forward to a long, peaceful, uneventful future in their sleepy banf village, which predictably was not to be.

The Adventure Continues . . . . . .

Seven Years On

Stars of sunlight sparkled through a swaying canopy of emerald leaves, to play across a cradle of wrinkled green boughs as a softly fluttering fusion of light and shade. Jonquil was lounging in the generous arms of a green oak on the trail to their village, in dreamy half slumber, a perfect picture of comfort and ease; a shallow trough lined with hoarded leaves for a nest.

His terragon companion, too hungry for idleness, was snuffling through the ground cover beneath the tree, convinced he had caught the scent of a Fallen Star.

As soon as Jonquil could summon up the energy he intended to mooch amongst the ferns and herb hedges for wild onion bulbs and root truffles to roast in a mushroom stew for their supper; but for the moment he just had to rest; for the sun was so warm and relaxing and the music of the breeze-kissed foliage so soothing that to move a muscle would have been a sin.

As a reward for their bravery, the Spring Wizard had bestowed his gift on Jonquil and Rattajack; a private Spring, in anticipation of the real thing that was to come, for the Kingdom of the Banfs. A gift of enchantment that filled the luxuriant canopies with birdsong and the verdant glades with flowers.

Jonquil and Rattajack had enjoyed re-discovering the many delights of their forest home since their return from the excitement of the Great Council. The happy years that followed had been spent in the blissful occupation of simply doing nothing but forage for food, climb trees, swim in the pools and rivers, doze in the filtered sunlight of a warm afternoon, and relish the company of friends and family.

Jonquil's feet occasionally itched to wander, when images from past adventures flickered uninvited to mind, but otherwise he was content.

The banf slowly stretched his languid body back to life and peeled open his sleepy eyes. A Spring butterfly tipped with orange flapped across his view, trying this way and that in its random, undecided journey. Jonquil followed it with his eyes until it drew his attention to the busy green form of the terragon, who seemed to have been hunting the same Fallen Star for the best part of the afternoon. Swinging his legs out of his comfortable bed, the banf carefully descended the broad trunk of the green oak and joined his friend.

They were just over half a days walk from Oak-Goldeneye, returning from one of their frequent sojourns at Merlion's oak palace, where they were able to hear the news from outside the forest, brought to the banf king by a regular succession of messengers from the Canvas City. Mezereon and his fellow fugitives were still at large, but the arm of the Alliance was long and extending further day by day, it was surely only a matter of time before the Dark Sorcerer was caught in Halmarand's tightening net.

The afternoon shadows were beginning to lengthen, the waning sun peeping through the crazed roof of the forest canopy to paint the leaf-strewn avenue that snaked on ahead between the trees with a delicate web of projected lace, winking here and there with occasional spills of leaked sunlight. The orange-tip butterfly had found a friend and was dancing a mesmerising, twirling duet along the slanting beams of golden light, the enticing pas-de-deux coaxing the two companions to follow them into the flourishing flora of the favoured forest.

Suddenly Rattajack stiffened to attention, and for an instant Jonquil thought he could hear it too; a shrill, resonant note, almost inaudible, and clearly emanating from a great distance. The banf and the terragon stared at each other for a while neither quite sure whether they recognised the sound or not, but when the note wasn't repeated, they were both inclined to forget it and set off into the undergrowth to find their supper.

The next morning saw a vibrant chorus of sweet birdsong rousing the two companions in good spirits, which soared to even greater heights when a victorious Rattajack trotted proudly back to Jonquil with his elusive Fallen Star in his mouth. An early morning gallop had ended with the terragon literally falling over the delicious mushroom that he'd spent long hours searching for the day before. Consequently Jonquil was able to prepare an unexpectedly sumptuous breakfast for them both to give an extremely handsome start to the day.

Unfortunately, Jonquil and Rattajack had travelled only a short distance along the trail before the bright sun of their happiness was assailed by a menacing cloud of darkness.

The two companions were deep in the throes of a particularly vigorous game of treevine football, neither protagonist above snatching the ball and flying with it into the lower branches, a manoeuvre that was definitely against the rules; and a foul that only Rattajack had been able to commit previous to Jonquil's wings. Then just as the banf was chasing the terragon who had the ball wedged firmly in his mouth, a desperate cry rang out in the distance.

Both stopped dead in their tracks. A voice so full of pain and anguish was never heard within the confines of the protected kingdom, and as such was unsettling and fearful.

The keen eyes of the two companions focused on the two figures of a banf and a terragon racing towards them along the trail. It was Peart, Meadolarne's young cousin, and his faithful friend, Jotterel, and as the banf and the terragon broke with their horse-play and hurried to meet them, they could see by Peart and Jotterel's obvious grief that they were burdened by the gravest news. When they reached the two companions the young banf virtually fell into Jonquil's arms and was so distressed and exhausted by his great exertion that for a while he could do no more than gasp for air.

When he finally caught his breath and could speak, he gripped Jonquil tightly by the arms and communicated his dreadful tidings to the banf . . . Meadolarne was missing.

Jonquil refused to believe his ears, but one look at the condition of the two young messengers, who had clearly run without rest all the way from their village, confirmed that Peart was in earnest.

"Missing!" Jonquil cried. "Peart, what are you saying?"

"I . . . I think she's b'been stolen!" Peart stammered breathlessly.

Despite a wave of panic threatening to engulf his senses, Jonquil did his best to stay calm and encourage the young banf to tell his tale, slowly and clearly. Then, after gleaning what information he could from the exhausted Peart, before the tearful young banf finally collapsed from his ordeal, Jonquil left the wilting youngster in the care of Rattajack and Jotterel, and flew like the wind along the winding trail that led to Oak-Goldeneye.

There was no sign of the banfina anywhere in the village or its outskirts. Her mother, Opolla and Old Yargle knew little more than Jonquil, and all of their searches had also proved fruitless. Peart, in his greatly agitated state, had kept referring to a 'dark lady' in the trees. It appeared that Meadolarne had been able to see this mystery figure but Peart had not. The banfina had claimed that the lady was in distress, crying for help, calling Meadolarne by name; and according to the young banf just before his beautiful cousin disappeared she had seemed distracted and distant; as if after hearing the secret voice, she could hear nothing else.

Whipping up a storm of old leaves, Jonquil tore into the outlying forest to search for clues. For the next few days he scoured every inch of the patch of forest into which the banfina was thought to have gone, but the veteran snow in the forest, which had remained unthawed since its falling, still bore the scars of the great battle that had been fought beyond the Ring all those years before. It was impossible to distinguish which tracks were fresh and which ancient. The banf couldn't help a shiver of fear as his eyes fell upon the giant prints of a charging gracklin. Even the blood of the enemy, which had soaked into the snow in deep, ruby stains looked as if it had been spilt only yesterday. A terrifying thought suddenly struck Jonquil but almost as soon as it occurred to him he dismissed it from his mind. Meadolarne was alive, he was sure of it.

Jonquil was just about to give up his search and return to the village to plan his next course of action when his sharp eyes saw something small and dark hanging by a slender thread from a low branch.

The banf gingerly approached, hardly daring to hope that it might be an artefact belonging to Meadolarne to aid him with his search. Suddenly a gasp of recognition burst from his throat and his shaking hand reached out to grasp Meadolarne's whistle, the one he had so lovingly carved for her from a slipper nut.

There could be no doubt that the whistle had been placed there deliberately, for its mushroom leather thong had been tied with a firm knot to the thin branch. The carved nut had clearly been left there as a sign for Jonquil, the only question was, by whom? Meadolarne or her abductor . . . the mysterious lady.

Jonquil gave a sharp blast on the whistle, half expecting Meadolarne's sweet voice to echo back to him through the trees in response; and as he did so he suddenly remembered the shrill note he and Rattajack had heard on the trail. He was almost certain that what they had heard had been the voice of the carved slipper nut; but had Meadolarne sounded it to summon help? Or had it been an act of defiance from the dark figure that had taken her.

Either way, Jonquil was certain the banfina was alive, and whatever the kidnapper's motives may have been, for the time being it seemed they intended to keep her that way.

Suddenly Jonquil remembered the seeing orb given to him by Orolan, and he raced back to Oak-Goldeneye to find the precious globe amongst his carefully stored gifts from Merlion and the Great Council.

Jonquil held the small orb up to his eyes and gently called Meadolarne's name. As he did so, the crystal interior of the shiny sphere filled with mist and then an image slowly began to build upon the pale screen.

The beautiful face looked drawn and pale, and large eyes dull and sad. The banfina's gorgeous mane of auburn hair had been wrapped in a servant's turban. These pictures were puzzling indeed, but at least they proved that Meadolarne was alive. Then Jonquil conjured up the face of her abductor and a gasp of shock burst from his mouth; the face looked exactly like that of Tuatara, and yet the banf could see that it was not Tuatara, although the girl's resemblance was uncanny.

After meeting up with Rattajack and Peart, Jonquil decided that his best course of action was to fly to Dragonskeep. Although he couldn't be absolutely certain, the banf suspected that Meadolarne had been taken by the enemy, and if so their exit from the forest would have been swift and pre-planned. Therefore there could be no merit in wasting time searching through the concealed wastes of the Green Sky. Jonquil knew that Halmarand was conducting the search for the remaining Winter Captains still at large at the great fortress in the north, and resolved to start his quest there.

Even in defeat, it seemed Vrorst's servants were still capable of inflicting their malice upon the innocent. At Dragonskeep, Jonquil hoped to hear news of the Winter fugitives, and possibly piece together a trail that might lead him to Meadolarne.

Rattajack, of course, insisted on making the long journey with him, and the banf tarried only long enough to put on his enchanted delsidian coat, his precious acorn-lantern and the pouch he had made to carry the seeing orb.

Before they left, Jonquil squeezed one of the terragon's long pointed ears and said to him with a sigh;

"Here we go again, Ratters!"

Then in a flurry of feathers and green, scaly skin, the two companions were gone.

The Beautiful Ale-Wench

The main room of the tavern was dim and thick with pipe smoke. The yawning mouth of the open stone fireplace, banked high with giant logs and rolling with sheets of fire, painted the beamed interior and the riotous crowds that filled it with a flickering amber glow. The outer walls of the main space were divided into clandestine stalls and cubby-holes, drenched in darkness and ripe for secrecy or felonious meetings.

Seated alone in the darkest of these threatening booths, the anonymous figure watched the room. Secreted within the blackest pool of shadow, his face buried inside a deep cowl, and wrapped with a drab, featureless cloak, the stranger almost achieved invisibility.

His eyes were drawn again to the tall, elegant ale-wench, who had previously caught his eye; so incongruous amongst her lesser peers. She gracefully picked her way through the romping clientele, aloof and serene, with an intriguing air of sadness, delivering foaming jugs of the foul beer they called Shashlick as if she was granting royal favours.

To the eyes of the stranger she was so unlike any of the other tavern staff, who were nearly all plump-cheeked, buxom and clumsy, and had to wrestle past a forest of clinging, groping hands, fending off drunken advances with brazen oaths, barn door swipes and well practised punches. The tall ale-wench seemed to glide through the uproarious chaos, unmolested and untroubled by the rough tribes of farmers and farmers' sons that clamoured and roared about her. They instantly responded to her cool demeanour and offered her only boyish smiles, rather than the hard slaps and lewd pinches they gave to the other serving wenches.

Even the proprietor of the bawdy establishment, who did little more than bawl and rage at all and sundry all evening seemed to treat her with special deference, politely asking her to serve their customers, rather than threatening her with a beating within an inch of her life if she didn't move her fat behind, like he did all of the others.

The quiet stranger was struck again by her loveliness and her uncanny resemblance to Tuatara, more profound than ever since she had grown to womanhood; the tall, statuesque figure, the pale, unattainable beauty, the long cascade of silky hair . . . the colour of star-spangled midnight.

During their time together at the Throne Citadel it had often been speculated amongst Vrorst's captains that the beautiful orphan was indeed the daughter of the Ice Witch, the rumours fuelled by the fact that Tuatara had no memory of her former existence before becoming a servant of Vrorst.

He called to the girl with his silent inner voice, her back straightened immediately and she turned to stare coldly into the dark corner where he sat. The girl stood frozen with apprehension, unmoving within a sea of flailing arms and swaying bodies, and then slowly, cautiously she started towards him, the crowd unconsciously breaking and closing around her as she stepped commandingly through them.

The dark figure feasted his eyes on the slender silhouette that stood before him, she had grown into a beautiful young woman, and it was that same uncommon beauty that would eventually betray her.

"It's been a long time, Hexerne," he said.

The girl visibly winced at the mention of that name and she threw anxious glances about her as if fearing imminent discovery.

"Seven years!" The dark stranger gasped.

"You are mistaken, Sir," she told him. "My name is Luth!"

The hooded figure said nothing for a few moments but then motioned to the seat opposite.

"As you wish," he said and then added the command. "Sit down!"

The girl hesitated, but then fear or intrigue or perhaps a grain of recognition persuaded her, and with another uncertain glance to the room lowered herself on to the wooden bench.

"You are not safe here!" The figure continued. "This is no sanctuary for you. You are too obvious."

"Who are you?" The girl demanded.

"Do you not know me?"

The girl's eyes narrowed with suspicion and her face tilted to scrutinise the black void that cloaked the stranger's features. His gloved hands lifted to the hem of his deep hood and slowly pulled it back a little to reveal his countenance. As soon as her bewildered expression changed to recognition, he let the hood fall back to its original position and extinguished himself once more.

"Vakari?" She whispered.

"Like you . . . er . . . Luth," he softly replied. "I find my former name no longer an asset to me!"

"Why have you come here?"

"I have come for you," he told her.

The girl's face became troubled and wary.

"They have accepted me here," she said after an anguished silence.

Vakari made no response but leant to one side to see past the girl into the smoky, firelit room, the crowds of intoxicated revellers more raucous than ever.

"An ale-wench?" he sneered at last. "Is that your future? To waste your life serving worthless peasants?"

Hexerne's gaze suddenly dropped to the table and her glassy eyes stared hard into the blank shadow of the wood, blinking hard to fight back the tears.

"Or perhaps you'll marry a farmer's son?" Vakari cruelly continued. "What an ambition! If that is your wish, I see you have the choice of many!"

The girl lifted her heavy stare once more to the black hole of Vakari's hood.

"I have no future!" she said in a flat, trembling voice.

The hooded man then grasped one of her slender wrists with a large gloved hand.

"There is always a future, Hexerne!" He hissed. "Be it black or bright! You must choose!"

The girl's eyes burned with alarm.

"Why do you say I am not safe here?" she asked trying to pull her arm free of his grip. Vakari released her and eased back from the table.

"This drunken rabble may be too blind with beer to find their way to the door, but do not make the mistake of thinking that they are ignorant of you. I have watched them. They treat you differently because you are different, they have eyes enough to see that.

Compared to these peasants and yokels, you shine! You shine like a jewel amongst clinker. They may be too drunk or too stupid to make anything of it now, but one day, Hexerne, your beauty and brightness will attract the attention of the more perceptive."

Hexerne's eyes already moist with despair, bore into the darkness of Vakari's face, wide with fear and pleading. This reaction was just what the hooded man had hoped for, and so he continued.

"There is a new sun burning in the sky, Little Sorceress. Every day it grows stronger and brighter, illuminating more and more of the world, and soon even this insignificant cluster of shacks, that you have chosen for your disguise, will come under its gaze." He paused to allow his words their full effect. "And then there will be no shadows left to hide you!"

The girl's face crumpled into tears and she buried her head in her hands.

"Oh, why did it have to be lost?" She cried. "Why wasn't it delivered to Mezereon as He commanded?"

A significant silence passed between them, every empty moment loaded with tension, then the atmosphere perceptibly chilled and when Vakari spoke again there was a definite note of anger in his voice.

"What makes you think he doesn't have it?"

The girl's tear-stained face lifted to him again, and her pain slowly grew into confusion, her red eyes trying vainly to perceive just what lay behind Vakari's question.

"Well . . . " she began uncertainly. "If Mezereon had it there would be no peace for these mortal fools to revel in," at this she casually gestured behind her to the sprawling celebration. "There would be war! The might of Winter rising again to take back what was rightfully His . . . !"

"Indeed?" Vakari sneered.

"If he had the Orb," she concluded.

Vakari leaned towards her across the table and as he did so sparks of firelight ignited in his dark eyes.

"Only if he was prepared to use it," he quietly stated.

Hexerne was bemused.

"How could he have it and not use it?"

"How indeed?"

This time it was Hexerne who reached across and grasped Vakari's arm, her sharp eyes incandescent with blue fire. How like the Ice Witch she looked now, the hooded man thought to himself, as a an involuntary rash of fear dashed along his skin.

"Are you saying that Mezereon does have the Orb?" she hissed.

Vakari quickly swept his eyes up and down the bar to make sure of their privacy.

"He has had it these past seven years!" came the frustrated reply.

Hexerne could restrain herself no longer and with a sudden burst of rage jumped to her feet and screamed "No!"

Vakari's nervous reaction to her outcry emphasised her folly and she quickly turned to the crowd to see if she had attracted anyone's attention, but she needn't have worried, the ale-blunted senses of the languid gathering had not been even slightly aroused. Half of them now unconscious, the other half engaged in singing mournful songs, oblivious to anything but their own wailing voices.

Vakari drew her back down to her seat and spoke to her in a low urgent voice.

"We found him several days ago in a tumbled down shack, high up in the mountains north of here. We have tried in vain ever since that time to persuade him to embrace the power of the Orb."

"How can it be?" Hexerne sighed wearily. "How can he have possessed the Orb all this time and not taken charge of its power. Seven years the enemy have had to heal their wounds, and now they've grown strong again. He should have used it the moment the dragon brought it to him!"

Vakari stared at her for a few thoughtful, silent moments.

"You must come with us!" He told her. "Now that you are . . . older! You may succeed where we have failed."

"We?"

"Wargren is with me. We have two snowdragons waiting on the outskirts of this wretched settlement . . . we leave before the dawn."

Vakari rose as if to leave but then halted as another thought occurred to him, he looked down at her to speak but this time his voice sounded distant and a little uncertain.

"It's strange," he began. "The Orb, it seems different now than when Vrorst possessed it, somehow . . . alive!" He paused as if waiting for some reaction from the girl. "It spoke to me. It told me how to find you."

"I knew the enemy did not have it!" Hexerne quietly declared, ignoring Vakari's disquiet. "I could feel it!"

Vakari made to move again.

"I have someone with me," Hexerne announced. "A servant!" She said unconvincingly. "Her name is Stobe."

"Servants are the least of our worries!" Vakari snapped. "Leave her behind."

"She is important to me!" Hexerne protested. "She may prove important to all of us. I will not leave without her."

The hooded man exhaled a deep sigh and shrugged his heavily mantled shoulders.

"Just as you please!" he crooned. "But she'll have to ride with Wargren. Remember, we leave before dawn!"

The cool draught of Vakari's departure rode across Hexerne's face and then she was alone. She sat in the shadowy booth for some time brooding on the tidings that her dark visitor had brought to her. A cold, raging fire was building in her breast, and her fixed stare was like a blast of icy wind. Soon the tavern melted away until all she could see was Mezereon's simpering face, and her strong nails dug into the grain of the wooden table until sharp splinters crackled from its surface.

The Lair of the Serpents

Judruff and a small flight of falcons spotted Jonquil and Rattajack and swooped down to accompany them over the last few wingbeats of their long journey from the Banf Kingdom.

The giant fortress spilled over the craggy, northern lip of the steep chasm and spread out across the cliff top as a grim mountain of towers and battlements; isolated turrets and tooth edged walls rising amongst the surrounding buttresses of rock as if its outer parts had been set adrift from the main heap, or been allowed to melt into the jagged face of the cliffs. Dragonskeep had an almost organic, uncontrived demeanour, as if its grey fabric and structure had not so much been built on the steep bastions of rock but had grown from them.

If Old Yargle had been trying to describe the great fortress for his fireside audience, he might have said;

"Imagine the great grey building bricks of some giant infant, lovingly and carefully assembled into tall, neatly built walls, with even turrets and immaculately raised levels; square, ordered towers in pristine lines . . . all rising and combining to form a magnificent, soaring structure . . . then imagine the whole lot suddenly cast into sprawling disarray by a titanic temper tantrum . . . that was Dragonskeep!"

The one feature of the great garrison that could not fail to impress however was the immense dragons carved by ancient hands into the smooth sheets of stone that rose from the broken floor of the canyon; the vast sweeping arcs of their wings shielding the feet of the clinging castle.

The small group of fliers banked into a gusting wall of wind and allowed themselves to be carried to the beckoning mass of the High Keep. Wearily the two companions fluttered down on to the wooden platform which protruded like an extended tongue from the yawning gape of a dragonport.

Within the hour the two companions were warming their toes before a roaring blaze in Halmarand's lofty apartments, studying an array of detailed maps of the surrounding terrain, and quizzing the general about the progress of the hunt.

Mezereon had still not been found but fresh news of him filtered through to Halmarand's spies with almost every day that passed, numerous dragonflights already having been despatched that very morning to investigate a clutch of promising sightings in far, remote settlements.

Halmarand listened sympathetically to their plight but unfortunately had little or no news of the whereabouts of the other Winter servants or the mysterious 'dark lady'.

The banf and the terragon took the opportunity to familiarise themselves thoroughly with the general's maps, somehow feeling that such detailed knowledge could be vital for a successful conclusion to their quest.

After they had absorbed as much as possible, Jonquil decided to visit with Judruff whilst Rattajack disappeared to parley with the wise and perceptive Agamanthra, and learn the dragon's perspective on their difficult situation.

The windsprite king welcomed Jonquil into a small, cosy round tower, with a roaring fire and two comfortable sacks, stuffed with woodshavings. Judruff hurriedly thrust a bowl of piping hot spearherb tea (no prizes for guessing where that came from) into the banf's hand, guided him to one of the large bags, sat him down and without even an attempt at preamble, knowing what an insatiable devourer of stories Jonquil was, proceeded to tell him all about the horrors of Dragonskeep.

It was a subject, the banf was later to discover, that preoccupied almost everyone who dwelled in the vast stone vaults of the castle, and with good reason.

As a last defiant gesture to the victorious allied armies, the Dark Sorcerer had thrown the levers which operated the doors restraining the most dangerous products of his evil imagination.

The malignant spawn of his experiments spewed forth from the black mouths of their cages and pits, to slither, crawl or stride into the torchlight; trolls with two heads and four arms; fire-breathing goblins with leathery wings; wolves crossed with dragons, dragons crossed with snakes, snakes crossed with men and men crossed with wolves; an unholy community of bloodthirsty beings whose only purpose for living, once freed, was to exact revenge on the unwary for the crime of their creation.

All these, Mezereon deliberately released from their cells to haunt the labyrinthine roots of the garrison and wage war on its noble conquerors.

The monstrous, unnatural fruit of Mezereon's labours made short work of the first brave souls to venture below the level of the prison cells, to explore the forbidden chambers of the sorcerer's laboratories; and afterwards there wasn't a single resident of Dragonskeep who hadn't lain awake in his bed at night, wondering what might be stalking through the shadowy corridors outside his firmly bolted door.

Before Halmarand had made Dragonskeep his headquarters, successive commanders had organised regular expeditions to plumb the dangerous depths and brave the wrath of the terrible creatures raging unleashed in the dark bowels. Many unfortunates had lost their lives trying to rid the great castle of its evil pestilence, descending the black stairwells to confront the murderous brood with only sword and shield to protect them.

Within one day of the great general's residency, all access to the lower levels had been sealed, and the deformed monsters left to fight it out amongst themselves. Halmarand couldn't see why anymore valuable soldiers should risk their lives fighting with the demons, when left alone they would quite willingly destroy each other.

Judruff described to Jonquil the blood-chilling screams and terrifying roars that had risen through the fabric of the castle as, just as Halmarand had predicted, the monstrous host did battle with each other. For a whole month the slaughter continued, the dreadful cacophony of shrieks and wails invading the tranquillity of the day and shattering the quiet of the night. The awesome noise penetrated every chamber, pervading the thick walls and hallways to the very highest pinnacle of the massive building; there was nowhere that could offer respite from the ghastly din.

Then suddenly the raucous clammering ceased, the last of the horrific cries fading to a dying moan and then melting into silence. As soon as all was quiet, the general sent in the troops to end the misery of the wretched survivors, but they encountered precious few, and those they did find were already dying from mortal wounds.

"But what they did discover," Judruff continued, in the sort of voice he probably used to frighten windsprite children on ghoststory telling nights, "was evidence that before the lower chambers had been sealed, some of Mezereon's spawn had escaped into the prison levels and then most likely up into the main body of the fortress."

"Have they ever been seen?" Jonquil asked nervously.

"No, but I've heard that a few guards have gone missing on isolated patrols."

Jonquil swallowed with difficulty and stared apprehensively into the leaping flames of the fire.

"Here," Judruff said as he reached behind him to open a large chest. "Take this!"

The falcon king offered the banf a short, sheathed sword. Jonquil drew its polished blade into the light.

"Keep it with you always," Judruff urged him. "And keep out of the shadows!"

Rattajack in the meantime had spent an equally harrowing session in conversation with Halmarand's charger. Agamanthra had spun a dramatic yarn of his own on the fearful subject of Mezereon's creatures, although he had concentrated on a different breed of monster to Judruff. According to Agamanthra, by far the worst crime the Dark Sorcerer committed before escaping from the clutches of the allied armies was to raise the bars on the most deadly of his malignant progeny; the tunnel serpents.

Their heavily fortified dens were situated outside the self-contained vaults of the laboratories, separated only by stout iron doors from the network of channels and passageways that spread into the very heart of the mountains, and included the boltholes of the dwarf rebels.

The heavy doors had risen with the high pitched purr of hauling chains, and then a monstrous hiss was spat into the darkness by the coiled occupants within. With the scrape of needle-sharp claws and the heavy rasp of scaled bodies, the mighty slithering creatures had eased their long lengths from the close confines of the narrow dungeons; sniffed the air for the scent of the dwarfs, bared their vicious fangs and raced into the meandering system of tunnels to hunt their prey.

By the time the two companions rendezvoused later that evening the deepening shadows of the stone walls had taken on a decidedly sinister complexion for them both.

Halmarand shook his head and could not help a smile.

"Every castle has its ghosts, Jonquil," he admitted after the banf and the terragon had joined him on the parapet outside his quarters, and Jonquil had conveyed the bones of his visit with Judruff.

"But you are wise to be cautious, my friends," the general continued more seriously. "Danger lurks for all of us around the unchecked corner. Complacency, my friends, that is the real enemy in a war situation!"

"Are we still in a war situation?" Jonquil asked.

Halmarand allowed himself a few moments to answer.

"Until the Orb of Winter has been recovered and delivered safely into the hands of the Wizards of Light, none of us should sleep too soundly in our beds!"

Jonquil, always a slave to his curiosity, decided to brave another probing question.

"Do you think Mezereon has it?" he ventured.

The general appraised the banf with a keen eye and seemed mildly amused by his interest. Then his sharp, grey eyes narrowed into a question.

"Of course, I was forgetting, you have had first hand experience of the Orb, haven't you?"

Jonquil suddenly tried hard not to remember but Halmarand only smiled and turned from the two companions to embrace the topaz-stained landscape of the gorge at sunset, and scoured the breathtaking sweep of burning clouds with his eyes.

"If he does have it," he said at last. "I don't know why he doesn't use it. I would if I were him. What else has he got?"

The general's jaw stiffened and his voice suddenly grew hard and determined; his gauntleted fist pounding against the stone of the battlement.

"We're close to him!" he growled. "I just know it! And getting closer all the time. One day soon we'll be just a breath behind him . . . and then we'll see the rabbit run!"

The banf and the terragon joined him at the view, and just as they did so, a rising thread of dragons lifted into the inflamed sky, their black profiles outlined with a blazing fringe of orange fire.

"Do you think he will use it?" Jonquil persisted.

Halmarand snorted with laughter and patted the banf warmly on the shoulder.

"That is not for me to say," the general told him as he strode through the archway leading to the firelit warmth of his chambers. "I am a soldier, and I dance to the commands of my betters. When they say, 'Halmarand! Find us the Orb of Winter!' That is as much as it is for me to consider."

The general suddenly struck a theatrical pose.

"Until Mezereon and the Orb are found, there can be no rest for Halmarand!"

Just before he twisted the iron ring and crunched the door open to the interior, the general raised his eyebrows at the two companions and added;

"I made that up myself, you know!"

Jonquil smiled, even though he would rather have replaced the words 'Mezereon and the orb' in the rhyme with 'Meadolarne and the dark lady'.

Jonquil and Rattajack passed a miserable week in the dark mass of Dragonskeep. News of the great hunt flowed fast and furious into the dragonports, but none of it concerned with the banfina or the mysterious 'dark lady'. The seeing orb had shown the two companions nothing of any substance, only that Meadolarne was still alive, which of course was a light of hope in their darkness. The banf was anxious for tidings and itching to engage in some positive action that might further their cause, or at the very least distract the two of them from the terrible silence of their so far fruitless search.

And so the banf and the terragon took to exploring deep into the far reaches of the sprawling castle. Jonquil had his sharp sword and his brilliant acorn-lantern to banish even the deepest banks of shadow, so they felt reasonably secure.

Judruff, who had clucked and worried over the two companions' wanderings like a neurotic mother hen, had insisted they carried a detailed plan of the maze of corridors and chambers with them, so that they might never get stranded or lost. The windsprite king was a firm believer in the 'stalkers', rumoured survivors from Mezereon's initial release of creatures that still roamed the outer fringes of the vast building searching for victims.

Some of the areas Jonquil and Rattajack investigated were abandoned and derelict and looked as though they had been that way for many long years. Sharp winds charging up from the cliffs below wailed in through the crumbling apertures of ancient dragonports, their wooden platforms and canopies long since left to rot and collapse, or be torn down by the violent tempests that regularly thrashed the old bones of the building. Timbers creaked underfoot, unfastened shutters slammed against stone, and the icy draughts swept along the doorless hallways, moaning as they burrowed through the warrens of empty rooms.

One day, Jonquil and Rattajack found themselves in the western arm of the fortress, discovering the old sorting chambers, where the raw power crystals were once deposited by the dwarfs to be cleaned and polished, before being transported by carrier-dragon to the Throne Citadel. Rows of old, dishevelled wooden stalls still stood where once a large population of dragons would have lived. Long oak tables, now cobwebbed and neglected showed where the dwarfs charged with sorting the precious crystals would have sat to carry out their important work.

Cracked barrels and abandoned stools were scattered furiously about the stone floor amongst torn sacks and smashed chests, and it suddenly became apparent that a violent mêlée had taken place with the occupants of this place of noble toil. Heaps of waste rock that had clearly once been collected into neat piles had been kicked over or hurled about the rooms, and now crunched loudly beneath the feet of the two visitors. Ugly rusted weapons of war; spears, axes, curved goblin scimitars lay amongst the more acceptable chisels and hammers; all the deranged debris shrouded in a thick skin of dust.

Jonquil picked his way carefully to the great opening of a disused dragonport, the rickety landing stage groaning ominously as he stepped gingerly upon it. Icy gusts flickered through his hair, tweaking tears into his eyes, his broad wings instinctively unravelling to test the strength of the wind and lifting him up on to tiptoe.

Long scars had been scraped into the timbers of the platform as if a series of heavy angular vessels had been dragged bodily across it and then presumably flung over the side into the plummeting depths of the chasm. The banf leaned over to see if there were any broken remains still visible on the jagged face of the cliffs, and at first saw only what he expected; the endless drop of the canyon walls plunging into a drifting milky haze. Jonquil edged a little further along the creaking length of the platform, feeling its fragility shaking beneath his feet.

Suddenly, a flash of gold caught his eye a little way down the cliff, a tiny star of amber burning from a shallow crease in the dull, grey rock. Almost without thinking, the banf threw open his wings and stepped into the air to investigate, the terragon tearing to the edge of the dragonport with a whine of terror, as his friend disappeared into the void.

Rattajack thought he would never get used to the idea of his lifelong companion being able to fly, even though the banf clearly had every confidence in his broad span of feathers.

With a volley of strong gusts threatening to dash him against the rock face, Jonquil skilfully tilted and angled his wings into the powerful draughts to manoeuvre himself safely towards the sparkling object. The banf seemed almost oblivious to the fact that he was hanging in the air above the unfathomable plunge of Dragongorge, with only the strength of his flight muscles to hold him there, so completely had his attention been seized by the shiny object.

Rattajack was watching him from the lip of the dragonport with bated breath, voicing the occasional whimper of anguish as Jonquil was jostled and shoved by the aggressive updraughts.

When the banf finally lowered himself to the source of the mysterious light, he found it lying at the mouth of a small cave, the rear of which seemed to disappear into the black hole of narrow tunnel.

Jonquil took a firm grasp on the cold skin of the rock and scrambled into the cave. It was a relief to be free of the bullying wind, and after shaking the chill from his wings, he rested on his haunches and crouched to examine his find.

Although this was the first he had ever seen close to, apart from the finely cut examples the Wizards wore on their robes, the banf immediately guessed that the shiny, amber fragment was a raw power crystal; and by its golden colour he knew it to be a shard of Sunfire . . . Orolan's enchanted gem.

As he held the glittering piece up to the bright screen of mist, Jonquil saw it sparkle with sunlight; but the golden stars were not borrowed or reflected, they emanated from within the crystal, for the sun itself was smothered by a thick ceiling of cloud. The banf could feel the energy of the small stone trembling against his fingertips; its innate power untouched and unfulfilled.

"There must be a whole day's worth of Summer contained within this little nugget!" Jonquil mused to himself, and he wondered how such a precious article came to be lying abandoned and forgotten in that cold, desolate place.

The banf could only assume that during the struggle in the sorting chambers high above, the assailants, who had no doubt been the servants of Vrorst sent to stem the flow of power to the Three Wizards after the Grand Betrayal, had ruthlessly flung the unsorted crates of freshly mined lode-rock into the chasm. The glistening lump of golden crystal must have been lying amongst the piles of jettisoned rubble, and lodged on the proud lip of rock when the crates were smashed open and their contents spilled all over the cliff face. Jonquil couldn't help wondering how many more priceless fragments lay undiscovered amongst the chinks and crevices of the rugged drop.

Rattajack piped with concern from above, for he could no longer see the banf, who was sheltering from the worst of the wind inside the cave entrance. Jonquil's smiling features then emerged from the sheer plane of the rock face and beckoned to the terragon to follow. Gathering his courage, for Rattajack was most unhappy with their head-swimming distance from the canyon floor, the terragon leapt into the wind and made a quavering, ungainly descent from the groaning tongue of the dragonport to the small, jagged opening of the cave.

Once safely gathered inside, Jonquil showed the terragon what he had found and Rattajack's eyes beamed with wonder, for without touching it he could feel the potent essence of the gem disturbing the air about itself.

Suddenly a terrific bolt of wind screamed along the wall of the chasm, bursting in upon the two companions and nearly bowling them bodily into the throat of the cave. Then the squeal of splintering supports was heard from the body of the ruined aperture above. The bones of the dilapidated structure, brittle through age and neglect, no longer a match for the violent charges of the Winter gales, and with a deafening rumble, the wooden jaws of the ancient dragonport were slammed shut and its shattered skeleton forced to surrender to the gorge in a thunderous avalanche of oak and stone.

The two companions leapt for the rear of the cave as a deadly curtain of sliding debris crashed on to the shallow ledge, two stout posts jamming into the entrance forming a funnel and guiding a ferocious stream of stone and timber into the cave. The bright disc of daylight was immediately extinguished by a billowing storm of dust, the confined space of the tiny cavern invaded by a hail of flying rocks. Jonquil threw himself across the cowering form of the terragon and was amazed to feel heavy chunks of rock bouncing off his coat of fairy mail like balls of paper, the enchanted layers of his delsidian armour living up to their remarkable reputation.

When the massive onslaught finally subsided, the banf and the terragon saw with horror that the cave entrance was completely blocked.

Jonquil and Rattajack slowly turned and stared with shivers of apprehension at the black mouth of the tunnel at the back of the cave waiting to swallow them; neither of them wanting to enter, but both of them knowing it was the only path open to them.

It was then that Jonquil discovered another blow of misfortune; his pouch containing the seeing orb was still sitting on the oak table in their quarters where he had left it the night before.

The banf dusted off the now tattered tunic which he wore to conceal his fabulous shirt, pressed the tiny clasp on his golden acorn and released an irresistible beam of bluey-white light that revealed the beginning of a meandering burrow of grey rock.

With a wry smile at Rattajack, Jonquil dropped on to his hands and knees, with the brilliant beam of light wafting to and fro before him from the swing of its golden chain, and crawled cautiously forward into the tunnel.

The terragon watched his friend lead the way, and for a moment envied Jonquil his ignorance of the terror that now dwelled in the tunnel system. The banf believed all of the dangerous creatures to be confined within the walls of Dragonskeep; Judruff's 'stalkers', the lingering laboratory escapees. He hadn't been told the tale of the tunnel serpents. To Jonquil, adventures beneath the ground meant cuddly creatures like peepers or friendly dwarfs, wondrous caves filled with glowing mushrooms and chuckling streams; the terragon prayed that they would not encounter anything on their imminent journey to spoil the banf's naive vision.

Neither the banf or the terragon knew if the tunnels of Dragongorge led back to the great garrison, the clifftops, the dwarf-mines or somewhere else. Unfortunately neither Halmarand's or Judruff's maps and charts had dealt with the subterraneous pathways; and so the two companions had to rely on guesswork, tempered by the keen senses of the terragon, to guide them 'upstream' through the weaving maze of ancient dry water channels that mingled and crossed on their gradual descent to the great chasm.

Eventually their chosen passageway broadened until it was large enough to stoop in, and then after a good distance forked into two equally capacious openings and presented the banf and the terragon with their first choice. The lantern couldn't reveal anything to favour one over the other so it was left to Rattajack's keen nose and intuition to decide.

The terragon sniffed, scratched, whined, pondered and finally settled on the left hand aperture; Jonquil gave him a reassuring hug and then followed the stark beam of the lantern into the chosen course.

The walls of the twisting sleeve of rock were, at first, jagged and treacherous to negotiate. Each step had to be carefully placed so as to avoid stumbling on to sharp points and ridges, and so their progress was slow and deliberate. Nevertheless the two companions continued in this careful manner for what must have been hours, although when deprived of the sun the gauging of time is difficult.

Jonquil hated to think what might have become of them if they had not had the acorn lantern to banish the darkness and guide their steps. The banf could not help remembering the last time he had walked beneath the mountains, before he was found by the peepers. After his final torch had died, a solid wall of blackness had suddenly rushed in to entomb him, and Jonquil could still recall the irresistible misery and despair it brought with it.

The strong, unwavering light of the tiny, imprisoned mushroom, threw up bold unnerving shadows from proud limbs of rock or boulders, which swayed or pounced across the walls with the movement of the banf's body, occasionally making the two friends start as their overactive imaginations turned the harmless shapes into looming malevolent beasts. However, both the banf and the terragon would not have hesitated to agree that the infrequent frights they got from the shadows were a small price to pay for the gift of light in the deep tunnels.

When the banf and the terragon eventually slumped from exhaustion after what seemed a lifetime of 'one step in front of the other', Jonquil estimated they must have travelled the best part of a league along their subterranean road; although almost certainly not in a straight line.

Luckily they had been carrying a small amount of food and water with them before they were stranded by the collapsing dragonport, another of Judruff's 'just in case' insistences. Jonquil made a promise to remind himself to thank the King of the Windsprites for what had seemed over-cautious nannying at the time, but had now turned out to be a lifesaver.

Whilst he was searching for the last of their provisions, Jonquil's fingers found a small lump of rock in the pouch of his tunic. The banf assumed it to be yet another lodged projectile from the force of the cave-in . . . he had removed several from his person during the journey so far . . . but when he pulled it out into the light he found it to be the piece of Sunfire.

Rattajack sniffed at it in disgust, after all wasn't it all because of that pretty nugget that they were imprisoned beneath the mountains? Jonquil couldn't remember placing it in his pouch but despite their regrettable predicament, he was glad he had.

They ate their food and were just about to scramble to their feet to attempt the next arduous stretch of their journey, when a harsh, sliding sound, amplified and distorted by echo, floated towards their large, attentive ears; they both suddenly stiffened in one motion.

"What was that?" Jonquil gasped, unwilling to raise his voice.

Rattajack looked blank and tried hard not to think of what it might be.

The disturbing noise was followed only by the oppressive silence, and so with slightly quicker heartbeats and a faster pace the two companions set off again, picking their way further along the rugged tunnel.

After a while the going became decidedly easier and Jonquil took a moment to examine the detail of their environment. The lantern revealed that the deep grooves and ridges of the water channels had gone, the surrounding rock more even, its relative smoothness seeming more deliberate than natural. Jonquil could not be certain but he felt the rippled texture of scooped facets covering the walls was the work of chisels rather than erosion. The surface underfoot was certainly more conducive to walking and before long, the two underground explorers were striding after the swinging pool of brilliant light with good speed.

The roundness of the tunnels eventually gave way to the arched profile of crude passageways. There were strange symbols carved into the dark grey rock at the junctions with other passages; secret signs, perhaps, that could probably direct those literate in dwarf-lore to a variety of destinations; the crystal mines, the secret paths to Dragonskeep, back to the gorge, to the surface. If only they knew how to read them, Jonquil couldn't help thinking, they could easily find their way out of that black labyrinth. The banf wished he had spent more time with the dwarfs and learned their language, for now a whole network of potential escape routes lay before them, and each one with a label they couldn't decipher. For reasons of secrecy the dwarfs hadn't used pictorial symbols in their writings, so it was impossible to guess what the complex arrangements of runes and designs were supposed to represent.

The banf and the terragon decided that it was best to ignore the signs and remain faithful to their current route. Apart from the carved words in the rock, there was very little evidence of occupation in the burrowed corridors. It was obvious that the neat little passages were the work of the industrious dwarfs, and equally plain that they had long since deserted that remote corner of their domain. The few discarded implements or shreds of clothing that the two of them encountered, were withered with ancient rust or mildew; every cold hallway, dark and silent.

After a while the beaming swathe from Jonquil's lantern melted into an arch of black, no walls reflecting the bright gaze of the lamp from beyond the curved profile. It was clear that they had reached an open space of some kind, and with a sudden eagerness to be free from the cramped embrace of the tunnels, the two companions scrambled forward to investigate.

As the light of the golden acorn swept into the darkness, the two friends discovered that they had emerged on to the brink of a huge divide. The great underground gap seemed infinitely tall and wide but proportionately very narrow, like a slim cavity between two massive walls of rock. The thin strips of floor and ceiling were both beyond the reach of the lantern, so there was no way of telling just how vast the fissure was. The noise of the two companions' whispers or shuffling steps was carried aloft by a pulsating rhythm of reverberations, even the slightest breath amplified until it was loud in their sensitive ears. The urge to call out, or make silly noises was almost unbearable for the both of them, for they were sure that the narrow acoustics of the great crack would have afforded marvellous echoes; but the silent menace that hung in the black air of that hidden realm persuaded them not to advertise their presence too blatantly.

The ominous scraping sound that they had heard some time ago, whilst crouched in the tunnel, had not repeated itself, and they had seen no tangible signs of danger; but the keen instincts that both of them knew better than to ignore, were screaming at the two friends to get out of that damp, desolate place as soon as possible. The air, which was beginning to acquire a slightly stale, musky texture, tasted of threat, and did little to encourage the banf and the terragon to linger.

Straddling the two opposing cliffs was the modest rise of a small hump-backed bridge, constructed from a basic arrangement of typically undecorated stone blocks. The curved platform began at their feet and reached across to another arched entrance on the opposite side. Although the ledge the two companions were standing on continued either side of them and might have led to a number of alternative routes, after a silent debate between their eyes, Jonquil and Rattajack agreed that their journey was to be continued on the other side of the great bottomless fissure.

Jonquil took the lead and placed a tentative step on the curve of the bridge. As there was no initial indication that all was not well, the banf slowly and warily began to climb the shallow arc of stone blocks. Jonquil held the terragon back with an outstretched arm until he was satisfied that the ancient structure had been fully tested by his weight. At last Rattajack was allowed to follow and the two of them cautiously began to negotiate the short distance to the opposite cliff.

The terragon was just about halfway across the bridge when the dreadful sliding noise came again, this time much nearer and sounding as if it might be emanating from the tunnel they had just left. Rattajack hesitated and turned to listen, his large ears hungry for more information. This time the noise did repeat itself, again and again, in a steady rhythm as if the author of the disturbance was moving with a purpose; a heavy scaled form scraping itself along the rough texture of the tunnel's wall. Of course the contours of the hollow passages were probably amplifying the sound, making it appear much nearer than it actually was, but as far as Rattajack was concerned if they could hear it at all it was already too close.

Jonquil forgot himself for a moment and joined the frozen terragon on the apex of the humped bridge.

"It's following us," he whispered to Rattajack. The terragon's fearful eyes were captured by the light from the golden acorn and Jonquil saw at once that Rattajack knew what the creature could be, and that they had reason to be afraid.

Suddenly, the two companions felt a profound tremor beneath their feet and heard the ominous grinding of stone against stone. A web of cracks sprang between them, and the small bridge, which had clearly feigned substantiality, proceeded to disintegrate under their combined weight. The clatter of evacuating lumps and fragments tumbling into the ravine, the gritty shearing of deteriorated blocks of stone and the coarse whisper of crumbling mortar filling the receptive space of the giant gap, blocking out all other sounds.

Jonquil instinctively gripped one of Rattajack's forelimbs and flung him bodily to the far side of the chasm. In the trembling light of the acorn lantern, Jonquil saw that the bridge stayed together long enough for the terragon to scramble over to the opposite ledge and reach safety. For the banf it was too late; thrown off balance by his exertion he toppled over into the blackness as the faltering arch finally ceased its efforts to hold together. The deafening roar of the collapsing bridge was sustained in the narrow confines of the chasm for a long time, the crashing shower of stone plummeting into the endless drop of the fissure, assaulting the steep walls with a violent cacophony of echoes on its long journey to the bottom.

The banf was thrown into a bewildering spiral, the fanned beam of his lantern slicing through the darkness to reveal bright slithers of the grey walls in wild spinning arcs. Jonquil was totally disorientated and no longer knew which way was up, it was as much as he could do to stop himself from crashing into the cliff faces as he gradually careered towards the floor of the ravine.

Eventually Jonquil's wings regained their mastery over the air and ceased his manic girating, bringing him fluttering safely to the ground. The banf was relieved to discover that the bottom of the narrow drop was dry, a weaving boulder-strewn bed that led off along its silent course into the roots of the mountains. The banf had no idea how far he had drifted from the site of his fall, and when he tried to locate the place with the lamp, he realised the one landmark that he was searching for, the bridge, was no longer there to aid him. Luckily, the residue of the collapse was still whispering down the cliffs, so Jonquil could be sure which way he was facing, and by the sound of it he had tumbled at quite a wide gradient through the air and landed some distance along the gap.

Jonquil resolved that the only thing to do was to fly up into the thin space between the steep walls and wait for Rattajack to see his light and call out to him; it was his only chance to relocate his friend. The banf was just about to leap up from the rocky bed when a strange sound caught his attention some distance above him. It seemed to originate from roughly the area where he estimated the bridge to have been; it sounded like something crawling down the cliff. At first Jonquil thought it might be a few loose rock fragments late on their way to the bottom, or perhaps Rattajack, unwilling to be left behind in the dark and attempting the difficult descent to reach him; he knew the terragon to be a creature of remarkable ingenuity and resource, but even so, descending a sheer rock face seemed beyond even his incomparable friend's enviable capabilities. Besides, the terragon could fly, why would he need to climb down into the ravine? He need only spread his leathery wings and glide down to Jonquil's light.

Then Jonquil remembered the creature in the tunnel, which with the trauma of the collapsing bridge had temporarily escaped his thoughts. Added to this, the banf recalled the look of terror in Rattajack's eyes when they had heard the sounds behind them; what had the terragon thought the creature to be, that it should inspire such fear?

Jonquil decided that there was no other course of action but to fly back to where he had left Rattajack, with danger lurking in the tunnels this was no time to be separated. The banf had the lantern and the slipper nut whistle about him, so he calculated his chances of finding the terragon again were quite favourable.

Without another thought, Jonquil spread his wings and rose into the thin gap, glancing the beam of the acorn across the height of the opposing cliff as he did so to try and locate his pursuer. Although the sweeping passes of the bright light revealed no monsters, there were numerous caves and crevices in the pitted face of the rock which flooded with dense shadow at his approach, any of which might conceal an enemy. The banf also fancied he could feel the glare of cold, malevolent eyes hungrily regarding his slow, ascending flight, following his course through the chasm with intense interest. This sensation might just have been the product of an over-worked imagination but Jonquil was in the mood to take no chances.

He had not proceeded very far when a reasonably small opening in the far wall was found by the lantern. Jonquil closed in and thought he recognised the roughly hewn archway to be the one that had once been served by the small bridge. There was a narrow ledge running along the cliff before it and a sister tunnel on the opposite side but the banf was surprised to see that all traces of the bridge had disappeared, and that the friendly, welcoming face of the terragon was not waiting for him in the mouth of the dark aperture. Before entering, Jonquil made a brief inspection of the surrounding wall area just to be certain that he had the right place, and then satisfied that there could be no mistake climbed inside.

Rattajack was nowhere to be seen. The new tunnel progressed further into the mountain in much the same manner as its predecessor had done in bringing them to the thin ravine. Jonquil covered a small distance and then paused to listen for any sounds that might lead him to the terragon. Rattajack would not have fled from the mouth of the tunnel unless something had scared him, and then Jonquil realised that if some monstrous beast had emerged from the first tunnel, the terragon would have been perched just opposite from it, across a not unconquerable divide. Had their positions been reversed would not he have retreated into the depths of the passage? After all, Rattajack was not to know that the creature would choose to follow the light, rather than attempt the leap across to him.

Jonquil explored a little further along the winding path of the tunnel, a few secondary passages led off from the main but the banf was unsure whether he should follow any of them. He was fast approaching the conclusion that the task was hopeless; if Rattajack had decided to hide, he could have been concealed anywhere, and Jonquil's chances of simply wandering through the maze of burrows and bumping into the terragon by accident were practically nil. The banf began to consider the merits of sounding Meadolarne's whistle; of course it would advertise his presence to any enemies that might lurk in the black corridors, but it would also be an unmistakable signal for Rattajack, to tell him that Jonquil was near.

It was a great risk, but then he had to find his friend, so where was the virtue in silence? Jonquil pulled on the leather thong about his neck and brought the carved slipper nut out from inside his tunic. He placed it to his lips. The banf only dared one blow, so it had to be a good one. He sucked in a good chestful of air and sounded the whistle. The sharp blast stabbed through the black silence like a piercing rapier, bouncing off the narrow walls about him and repeating far into the distant warren of empty passageways. Any creature within a league of the banf would have heard the shrill, powerful note, and Jonquil prayed that the only being it lured to him was his friend.

For a few long moments, after the last trace of the whistle's echoes had faded, there was a deep, tense silence as if the whole world was holding its breath with Jonquil waiting for a reply, the banf even felt his heart had stopped beating to listen for a response.

Waiting was agony, and all the time he crouched there in the darkness, the banf's imagination kept inventing happy scenarios of Rattajack piping his cheerful greeting and emerging sheepishly from one of the side passages to be reunited with his friend. Unfortunately this was not to be and Jonquil was just about to admit failure and try to devise another plan, when he thought his large ears caught the faintest whining sound far off in the distance.

It might have been Rattajack's voice but it had really been too indistinct to tell. Then another sound drifted along the walls of the passageway towards him . . . the sound of movement.

It had to be Rattajack, Jonquil kept telling himself, even though the sound was more of a scratching noise than a shuffling, and the terragon's soft fleshy feet would really shuffle not scratch. Then a scraping noise began to accompany the scratching; a rough, scales against rock sort of sound, as if a long body was being hastily hauled through the chiselled tunnel. Despite the fact that Jonquil was still trying to convince himself that it was his terragon friend approaching through the blackness, the banf's feet clearly had other ideas, for almost independently of his will, they began to move Jonquil into the opposite direction.

Even the terrifying hiss that suddenly swept along the passage after Jonquil failed to persuade his stubborn reason that this was not Rattajack, but the banf's feet refused to slow their pace and before he knew it Jonquil was running for all he was worth along the twisting bore of the dwarfs' tunnel. Jonquil's pursuer seemed to sense his sudden burst of speed and soon the vague scratching became the dreadful screech of needle-sharp claws grasping for purchase against the hard rock, the buzzing rasp of its long, wriggling trunk of scales scraping ever louder against the textured walls as it slithered more swiftly to match the banf's progress; but it was the terrible hiss of the creature that almost caused Jonquil's knees to buckle every time it spat its breath at the banf, the monstrous sound tearing after him, filling the slender space of the stone passage with a petrifying din.

Jonquil snapped the golden acorn shut and buried himself in darkness, for he now feared the creature was close enough to hunt him by sight, and he wished to give it no aid in doing so. With arms and wings outstretched either side of him to feel his way along the walls, the banf sprinted on into the black bowels of the mountains. He had no idea what manner of beast it was that pursued him, but he knew he was running for his life.

The banf's legs pumped hard against the solid floor of the tunnel as he tried to escape the monster, but with every step Jonquil could feel the creature drawing closer to him. The noise of its furious chase, as it streaked along the sculpted walls, seemed very near; its sharp, rasping breath snorting into the tired air he had passed through only moments before. Jonquil's nostrils told him that the creature was no stranger to the deep passages, the pungent musky taste that had hung in the air ever since they had arrived at the slim chasm seemed to be growing stronger, and the banf had the terrible feeling that the extensive maze of burrows that he and Rattajack had crossed in to, were all part of a massive lair.

The approach of the slithering beast was now horribly loud in Jonquil's ears, its tugging claws screaming against the rugged stone, and the scrape of its scaly flanks assaulting the curved walls just behind the last bend. Suddenly the banf's blind feet snagged against a raised lip of rock and he was thrown forward into the void, legs and arms flailing in a wild, hurtling dive. Without his wings Jonquil would have crashed headfirst on to the rough base of the tunnel, inflicting grievous damage upon himself, but the instinctive spread of his feathered limbs carried the banf into a gentle glide which deposited him safely on the ground.

The awesome grinding of the monster's scaled length rose into a violent churning crescendo and then abruptly ceased as Jonquil slowly stumbled to a halt and fell back against the curve of the passage. As his body was jarred by the stone wall the clasp on the banf's golden acorn flew open flooding the enclosed space of the tunnel with an immediate brilliance. Jonquil's eyes almost burst from his skull as the terrible form of his pursuer was suddenly exposed in all its malevolence before him, poised to strike out of its tensed coils like an arrow straining in the bow.

The light of the lantern was reflected by layers of gleaming scales sweeping

up into the menacing arc of a huge snake-like shape. Cold, black eyes sparkling with two bright stars were set above a fierce, dragonish gape, armed with thin, curved spikes that glistened like pale thorns. Two long flags of leathery skin flared out from behind its crested head to magnify its threat, and positioned far apart on its strong, muscular trunk were its diminutive arms and legs; sinewy and powerful almost like an insect's limbs, its slender digits furnished with long stiletto claws, its fore-limbs now hovering in the air above Jonquil like two deadly spiders. It was Dromeliad, one of the four ferocious tunnel serpents Mezereon had managed to release into the dwarf tunnels before he had to flee from the great fortress.

The creature was superbly adapted to hunt the narrow channels and pipes of the mines, having the ability to slither at great speed like a snake and climb swiftly with the aid of its small but mighty limbs like a lizard; fastening itself to the textured rock faces with the formidable spans of its rapier claws. The tunnel serpents could propel themselves through the smallest apertures, indeed specially designed by the malicious sorcerer so that any opening that was large enough to accommodate their prey would also be accessible to them. Little wonder that the remaining dwarf rebels had evacuated the burrowed passages near to Dragonskeep and hidden themselves in the deeper more remote bores of the mountain roots, praying their barricades would hold against the sliding monsters that were bred to follow their scent and annihilate them.

A mind-shattering hiss burst from the coiled creature wrenching Jonquil to his senses, and when the serpent lunged at where he had been crouched, it found the banf already on his feet and sprinting away down the tunnel. Jonquil knew that his only chance was to keep running and to change direction whenever possible. Luckily he was now in a part of the tunnel system that was served by a busy exchange of short corridors and pipes that enabled the banf to dodge and swerve from the path of his hunter, denying it a clean strike. Unfortunately it also meant that he needed his lantern to aid him thus giving the serpent an easy task to follow him.

The rage of the creature seemed to increase with every blast of its piercing breath. Jonquil was now a bobbing, winged shape for the serpent, silhouetted against a wildly rolling pool of light and framed within the tight embrace of the narrow passageways. The creature flowed into a succession of tight bends, its supple length dragging against the rounded corners, eating into the hard rock with the teeth of it scales, only to catch the briefest glimpse of its flickering prey before it disappeared into another opening. Exhausted as he was Jonquil never slackened the pace, every dark aperture that presented itself to him he ducked into, blind to where he was running, only mindful of the pale fangs that seemed able to pursue him through even the tightest burrows. Whenever he threw a swift glance to the rear before taking a new direction, the monster was always fast approaching just beyond the light, its cruel eyes sparkling in the blackness.

The chase continued at a frantic pace through a mesmerising maze of channels, the tunnel serpent never close enough to end it with a successful lunge, and Jonquil never far enough in front to rest.

The desperate banf hurled himself down a worryingly long straight corridor, leapt a short flight of crudely hewn steps and darted suddenly into a black arch that loomed quickly to his right. The doorway led Jonquil to the initial rise of a bridge but too late his lantern revealed that this ancient construction had also fallen victim to the decay of time, and had long since collapsed into the deep belly of a wide, expansive cavern. Jonquil's legs were carrying him far too swiftly to respond when the curved ramp suddenly ended before him, so rather than hesitate or falter, the banf instinctively ran harder and launched himself into the void, his broad wingspan unravelling to carry him into a graceful swoop beneath the spiked ceiling of the large chamber. The light from the acorn found the corresponding doorway on the opposite end of the vanished bridge and Jonquil made a safe landing on its ruined promontory.

The banf turned to see if the serpent would be able to stop itself from tumbling into the pit of rock spears that rose from the wide basin below. Jonquil shone his lantern at the far entrance to the cavern but no serpent appeared. The banf was perplexed, the creature had been so close behind him it should have entered the chamber a few moments later but there was no sign of it. Jonquil swept the pool of light from the golden acorn over the jagged floor, wondering if the creature had already fallen silently to its death whilst he had flown to safety; the lantern revealed nothing.

Then a horribly familiar clawing sound drew the banf's attention above his head, and the beam of the acorn found the weaving form of the serpent, snaking through the inverted forest of rock spikes, moving at speed upside down across the thorny expanse of the ceiling.

Jonquil cried out in despair and incredulity, the creature must have streaked up the walls and started out through the stalactites without even stopping to draw breath; and the banf saw with a sinking heart that the serpent was in no way handicapped or impeded by its inverted state, its progress as swift as ever.

Jonquil turned and fled into the honeycomb of passages once more, his legs aching in protest at the prospect of another chase. However this time his brief flight had given him a narrow lead and he was able to put a short distance between himself and the monster. Jonquil knew that once the serpent had lost sight of him it would have to follow his scent trail, and that would inevitably slow it down a little.

After turning a sharp bend, the banf had to struggle up a slim, tightly bored tunnel which rose steeply and then levelled out into a rugged, roughly hacked corridor. The passages were beginning to look more uneven and natural again, as if Jonquil had come to a point on the edge of the dwarfs working domain where they had simply re-connected their neat little network of burrows to the pre-existing meandering system of ancient water channels. A terrible chill crept over the banf as he recalled the slow progress such pathways had caused when he and Rattajack had first entered the tunnels from the gorge, and he knew that such a pace would make him an easy catch for the approaching hunter.

A little way on from the summit of the steep tunnel Jonquil came across a large boulder sitting tightly against a crevice in the craggy wall, he was just about to run past it when an idea suddenly sprang to mind. The furious hiss of the serpent whistled up the slender pipe as the dreadful creature squeezed its long trunk around the tight bend and began the ascent to Jonquil. The banf quickly put all of his weight against the rear of the boulder, which was almost as large as himself, in an attempt to move it towards the slope. Jonquil pushed with all of his might, every muscle of his back and shoulders straining with the effort; but it was no use, the boulder simply refused to yield.

The clatter of the serpent's needle claws grew louder in the tunnel, and the banf knew it was only a matter of moments before the creature reached him.

Then Jonquil saw a long, stout wooden prop lying idly on the floor nearby, which, the banf assumed, may have been used to position the great ball of rock in the first place. When he returned with it Jonquil saw something else which gave him heart; for hammered into the curve beneath the boulder was a series of wooden pegs, clearly put there to keep the rock firmly in place against the wall. Neither the wooden stave or the pegs were deteriorated by age, so the securing of the large stone was plainly a recent deed.

With a burst of industry that could only have been achieved by the desperate, Jonquil wiggled most of the pegs loose and then thrust the conveniently sharpened end of the heavy wooden lever at the foot of the boulder and heaved with every ounce of energy he had left, even pushing against the opposite wall of the passage to gain more force.

The boulder grumbled deeply and eventually eased away from the crevice to move at a sedate, leisurely pace towards the brink of the slope. The serpent was now close enough to cast its awesome shadow in Jonquil's light, but the banf closed his eyes to it, dropped the heavy stave and charged the liberated boulder. The ball began to tip into the slope but was then caught by the strong fore-limbs of the rising monster. Suddenly the head of the serpent arced over the top of the giant stone and struck hard against the fold of Jonquil's right wing. The banf screamed in agony as sharp fangs sank into his feathered limb and in a surge of pain he relaxed his efforts on the boulder. The creature shook him violently and attempted to drag Jonquil up and over the large obstacle and down into the steep tunnel; but the great stone was already committed to the slope and the more the monster tugged at Jonquil the heavier the mass of rock became.

Finally, the creature could support the falling boulder no more and in a dreadful screech of sharp claws steadily losing their purchase and being dragged along the hard rock, the serpent was pushed back down into the tunnel. A terrible roar burst from the creature as its neck was sandwiched against the roof of the aperture and Jonquil was suddenly thrown backwards and released. The boulder charged against the cramped coils of the serpent and drove it bodily down the length of the slender slope, the crash of its eventual arrest muffled by the monster's trapped form.

When Jonquil finally found the strength to crawl to the edge of the incline, he held up the lantern and saw by the true beam of the mushroom light that the vicious creature was wrapped around the great globe of rock in a deadly crushing embrace, its long, glistening coils smashed against the tight bend of the wall at the bottom.

A deep, tremulous sigh escaped from Jonquil's lips and he slowly hauled himself to his feet. There was no going back that way to look for Rattajack, the banf would have to find another route to reunite him with his friend.

As Jonquil stood there quietly for a few moments, trying to collect his thoughts and nurse his burning injury, his sensitive ears thought they could detect a faint rushing sound from far away. It sounded like the movement of fast water and it had to be emanating from the rugged tunnel ahead for there were no other routes open to him. Then Jonquil's eyes fell upon the place where the large boulder had stood and there he saw the small black mouth of a hidden tunnel. Could it be the opening to a secret passageway that the dwarfs had tried to conceal for some reason? Perhaps it was a short cut to the crystal mines or the dwarfs legendary treasure vaults that were reputed to be stashed with the most breathtaking collections of gold and jewels. Being the slave to adventure that Jonquil was, he resolved that he couldn't pass by the hidden aperture without even the briefest investigation into its secrets; his insatiable inquisitiveness temporarily banishing his pain.

So, carefully easing his head and shoulders and the injured fold of his right wing into the small hole, the banf pulled his acorn lantern forward and shone it into the dark throat of the tunnel. As he did so a sharp hiss of furious breath greeted his curiosity and Jonquil choked in horror when his eyes focused on what lay before him.

The boulder hadn't been concealing the entrance to a secret treasure passage as the banf had hoped, it had been incarcerating a terrible prisoner.

The modest opening led to a narrow, cramped cave . . . an old dwarf grain store . . . and languishing inside, its long body filling the confined space in thick, twisted coils, its barbed jaws now opening in an evil, voracious snarl was Zadragul; another of the four deadly tunnel serpents released by the Dark Sorcerer. This second terrifying beast had been lured into the grain store by the dwarfs three days before and then quickly entombed with the heavy ball of rock. Now Jonquil understood why the boulder had been wedged so securely in place by the wooden pegs, and couldn't help pondering on the cruel irony of having employed the great stone in the destruction of one awesome serpent only to accidentally free another.

Zadragul had been squeezed into the tiny cave for three days and was now ravenous and very angry; its black, sparkling eyes slowly moved towards him, and Jonquil could see that it lusted only for revenge and murder.

Jonquil quickly pushed himself back out of the narrow opening and began to retreat along the tunnel, his eyes never leaving the black hole of the small cave. The head of the serpent swept into the passage, leading the rest of its snaking form out of confinement. Its monstrous snarl never lessened, and with an almost hypnotic, liquid curling of its body, Zadragul drew itself from the opening and tightened into a primed knot of coils, its long neck stealthily arching backwards to strike.

Rattajack, with his superior sense, both common and supernatural had considerably more success in the tunnels than his banf friend. With surprising ease, despite the terrifying handicap of being abandoned in a pitch black wilderness, the terragon worked his way through the seemingly endless burrows and passages; smelling each opening to find the ones with the freshest air and following that method faithfully through the bewildering subterranean maze. Until after a laborious day and a half of struggling through what was for both Jonquil and himself a most unnatural environment, the steadfast, remarkable terragon eventually emerged into a cave that opened onto the dazzling white footslopes of the mountains rising just above the sprawl of Dragonskeep.

Without pausing to rest, Rattajack unfurled his wings and glided down to the nearest towers of the great fortress to summon aid, a mere two days after he and Jonquil had set forth to explore the western reach of the ancient garrison.

The Rabbit in his Burrow

The icy peaks north of the Marble Fortress stood proud and resolute against the awesome visitation of a rampaging snowstorm. The snow-laden winds roared into the deep cleft of a high, remote valley, swallowed by the deep blue of the Winter night. The teeth of the storm blasted the steep slopes with a biting blizzard; the great freezing torrent sweeping through the narrow space between the tall shoulders of rock like the stroke of a mighty white scythe.

Clinging to a thin shelf, high on the valley sides, its ramshackle, flimsy construction belying its grim strength, the tiny shack braced itself against the howling assault. Thundering gales rammed its threadbare boards. Thrashing belts of hail and snow tore at the dishevelled fabric with icy claws; aided by the charging winds in their efforts to tear the shabby roof from the walls.

The steadfast little goatherd's shack knew only too well the arrogant ambitions of the mountain tempests, it had braved the acquaintance of many in its time in the bleak valley, as they had vented their wrath upon the cliffs and gullies of the higher vales.

The violent wind snatched a thin trail of wood-smoke from the squat chimney and drew a snaking blue-grey line across the shadow of the snow-clad slope. Apart from two tethered snowdragons, the wispy plume of smoke was the only evidence that the lonely dwelling was inhabited. The two dozing creatures were hardly discernible from the white groundscape, facing into the wild onslaught with complete indifference.

A storm of equal ferocity was raging inside the rattling walls and shutters of the formerly deserted cabin. Whilst the hissing sheets of snow battered the eaves outside, another bombardment was taking place within the cramped confines of the crude shelter.

Bathed in the soft, orange light from a modest fire, three figures stood around the cabin's one table in a state of extreme agitation. A fourth, seated on the one stool, the focus of their aggression, sat stiffly upright, rigid with indignance. A fifth, diminutive figure, smaller, it seemed in both stature and significance, huddled forlornly on the edge of the fire's glow, her impassive, green eyes staring vacantly into the heart of the flames.

In the darkest corner of the small interior sat an ominous bundle, a large, round shape loosely swathed in dirty sacking. The wretched, trembling figure by the fire feared to go near the mysterious object and cringed in terror when long tendrils of pale blue light permeated the open weave of its wrappings and crept inquisitively into the air or across the floor. The four figures around the table seemed not to notice the effervescent activity emanating from the corner, oblivious to anything save their own argument.

Mezereon's face was drawn and shadowy, and although not vulnerable to the passing of time like a mortal man's, the long years since Vrorst's demise lay heavily on his weary countenance.

His had become a wretched existence. Since fleeing the luxury of his sumptuous apartments at Dragonskeep, the Dark Sorcerer had been forced to suffer the ignominy of hiding in dark, lowly places like a common criminal. For years now he had not dared to show his face in daylight, but skulked under the cover of darkness from place to place, constantly living in dread fear of discovery and apprehension. The deserted goatherd's cabin that was now his home was the last in a long line of similar, disreputable abodes, but despite the austerity and harshness of its accommodation, he had at least thought its insignificance and remoteness safe from discovery. That was until Wargren and Vakari had hammered upon his lonely door one dark, stormy night and violently ended his long, silent hours of self pity and solitude.

"For the last time, Mezereon," Vakari pleaded, "embrace the power that has been left to you. What future do any of us have if you do not?"

The Dark Sorcerer suddenly straightened his back and fixed all three inquisitors with a steely stare, his face a picture of arrogant defiance.

"Since when has the responsibility for your welfare lain on my shoulders!" Mezereon roared. "We are all the captains of our own destinies. It is not for me to adopt the role of saviour!"

"You are Vrorst's heir!" Wargren wailed. "His named successor. How can you simply hide like a quaking coward and do nothing?"

Mezereon suddenly oozed with false amity.

"My dear Wargren and Vakari," Mezereon began, with a slightly condescending tone. "I fully understand your passions, but what you fail to understand is that it is not possible for me to receive Vrorst's Orb of Power."

"Why not?" Wargren snapped, almost every word he addressed to the sorcerer now forced through tightly gritted teeth, his patience clearly beginning to fray.

Mezereon waved at the air expansively.

"Because sorcerer's and their orbs are unique to each other, they cannot be interchanged." he slowly replied, as if addressing small infants. "They are like a key and a lock, each useless without the other. And as no other key may fit the lock, so no other lock may be opened by the key. That is the way of things, and only doom and disaster await the arrogant sorcerer who tries to adopt the orb of another!"

"Unless," Hexerne said boldly, her eyes boring into Mezereon's pompous face, like an eagle fixed on a rabbit. "It's owner is dead and the orb has been freely bequeathed to the other."

Mezereon visibly deflated and hurled daggers at the girl with his dark eyes.

He had forgotten that Hexerne had been Vrorst's pupil for a time, and had inevitably been schooled in the lore of sorcery.

Vakari, who like Wargren, was a former high officer not a sorcerer, but had spent enough time in the Ice Lord's service to glean a superficial understanding of the way of wizards, turned thoughtfully towards Hexerne and after a few pensive moments his eyes brightened.

"Hexerne is right," he said. "Vrorst made you eligible to receive the Orb with his dying words! He bequeathed it to you. It's yours for the taking, Mezereon!"

Wargren cried out in agreement and an almost imperceptible smile of victory played softly on Hexerne's lips. Mezereon's eyes glanced nervously from face to face, and his long fingers began to fidget. His defences were steadily being torn down one by one, and all that lay behind them was the ugly face of cowardice.

Mezereon saw no shame in admitting the truth to himself . . . he was afraid. He greatly feared the Orb of Winter and its awesome, malevolent force.

During his long years of seclusion, he had carried the priceless globe faithfully from one hiding place to the next, but he had always been careful to keep it covered and his hands gloved, never allowing his skin to come into contact with its cool, glassy surface. Mezereon could sense a dark, powerful presence dwelling within the large Orb, an entity that was hungry for him; it constantly called to him, lured him, tried to seduce him, its icy voice tempting him with promises of untold power and riches.

Sometimes when he was alone with it, he saw eerie lights peeking out from beneath its sacking shroud, and long, ethereal limbs that snaked into the air like liquid moonlight, reaching for him, beckoning, grasping. Mezereon even fancied that at times he had seen strange shapes rising against the coarse material, pushing and clawing at the loose covering like small, unnatural creatures trying to find an opening.

The Orb wanted him to lift it from the shadows, tear off its filthy wrappings and lay his bare hands upon its freezing, burning skin; and there were times when the whispering inside his head, the tugging at his sleeve, the promises, the ghostly shades, the colours, the desire, almost made him do it. After all, the longer he refused its embrace, the longer he would have to continue living in the gutter like a rat.

A Mezereon with Vrorst's power at his fingertips could have the choice of a hundred palaces in which to lay his head, instead of only a few flea-infested hovels. And wasn't that what he had always dreamed of? Succeeding Vrorst? Now all of that power and majesty was his for the taking, all he needed to do was reach out and grasp it . . . but always at the last, something stayed his hand.

Could it be that his innate, cowardice was stronger than the Orb's enchantment? Whenever he thought that he might surrender to the globe's lure, he remembered the lake of blue fire that burned deep within it. Somehow he knew that the moment he laid aside his shield, and opened himself to its touch, he would be consumed by it, devoured, destroyed.

He was no replacement for Vrorst! He was but a pale shadow of the Ice Lord's stature. How could he a lesser sorcerer, an underling, a feeble dabbler in biological corruption, ever hope to withstand or more importantly direct the magnitude of a force that could split mountains and ignite the skies.

Mezereon could only speculate as to why the Orb wanted him so much, or what devious plots or preparations Vrorst had invested in the Orb in the moments before his death, if there had been time. He only knew that the Mezereon that entered the lake of freezing fire would be very different from the Mezereon that returned from it, and he suspected that the manner of being he knew and recognised as himself would not be the one to survive the ordeal.

And still the menacing shadows on the wall beckoned him to undress the ragged bundle seething in the corner.

Mezereon's gaze turned to the fire, the flickering colour playing across a face haunted with anguish.

"Vrorst was insane to even consider declaring war upon the brotherhood," he spoke bitterly. Their power is too old and strong. They cannot be defeated!"

Wargren leaned across him menacingly.

"And yet, you were more than happy to share in the spoils of victory, along with the rest of us, at the time!" The general glowered. "Strange that I can't remember you voicing any of these opinions whilst Vrorst was alive." Wargren continued his voice heavy with poison. "I don't believe the Three Wizards possess even a fraction of the power that you profess. I believe Vrorst came this close to victory." He held up a tiny gap between his thumb and forefinger. "And but for a cruel twist of fate, he would have succeeded! It wasn't until the Winter Vessel was destroyed that the enemy gained the upper hand! Up until that moment the Three Wizards and their sympathisers were staring into disaster.

You forget, Mezereon, whilst you were safely relaxing in your comfortable apartments at Dragonskeep, hundreds of leagues away, I was there in the forest in the thick of battle! I saw it happen!"

Vakari began to fear the advent of Wargren's fury and any incidents that it might inspire. The long-serving general was already fractious with pain and fatigue. The legacy of his injuries sustained at the Battle of the White Ring had been especially cruel to him of late, causing much suffering and depriving him of sleep. His temper, short and fragile at the best of times, seemed to grow more volatile with every passing day.

Vakari realised with disquiet, that Wargren was mindful of the fact that Mezereon, with the power of the Orb at his disposal, could cure all his ills at a stroke. The possession of this knowledge did little to improve Wargren's intolerance of the Dark Sorcerer's inflammatory attitude.

Suddenly Wargren grabbed the sorcerer by the collar of his robe and dragged him bodily to his feet. Mezereon's wide, fearful eyes slowly drew level to Wargren's narrowed, malevolent stare.

"Use the Orb, Mezereon!" he demanded in a growling whisper. "It was the

Ice Lord's last command! You cannot refuse! With its power behind us we can make a new beginning. If you raise anew the banner of Winter, thousands will flock to our aid . . . "

The sorcerer suddenly shrieked with hysterical laughter. "He's dead! It's over! Don't be a fool, Wargren! Just find a rock to crawl under like the rest of us!"

Wargren began to shake with rage, and then with a surge of violent strength hurled Mezereon from him. The sorcerer stumbled back through the darkness and crashed against the far wall. Mezereon let out a pitiful cry of fear as the general's sword screamed from its scabbard and a shard of firelight glanced across its poised blade.

"Prepare to die, Mezereon!" Wargren roared. "For you are not worthy of life!"

Mezereon sank to his knees, wailing like a child, his hands held out in imploring submission.

"Wargren, no!" Vakari cried, rushing forward to grasp the general's prone sword-arm.

"Unhand me, Vakari!" The general growled. "And let me cleave this cockroach!"

"No, Wargren!" Vakari held firm, his broad hand clamped tightly about the general's raised forearm. "If you kill him you forfeit your own life! Listen to me, Wargren. A mortal cannot strike a sorcerer and survive the blow himself. To do this, Wargren, will mean your death!"

Mezereon said nothing, for he wisely perceived that just one loose word from his lips would be enough to bring the general's sword flying out of Vakari's grasp and crashing down upon his head; it was clear that Wargren's sanity was poised on a knife edge.

"What difference would it make, Vakari? Are we not dead already?" Wargren screamed, the muscles in his arm still tensed to strike. "This is not living."

Mezereon slowly shrank into a quivering ball under the general's murderous stare, his long, shaking fingers still clawing the air, begging for mercy. The burning hatred in Wargren's eyes gradually changed to weary disgust and his stiffened body began to soften a little. To Vakari's relief, he felt the pressure of Wargren's sword-arm against his hand relax and grow limp. Vakari released his hold on the general and the tip of Wargren's sword thudded into the wooden floor.

"It would be better if we were all dead," he said finally. "For if this snivelling coward refuses to accept his destiny, what hope is there for any of us?"

Vakari gripped Wargren by the shoulder and turned him to look into his hard eyes, "Whilst we live, there is still hope."

"Then you'll have to hope for the both of us, Vakari," Wargren groaned. "For I am immune to the stuff!"

Wargren grudgingly sheathed his sword and staggered lamely towards the door of the shack. Before lifting the wooden bar and inviting in the fierce night, he turned back to speak his final words to Mezereon.

"I only hope I live long enough to see you captured. To see them strip you of every last ounce of your power, and release you into the world as a miserable old, mortal man. I want to see your expression when you remember this night. The night you could have made a difference. The night you could have saved us all!"

A chilling smile enveloped the general's steely expression and then he turned to the other mortal. "Come Vakari! The smell of this place sickens me!"

With that Wargren threw open the door letting an onslaught of furious snow burst into the room, he stooped into the wind and limped out into the blackness.

Vakari slowly approached the still kneeling sorcerer and with an almost pleading expression in his eyes said, "Is there nothing I can say to make you reconsider?"

Mezereon did not answer but lowered his eyes to the floor and grimly shook his head. Vakari gave him a look of thinly veiled contempt and then turned as if to leave, but hesitated when he drew level with Hexerne.

"Come with us," he asked the girl. "We still have friends in the north that will help us. We can offer you a considerably more comfortable rock to hide under than this."

Hexerne did not look at Vakari, her eyes were still glued to Mezereon, but she shook her head. "I shall stay here," she said finally.

"Go with them, Hexerne!" Mezereon snapped. "You have no place here!"

Hexerne eyes never left their target but her lips moved once more. "I wish to stay here."

Vakari allowed his stare to follow that of the girl's and his eyes drifted back to the sorcerer. When he spoke, his voice was flat and dispassionate, as if he was calmly discussing the fate of some miscreant knave of little importance.

"He will be caught, Hexerne," Vakari said. "Because of the Orb. It will lead them to him, wherever he is. He must either use it, or abandon it! For the Orb of Winter can be a saviour or a betrayer, one thing it cannot be . . . is ignored!"

Vakari turned back to the girl, even in the weak light from the modest fire her beauty shone like a beacon.

"Come with me, Hexerne," he breathed. "You need not share his fate."

For the first time her eyes lifted from the sorcerer and turned to face the man. She held his gaze for a long moment but there was no warmth in her pale, exquisite features.

"My name is Luth!" She said coldly.

The titanic storm that terrorized the night had departed by the first glint of morning. The bright ball of the sun climbed above the gleaming shoulders of the mountains into a pale sky thinly screened by the barest scraping of white cloud. The fierce, load-bearing tempest had dumped a huge cargo in its wake; a thick, dazzling cloak of snow laid heavily across the sharp valley.

As soon as the first shafts of searching sunlight speared through the gaps in the rugged walls to wake the inhabitants of the battered shack, a small, reluctant figure was pushed out into the snow to find more logs for the fire.

A terrified Stobe edged step by step along the side of the tiny building with her back pressed hard against the weathered boards; the great yawning chasm of the steep valley dropping away into oblivion only a few paces from her trembling feet. Although the poor disorientated creature could remember nothing previous to being the servant of the dark lady, she knew she was terrified of heights.

The snow-mound on the far side of the shack had been channelled by the spiralling winds into a huge slope that rose perfectly smooth to meet the apex of the roof. The wood-store was now buried deeply beneath a glistening white hill. With a shivering sigh, she smartly rubbed her hands and arms against the chill, and started to dig a tunnel through to the logpile.

Inside the goatherd's modest abode, Hexerne was staring forlornly at a meagre display of food lying on an unfolded piece of muslin that was to serve as breakfast. Mezereon rose stiffly from the floor where he had lain during the night and cast only a cursory glance at the food on the table.

"How do you expect to survive with no food?" Hexerne asked him.

Mezereon sniffed with irritation and shuffled over to a large shuttered window. "I wasn't expecting company!" He growled at her as he lifted the wooden stave and thrust the shutters open, dislodging a wall of snow and allowing a bold shaft of morning light to pierce the gloom of the interior.

The brilliant swathe cleaved the dark room in two, spilling directly across the table and catching Hexerne full in the face with its glory. The girl blinked against the sudden glare, and Mezereon, standing just outside the broad beam, now in even deeper shadow, took advantage of these few privileged moments to steal a private view of his uninvited guest.

The girl's beauty astonished him. The sorcerer had been far too preoccupied with saving his skin the night before to take much notice of the child; it was strange, but even after seven years, he still thought of Hexerne as 'that child'. Even so, gone was the awkward, sickening precociousness of childhood, he remembered. The seven years of hiding and anonymity that all of Vrorst's former high-followers who had managed to evade capture had been forced to undergo, had made her a woman of haunting loveliness.

But it was the stunning resemblance that really impressed him; the same tall, elegant finely sculpted figure, the high cheekbones, the piercing eyes, the full mouth, the long silky black hair. She was the very image of her mother.

"Why did you stay here?" Mezereon asked the girl.

Hexerne's eyes fluttered as she tried to focus on the dark figure cloaked in the deep shadow. She stepped from behind the table and moved out of the brightness to the opposite side of the window. In one motion, the two of them invaded the bright band of sunshine to stand face to face.

"I need your help," Hexerne told him.

"If you think that you can succeed where those two barbarians failed then I'm afraid that . . ."

"That is not why I stayed!" The girl interrupted him. "I believe you. I think the Orb is too powerful for you, as it would be for anyone, other than Him!"

Mezereon studied her warily, he didn't trust this abrupt change of heart. Hexerne's face suddenly lit up with an expression of rapture.

"It spoke to me, Mezereon!" she said at last.

The sorcerer visibly flinched at her words.

"I know you hear it too," she said.

Mezereon turned away into the gloom, his shoulders tense again, and his eyes wild and troubled as before. The girl watched him as he paced nervously about the room, and then she turned back to the splendour of the view.

"I had a strange dream last night," she whispered.

"Pah! Don't talk to me about dreams!" Mezereon snapped.

Hexerne moved fully into the window and took in the whole of the snow-capped vista with one, great devouring sweep of her sapphire eyes. The stunning panorama of frozen peaks marched away into the hazy distance in all its mountainous majesty and for a few moments the girl was rendered speechless by the sheer cruel beauty of their cliff top environment.

"I've never dreamt anything like it before," she said softly. "It was so real."

Hexerne leaned against the window frame and proceeded to relive the experience of her dream, her eyes sparkling in the brilliant light, her attention still fixed on the immense mountainscape.

"I was in a vast hall of ice," she began. "A great corridor of towering columns rising either side of me into an exquisite, vaulted ceiling, almost too high to see. But it wasn't dark like the inside of a palace can be, it was pierced by long radiant beams, and every part of it; the walls, the ceiling, even the floor was pervaded by a pristine, glistening light.

Before me, there rose a long, glowing flight of crystal steps, and at the summit, a single throne, bathed in the brightest shaft of blueish light.

I began to climb the long stairway, and as I did I noticed that I was no longer wearing the drab garb of an ale-wench, I was dressed in a long, queenly robe of shimmering white silk and furs. Soft slippers embroidered with pearls were on my feet, and my hair, rich and shiny with well being, was threaded with silver.

As I climbed the steps the air began to glitter with tiny snowflakes, they floated all around me like soft tufts of down, turning and tumbling, and sparkling like tiny stars as they caught the light.

As I reached the last step, streaks of blue lightning began to flicker through the frozen fabric of the throne. I turned to look back into the immense reach of the bright cavern, and for the first time I saw that it was filled with a pale multitude; all of them silent, expectant."

Hexerne strode majestically from the window, her head proud and her back straight. She reached the stool, and with an elegant flourish of an imaginary ermine cape spun around to face the light once more, and then gracefully lowered herself on to the wooden seat.

"I sat down upon the throne," she continued. "And as I did so, within the wide, blue shaft that shone down from above, a brighter, inner beam was ignited, falling like silver moonlight upon my head. Then I looked up and saw, floating down within the pale beam, a crown of ice; gently rotating as it descended, seizing the intense brightness and sparkling like diamonds.

The instant the crown came to rest upon my head a great exclamation swept through the crowds, and they cheered and cheered, praising my name over and over until the walls shook with their voices."

Hexerne's jubilant tones suddenly dropped.

"And then I awoke, and I was here in this dark, stinking hovel! My beautiful robes replaced with dirty, peasant rags!"

Mezereon gave a snort of recognition, he knew these dreams well. After suffering seven years of the Orb's cruel taunting he ought to have done. The girl had upset herself with her reminiscences and now her radiant eyes were watery with tears.

"It's just a cruel illusion, Hexerne," the sorcerer told her. "One of the nice little tricks the Orb likes to play on us. You get used to them after a while."

Hexerne rounded on him with a surprising rush of venom, her tearful eyes blazing.

"It was my destiny, Mezereon!" she raged, and then with a sudden weakness, "Before it all failed!"

Hexerne flopped down on to the stool again, her head lowered in despair.

"I was to be his queen. Queen of the World! How can I go back to yesterday, and become the wife of a farmer's son? How can I ever live with the knowledge of what might have been?"

"It's easy, child," Mezereon told her in a low, whispering growl. "You just forget! Forget everything but what you have now. I've had to, and just think what I've lost!"

Hexerne raised a desperate face to the sorcerer.

"I can't!" She cried.

Mezereon was unmoved.

"Then every day for the rest of your life will be torn with misery! Believe me, I speak from experience."

"Mezereon," the girl said in a markedly different voice. "My destiny was to become Queen of the World, such was Vrorst's desire. Your destiny was to inherit the Orb of Winter, such was Vrorst's desire. It seems now that both our destinies may fail. But I believe that the Orb itself has a destiny, and it is up to us, you and I, to see that it is fulfilled."

Mezereon regarded her with a chilling blend of suspicion and confusion.

His instinct was always to distrust, and his previous experience of the adolescent Hexerne gave him little confidence that any scheme of hers would be likely to advantage him.

"What are you saying?" He asked warily.

Hexerne's eyes brightened.

"That place in my dream, Mezereon," she began. "It was a place of great beauty and power. Cascades of glistening daggers hanging in the air like frozen fountains.

It wasn't regimented and controlled like the Throne Citadel or the old frozen palace. It was free, untouched, unspoilt . . . !"

Mezereon's face was a perfect portrait of bewilderment, he found the girl's poetic raving most unsettling.

"I believe that such a place really exists!" Hexerne proclaimed.

Now the sorcerer really was worried and found himself taking an involuntary step away from the girl.

"What?" He gasped.

"I believe it is called the Spire of the North!"

"The Spire of the N . . . "

"Vrorst once told me of a place," Hexerne continued. "A place he had built when he first came to Enchantica. A place of powerful enchantment! A place where if all should fail he could find sanctuary. A place beyond the reach of all his enemies! Where he was safe, untouchable. A place to restore himself and grow strong again. He called it the Spire of the North. Did he ever speak to you of such a place, Mezereon?"

The sorcerer's expression had changed from one of confusion to one of extreme agitation, the girl could see that she had struck a nerve.

"Did he?" she asked again.

"It . . . It was . . . just a rumour, a legend, a myth." Mezereon murmured. "None of us really believed in it. We couldn't understand how Vrorst could ever have need of such a place."

Hexerne gently touched his sleeve.

"We have to go there, Mezereon," she said.

A flash of rage sparkled in the sorcerer's dark eyes.

"What?" he snapped.

"We have to take the Orb there!"

A tense moment suddenly exploded between them, the sorcerer's face rapidly filling with horror and fury, his eyes boiling with resentment.

"Are you mad?" Mezereon wailed. "Why? For what purpose?"

Hexerne grew very calm and confident.

"Mezereon," she said, "I have heard the voice of the Orb, felt its touch. It is Vrorst's voice that speaks to me. His touch that I feel! There can be no mistake, the force that dwells inside the Orb is the same as that which dwelled in Vrorst. A part of him lives still, Mezereon, within that mighty globe. Therefore, I must serve the Orb as I would Him were he alive. I cannot help myself, I am and have always been His; body and soul!"

"Hexerne . . . ," the sorcerer tried to stop her.

"You must serve him too, Mezereon!" The girl cried. "He will not allow you to do otherwise!"

"Hexerne!" The sorcerer roared, seizing her arms and pulling her towards him. "You must not allow yourself to be swayed by the treacherous whisperings of that deceitful object! You have spent but one night in its company, I have lived with its tricks and confusions for seven long years! I have resisted the power of its voice for all that time!"

"And you were wrong to resist it!" The girl shrieked with a torrent of escaping rage. "My heart weeps when I think of all the opportunities we have missed!"

Mezereon was stunned into silence by Hexerne's emotional outburst, and for the first time since she had arrived at the weatherworn shack, the girl thought she saw a twinge of shame colour the Dark Sorcerer's cheeks.

A moment of doubt surfaced on his dark face, but it was short lived, for then he collected himself again and his venomous strength returned. He tightened his grip on the girl's arms, massed his determination to escape from any grand schemes the girl might be planning, and drew her even closer to him, his eyes gleaming with menace.

"Do you have any idea of the manner of journey involved in such a quest? Do you?"

Mezereon dragged her over to the brilliant mountainscape.

"Look out of that window." He demanded. "If you think traversing terrain such as this would be difficult, wait until you see the ice chasms of the far north. A hostile, inaccessible environment cloaked in mists so dense that not even the keenest of my snowhawks could penetrate them. If this place really does exist, which I seriously doubt, then you will have to journey to the very roof of the world to find it. As far north as it is possible for a soul to go! Your chances of making it alive are close to zero!"

"And what of your chances, Mezereon?" Hexerne swiftly responded. "What are your chances of finding a hole, deep enough, dark enough and secret enough to hide you from the growing eye of the Alliance? How many more tumbled-down shacks on lonely mountain sides do you think there'll be before they find you?

Perhaps you are right. Perhaps the Spire of the North is just a false legend. Perhaps we would both die trying to reach it. But isn't that better than hiding here, just waiting for the end? At least with the North Spire we have a chance, however slight it may be. And if it is there, and by some miracle we find our way to it, we'll be safe, Mezereon, beyond the reach of all our enemies! And who knows what wonderful things may happen once the Orb has been placed inside the enchanted ice cavern."

Hexerne's voice was filled with light, musical tones of hope and her eyes were bright with excitement. The Sorcerer stared at her thoughtfully, his eyes heavy with contempt.

"We could always abandon it," he said. "Then they might never find us."

"Abandon the Orb!" Hexerne cried in horror. "Can you honestly tell me that you could stand to leave it behind? For let me tell you, Mezereon, I could not! I could no more leave the orb here and walk out of that door, as tear out my own heart! We are both bound to it . . . to the bitter end! If I am sure of nothing else, I am sure of that!"

Mezereon said nothing more, but strode purposefully away from the window and began to gather together his few belongings. For a short while, all of which was sheer torture for the girl, the sorcerer remained silent.

"Mezereon?" She murmured. "Isn't it worth a try?"

The sorcerer fixed her with a disapproving stare.

"You must learn to speak for yourself, child," he said at last.

"Will you come with me?" Hexerne asked anxiously.

"If I do," the sorcerer began, "it is by no means an admission that you are right. Furthermore, I refuse to commit myself to this hopeless quest!"

Hexerne's face dropped.

"However," Mezereon continued. "I will start it with you. If there is a safe hiding place to be found for one such as me, I believe it lies much further north than here. But I say to you now, once and for all, I do not believe in the Spire of the North . . . this frozen sanctuary at the top of the world! It is a vain dream and I will not be seduced by it. But it may be that we can share part of the journey there together."

The girl was not sure whether to be pleased or not. At least she had succeeded in persuading Mezereon to do something, and that was more than Wargren and Vakari had managed to do.

"Oh, and another thing," the sorcerer continued. "That slave of yours . . . erm . . . "

"Stobe!" Hexerne told him.

"Yes. What is she? An elf?"

Hexerne considered the delicate situation, and decided to lie.

"Er . . . yes!" The girl told him. "She is an elf!"

"Get rid of her!" Mezereon commanded. "She'll only slow us down."

Hexerne struggled to think of a strong reason to protest.

"She is important to me," She said in desperation. "She may prove important to both of us. I will not leave without her!"

Mezereon was just about to pursue the matter further when the door to the rugged cabin creaked open and a very red faced Stobe, gasping with exhaustion, her headdress and clothes matted with great clods of snow staggered inside, her legs bowed under the weight of three very heavy logs.

To Hexerne's horror, Mezereon was studying the diminutive servant with acute interest.

For a few moments the poor creature was too shattered to move, her slight figure was stiff with cold and her arms felt incapable of releasing the logs.

Mezereon's eyes had narrowed in suspicion.

"Stobe?" he called to the shivering figure.

Hexerne foolishly exposed her fear by clumsily intervening.

"Stobe, drop those logs, and then gather my things together. We're leaving!"

Mezereon turned warily to Hexerne, suspicion growing in his eyes. He slowly approached the girl, who began to fidget nervously. When he spoke, his voice was calm and commanding, his eyes piercing her soul like cold steel.

"Who is she, Hexerne?"

The girl began to tremble.

"Her . . . her name is Stobe, she . . . "

"Don't lie to me!" Mezereon roared. His voice wrenching through the stillness like a hammer blow.

"Who is she?"

Hexerne was now quavering with anguish, her tearful eyes no longer able to hold the sorcerer's stare.

"She . . . she is under my spell. She is quite safe!"

The air grew decidedly chillier.

"Who is she, Hexerne?" Mezereon growled again.

The girl's breath was becoming laboured, and her shoulders began to hunch.

"She . . . she . . . she is a . . . banf!" The last word fell from her lips with the weight of lead.

The Dark Sorcerer's eyes grew wide with apprehension.

"A banf?" He hissed.

The girl nodded. Mezereon stared at her with incredulity.

"Like he who slew Vrorst?"

Hexerne winced at the connection and then nodded, her eyes cast down upon the floor like a naughty child. Mezereon threw an anxious glance at the banfina, who was dreamily oblivious to the drama.

"Why her?" The sorcerer asked at last.

Hexerne's tear-streaked face lifted miserably.

"She is his," she said simply.

"What?" Mezereon snapped.

The girl swallowed with difficulty.

"She is his female."

A mountain of rage rose into the sorcerer, and when he seized Hexerne by the shoulders he almost lifted her off the ground with the violence of his response.

"You fool!" He bellowed. "You little fool!"

"I thought she would come in useful!" Hexerne pleaded.

"What possessed you to do such a thing? Have you any idea what you've done?"

Hexerne's pale hands gripped the sorcerer's wrists and tried to loosen his hold. Such was his fury that he was crushing her shoulders.

"Is it not enough that we have the hounds of the Three Wizards baying at

our heels? Do you wish to bring the banf, his winged friends and the whole of Enchantica down upon us also?

Hexerne struggled to speak.

"I thought . . ."

"He is Jonquil the Hero! The Wizards' pet! The saviour of the world!" Mezereon suddenly threw Hexerne bodily against the faded boards of the wall. "And you have stolen his female!" The sorcerer's voice faded to a hissing whisper. "What were you thinking of?"

Hexerne shook fearfully and slowly crumpled to her feet. Her voice was heavy with sobs.

"I only thought if things went ill for us, we could trade her for our freedom."

Mezereon was never moved by tears.

"Liar!" He spat. "You wanted revenge! Revenge for Vrorst's death! Revenge against Jonquil the Hero!"

Hexerne threw a wild watery stare at the sorcerer, and he knew that it was true. He cast another anxious glance at the transfixed Stobe.

"Keeping this creature will not further our cause. She can only confound it!"

"Then leave her here and have done with it!" Hexerne bawled.

Mezereon's eyes blazed anew.

"Leave her here . . . to die?" He asked incredulously. "That will go well for us at the final reckoning!"

"Then . . . what?" The girl screamed.

The sorcerer picked up the large bundle of the Orb and his small pouch of belongings and strode purposefully for the door.

"We keep her with us until the first sign of civilisation. Then we dump her! Now come on!"

With that the Dark Sorcerer swept out into the snow, leaving a sobbing Hexerne and a motionless banfina. The girl sniffed and wiped the droplets from her cheeks. Then her eyes fell on Meadolarne; her small delicate figure wrapped tightly in thick furs, her soilworn turban slightly unravelled to reveal snaking wisps of auburn hair; and her large, soulful eyes, vacant and unfocused. The girl stared at her for quite a while, but the pathetic creature before her stirred not a drop of pity.

"You!" She snapped, Meadolarne flinched. "I thought I told you to gather my things together. We're leaving!"

Mezereon stepped cautiously to the lip of the steep chasm, threw wide his arms and began to mumble an almost inaudible chant. Suddenly a sharp updraught filled the Dark Sorcerer's black robes and surged over the cliff to buffet the girl and the slave. Then to Hexerne's astonishment, from the hidden depths below, a huge white shape lifted into view on the new surging wind. Its massive wings blotting out the sky as it neared the cliff. Hexerne's face exploded with joy as the giant shape folded itself about them.

"Grawlfang!" Hexerne tried to cry but her voice was stolen by the wind and emerged as barely a murmur.

"Like you, he's a slave to the Orb!" Mezereon cruelly taunted. "I know what you're thinking but don't raise your hopes! We can only use him for the first part of the journey, after that this great brute will prove too easy a target for my sharp-eyed snowdarts."

Hexerne tugged his arm.

"But what do we do after that?"

The Sorcerer flippantly shrugged his shoulders and gave the girl an arrogant sneer.

"We think of something else!"

The Orb and their own small collection of bundles were secured to the dragon. Then Hexerne and the oblivious Meadolarne climbed across Grawlfang's powerful shoulders.

After all were secure, the great white dragon swept from the cliff, causing a vast tidal wave of disturbed snow to roll into the narrow cleft in his wake. Then he climbed into the web of thin cloud and was gone; carrying his precious cargo northward.

The Fury of the Dragons

Zadragul released the tension of its powerful coils and flew at Jonquil's head, the tunnel serpent's cruel fangs bared to do lethal injury to its prey; and the banf met it with a crunching blow from the heavy mine prop that had somehow found its way into his hands. Jonquil wielded the hefty wooden stave with an explosion of furious energy; his wing was painful and for some reason that he would never be able to explain, it gave him the courage to stand his ground against Zadragul's opening strike and let the monstrous serpent share in a little of his discomfort.

The lunging head of the evil beast was whacked from its deadly course and slammed against the jagged wall of the tunnel. It crashed into the sharp rock and was swiftly followed by a sprawl of writhing coils and a seething riot of piercing curses that profaned the still air in a great hissing blast.

By the time the serpent had gathered itself again, Jonquil had already staggered and stumbled out of sight along the rugged course of the old water vent. Zadragul spat its vehemence at the fading flicker of the disappearing silhouette, flared its head-flags . . . which now burned with livid colour . . . and launched itself in a raging blur after the banf, every fibre of its loathsome being screaming for vengeance.

As the banf had feared, progress through the decrepit water pipe was painfully slow, and although he stepped as lightly as he could, it was impossible to move with any speed. The dull roar of rushing water was louder now and seemed to grow ever more so the further he pushed on through the difficult passage.

Jonquil heard the coming of the furious tunnel serpent like the approach of a titanic storm, its incensed hisses and snarls assaulting his ears in a terrifying volley of screeching sound. The noise of the underground stream was swiftly drowned by the screaming roar of the attacking serpent and Jonquil turned just in time to see the monster fling itself once more at his head. There was no time to launch a swing with the wooden stave, so Jonquil just held it up in front of his face and watched in terror as the flying jaws of the monster struck like a battering ram against it. The banf was punched backwards by the blow with such force that he staggered off balance for some distance still holding the stout prop and the clamped jaws of the serpent in front of him, before finally losing his feet and toppling over; however, he didn't crash down on to the bone-breaking ridged surface of the tunnel floor as he expected, he fell backwards into a well of open space.

Jonquil had tumbled into a vertical shaft, one of the surprise dangers of the mountain tunnels that the peepers had warned him of on his earlier visit to the undermountain; many unsuspecting travellers had plummeted to oblivion down such hidden pitfalls, situated as they were in the most unexpected places. Jonquil was just about to be grateful for being saved the savage death at the claws and teeth of the tunnel serpent for the quick drop of the dark shaft, when he came to a sudden, bone-jarring halt. The wooden prop was too long for the diameter of the shaft and had slammed across the opening with Jonquil thrown about below against the walls of its dark throat, his hands still tightly gripped to the stave.

For a few terrible moments the banf just dangled there, staring up into the snarling features of the serpent, the creature's fangs still clamped to the wood, its eyes narrowed and murderous. Jonquil couldn't think what to do at first, he was stuck; and then his traumatized brain slowly realised why he was still hanging there. The banf turned his attention to the frozen white-knuckle grip of his hands and gradually persuaded them to relax. With one last look at the monstrous countenance of the serpent, Jonquil flexed all of his digits and released himself from the wooden prop.

The creature was mortified at the prospect of losing its quarry and in a movement like lightning struck down at the falling banf, two thirds of its scaled length unravelling to dive into the vertical hole. The serpent just managed to grab the tip of Jonquil's left wing as the banf plummeted into the darkness, its strong jaws crumpling the longest of the banf's elegant flight feathers bringing him to yet another sudden arrest.

The rush of the hidden mountain stream was stronger than ever now, and for the first time Jonquil thought he could detect the faintest trace of fresh air drifting up the shaft from far below.

Zadragul began to haul the banf back up through the shaft, and even though its fangs had not penetrated Jonquil's flesh, the pain of his weight pulling against the roots of his flight feathers was excruciating. However, Jonquil was determined the creature was not going to have him, so despite his agony, the banf screamed his defiance and thrust his back against the rock, braced himself on all sides of the narrow width with his arms and legs and held himself firm against the efforts of the monster. The serpent was infuriated and hissed its frustration through clenched fangs, for tug as it might it could not wrench the banf free from the deep hole, and it dare not loosen its grip to try for a better lest the banf should drop away from it altogether.

Suddenly a spear of pain lanced through Jonquil's tortured wing as the ravaged primary feathers tore from his body. The banf immediately curled up in agony and dropped like a stone into the well of darkness; his plunging descent accompanied by the piercing screech of the disappointed tunnel serpent.

Jonquil was eventually caught by a gentle bend in the vertical drop, smooth and lined with moisture, not rough and scouring as he might have expected. The banf's vision began to grow blurred, the beam of the acorn lantern becoming opaque and hazy, and then Jonquil saw that the chimney of rock was filled with a thick milky mist. The damp shaft carried him down a short succession of shallow twists and spirals and then suddenly disappeared, relinquishing Jonquil into a short lived pale void after which he plunged into the surging torrent of an urgent underground stream.

To the banf's utter amazement the brisk body of water was warm, which explained the billowing clouds of steam enveloping it, and the misty palls which were driven up into the occasional vertical shafts rising from its burrowing course.

Jonquil had heard about the hot springs from Judruff; bubbling pools of steaming water that rose through the rock all over the Marble Fortress, and the banf and the terragon had seen for themselves the occasional misty plumes lifting from tumbling strands of silver water that emerged from the cliffs of the gorge. How the water became warm no-one seemed to know, although the learned spoke of great fires that burned far below the mountains, too fierce for any living being to suffer. They believed it was these vast submerged infernos that heated the underground river systems.

The light from the golden acorn still blazed valiantly even though it was for the most part submerged in the crystal clear water. Jonquil had to struggle to keep his head above the excited surface of the stream, and the clearance between the rippled waves and the curved ceiling of the water tunnel in places was not great. The acorn lantern provided an orb of illumination about the banf which was carried by the vivacious water through a smoothly worn tube that wriggled and twisted, dropped and reared, spiralled and looped in a seemingly endless sweeping ride through the ancient pores of the mountains. Jonquil's innate lust for life meant he couldn't help but enjoy this unique experience; sliding along the rounded pipe, sometimes feet first, sometimes head first, shooting round bends and tight curves, diving down great slides to be propelled over successions of hills and bumps; vigorously pushed along by the gushing downpour, accompanied at every turn by the constant rousing rush of loud water. Jonquil quickly forgot his pain in the warm torrent and soon felt restored and invigorated by his exciting passage, his only twinge of regret was that Rattajack was not there to share it all with him, for he was certain that the terragon, with his lifelong adoration of water, would have been enraptured by the thrilling ride in the buried stream.

Gradually the dark water beyond the incandescent sphere of the mushroom lantern began to lighten, and after rounding two wide, sweeping bends, Jonquil's stream was joined by several others until the banf was being carried along by a forceful river sparkling with the first rays of daylight. The acorn lantern was extinguished just before the banf was brought within sight of a yawning mouth of dazzling white, the effervescence on the water shot through with glittering crests of stars. Jonquil's eyes stang with the intense brightness of the approaching disk of outside world, and soon he found himself racing through a shallow cave, its arched ceiling painted with a rippling web of pale lines thrown up from the calmer water in the shallows. The main thrust in the middle of the river was driving forward to meet the opening with increased vigour, propelling the banf towards a rapidly enlarging wall of white.

Suddenly all Jonquil could see was a blinding mass of sky and the body of the industrious river disappearing over the jagged line of a rocky ledge. In less time than it takes to blink Jonquil realised where he had emerged and what was coming next, and before he was swept away into the milky void, the banf scrambled across the powerful current of the water and dived for a prominent tooth of rock. Jonquil's fingers closed on the rough textured stone and his body was turned forcefully by the river until the banf was facing back into the water cave, his legs dangling precariously over the edge of the roaring fall. The river tried with all its might to take him with it into the gorge but Jonquil's fingers were clamped like a vice on the rock and they refused to yield. At that point the banf would have given anything not to have had wings, for his large feathered limbs, now heavy with water, stood out against the current and only aided the river in dragging him down.

Painfully and laboriously Jonquil began to ease himself away from the lip of the chasm, hauling his body through the onslaught of warm water, steadily reaching for one safe hand grip and then another.

Suddenly a bloodchilling screech rang out from inside the cave and Jonquil's eyes widened with horror as the flared crests of Zadragul sailed into the light. The serpent had followed him into the underground stream and was now surging towards him in the flow of the river, its sharp claws paddling frantically against the waves, its long weaving tail thrashing to give it dominion over the current. Jonquil sucked in a chestful of breath and pulled himself flat to the rocks, allowing the full weight of the water to charge over his back. As the banf hoped, the serpent was more intent on seizing him than securing itself against the power of the waterfall, and by the time it realised that the river was stronger it was too late to struggle. The tunnel serpent was too large and ungainly in the water to resist its potency and with the greatest of ease the cataract swept the squirming creature right over Jonquil's submerged body and into the mighty jaws of the chasm, a strangled hiss of defiance rising from its throat before it disappeared over the edge.

Jonquil pulled himself clear of the torrent and as he did so a great flash of white and a roar of icy wind flew over him drawing his eyes irresistibly to the gorge, a large shadow sweeping down the face of the cliff at the same time; and then the banf watched in trembling awe as the magnificent form of a snowdragon rose majestically on the updraughts, the writhing form of Zadragul wrestling with its talons.

The banf watched spellbound as the graceful span of the snowy dragon carried it away into the gorge, its long slender sails of gleaming white skin hardly beating as it slipped effortlessly through the air. Then Jonquil's eyes were drawn to a tumbling pale streak stooping with a purpose towards the leisurely dragon; it was a robber, somewhat smaller than the first white dragon, rushing in to steal its victim's wriggling prize. With a flick of its long wings the larger snowdragon threw itself into a dive and plunged into the thick blanket

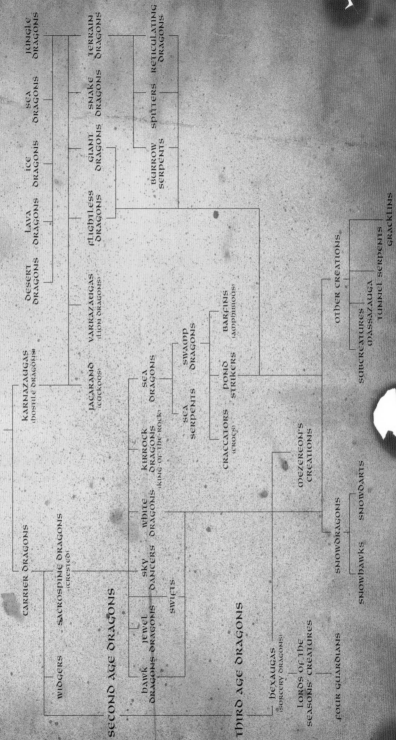

of mist smothering the canyon floor, its smaller assailant easily matching the rapid burst of speed, and all the time trying to snatch the tunnel serpent from the first dragon's grasp.

For a few moments Jonquil stood spellbound and watched the gleaming white shapes grow smaller until they finally melted almost imperceptibly into the milky haze that filled the vast course of the trench like a steamy pale river.

It was hard for a simple forest dweller to take in the full grandure of a natural wonder like Dragongorge. The great chasm of the dragons was a massive tear in the mountains that ran through the towering peaks like a weaving, ragged snake. Smaller chasms frequently sprang from its ancient bones like the roots of a tree, eating into the flanks of the Marble Fortress, and then plunging into titanic drops, leaving razor precipices and crumbling cliffs in their wake.

The mother of all canyons was also the mother of all dragons. An isolated universe with its own diverse climates and environments, all supporting a breathtaking selection of flora and fauna, which in turn supported an astonishing inhabitation of awesome dragons.

By far the most common group of dragons were the cliff dwellers. These tended to include many of the most fearsome species, and were usually to be found in the more barren, rocky stretches of the gorge such as the long, craggy reach containing the sprawl of Dragonskeep and beyond.

The sacrospines or crested dragons were the largest group. They included the greatest fighters and hunters; like the hawk, jewel and kirrock dragons; the sky-dancers, graceful broad-winged dragons that performed stunning aerial courtship displays; swifts and white dragons, who Mezereon had combined to form a basic creature from which to engineer his murderous races of snowbeasts.

There were dragons to suit all environments, and environments to suit all dragons. At various points along its mighty sweep, Dragongorge was lined with jungles and swamps; lakes and rivers; forests and verdant plains; glaciers, deserts, and even its own submerged mountain ranges. Dragons of all shapes, colours, characteristics and needs; strode, swam, flew and roared, in the caves, trees, marshes, dunes, ice-flows and pinnacles that lay within the monstrous rift that was Dragongorge.

A sunken world, separate from the body of the Commonlands and yet throbbing with an intense flow of life like a major artery running through it.

Jonquil cast his eyes into the blustery depths before him. The muscular winds which terrorised the rugged cliffs must have delivered a snowfall during the banf's underground adventure, for all of the crumbling shelves and ledges of the towering jagged walls had been caught with white, the stark contrast between the snow and the dark grey rock creating an almost mesmeric marbling effect that plunged into the soft body of the canyon's pale floating shroud.

Suddenly a menacing shadow fell across the banf and a terrible crushing pain drove sharply into his wings. Jonquil cried out in shock and then his eyes exploded into incredulous saucers as the rocky ledge of the waterfall dropped away from his feet; a powerful force lifting him into the air and then sweeping out over the vast trench of the canyon.

Jonquil tried to see what manner of beast had seized him, but all his eyes could reach from his dangling, horizontal situation was the pointed tips of long, white wings beating down either side of him. The dragon held the banf torpedo fashion and swung across the wide embrace of the gorge to bank into an oncoming storm of wind and shoot like an arrow back towards the rise of the white mountains.

Despite his flailing, dizzy ride, Jonquil was able to observe a brief glimpse of the land below him. He saw the snaking plume of steam that rose from the emerging warm river that he had ridden in, and that it poured from an unfamiliar rock face in the great chasm's north cliffs; the dark friendly heap of Dragonskeep was nowhere to be seen east or west of him. The banf could hardly believe that he had travelled so far beneath the mountains, or that he had been in the dark tunnels for so long, for the pale circle of the veiled sun told him that this was the afternoon of the next day.

The dragon bore Jonquil over the jagged northern lip of Dragongorge and up into the eastern sweep of the majestic snow-clad walls of the Marble Fortress. The great mountain range speared the threadbare ceiling of attendant clouds with a soaring armoury of gleaming points. The fractured shafts of sunlight, that somehow lacked the conviction of those that blazed in the south, stole through the shifting screen of cloud to dapple the broad shoulders of the mountains with a rolling patchwork of dazzling white islands in a sombre grey sea. Jonquil's abductor brought him down into this immaculate landscape, gliding low over the sweeping cloaks of snow that draped across the weaving feet of the giants. Eventually the progression of tight valleys were cleaved by a dark rift, splitting the white folds and plunging deep and narrow into the bones of the world. The sharp fissure was one of the many offshoots from Dragongorge that wrenched their way between the toes of the mountains and provided secluded cliffs for isolated populations of dragons. The chasm which opened up below Jonquil's feet was alive with winged shapes, swooping and circling about the severe rock faces in a shrieking, industrious cloud. The cliffs were layered with clefts and ledges, the ragged sheets of dark rock pitted with cracks and caves and it was to these perches and apertures that the wheeling population kept returning. The winged beasts down below were not the same as the one which had snatched the banf, they were coloured with earthy tones of red and orange, and their wings and bodies were somewhat heavier and broader.

Swift white dragons flew amongst the flocks of their darker counterparts, chasing and harassing them, stealing their food, or stooping cruelly at brooding females on the ledges trying to scare them into abandoning their vulnerable offspring.

These smaller, speedier versions of the snowdragon, had been named snowhawks by their dark creator, Mezereon, who had been obsessed with the breeding of faster and faster dragons. He called them hawks because of their vicious temperaments and formidable jaws and talons. They had earned themselves a dark reputation amongst the indigenous populations of Dragongorge since great murderous gangs of them had been irresponsibly released into the wild to wreak utmost evil and destruction upon the noble peoples.

The awesome snowdarts, an even swifter creation and a blue-fire breather too, of which mercifully only a few had been spawned, including the magnificent Snowthorn, had originally been given to Wargren to lead Vrorst's offensive against the Wizards of Light. However, these superlative fliers had since been captured and commandeered by Tuatara for her dragonflight; these spectacular dragons now, ironically, being employed to hunt their creator.

The snowhawk that had snatched Jonquil was now lifting him away from the gape of the chasm towards a ridge of high spearing ramparts upon which was housed a menacing rookery of its fellow creatures. The snow-dusted precipice provided a perfectly camouflaged striking perch for the agile killers. Every movement to and fro could be observed from on high, every creature passing through or over the dark fissure followed or targeted. These white scourges of the frozen mountains had now claimed the snowy uplands as their own; and even though as individuals they were not invincible, when their unnaturally keen hunting skills and ferocity were coupled with their innate flocking instincts and teamwork, they could gain superiority over all other dragons. Luckily for the rest of Dragongorge's more peaceful populations, the snowhawks' competitive and spiteful natures meant that they were not always willing to aid each other in their evil endeavours.

The powerful span of talons that was clamped on to Jonquil's wings tightened as the fleet dragon approached the habitat of the snowhawks; it clearly feared theft. The increased pressure did little to alter the banf's discomfort as he had lost all sensation in his wings shortly after being snatched from the steaming cataract; and dared not think what might happen if he was suddenly dropped by the dragon and had to rely on his numbed flight muscles to fly him to safety; even though that was probably a better prospect than what lay in store for him when the snowhawk finally reached its intended destination.

The dragon banked away from the high bastion and tried to skirt low and unseen over the snow-covered lip of the towering cliffs. By craning his head to look upside down between his legs Jonquil saw that the rows of white dragons perched on high hadn't seemed to notice their snowhawk brother with its talons full of food. Even though it could have been a very foolish thing to do, Jonquil decided that the only way to interfere with the evil intentions of his captor was to announce himself in the loudest possible terms to the other dragons and invite their intervention. His first vocal attempts were decimated by the blustering winds surging up from the chasm below, and then Jonquil remembered something far better. Before the snowhawk achieved too much of a lead, the banf breathed in a vast amount of cold mountain air, pushed the carved slipper nut into his mouth and then emptied his lungs into it for all he was worth.

The voice of Meadolarne's whistle sliced through the urgent breezes and bounced in a squealing echo off the stark towers of grey rock. The dozen or so dozing snowhawks slumped on the high ridge awoke and turned to regard the source of the strange sound as one dragon. An eruption of white wings spewed into the sky as the snowhawks' keen eyes spotted their evasive brother and the cargo of food swinging from his claws. With a cacophony of screeching cries, the dragons harnessed the swiftest of the draughts and raced after the fleeing snowhawk and Jonquil.

As the banf was hurriedly stuffing the nut whistle back into his tattered tunic his hand fell upon the cold metal scabbard of the short sword that Judruff had given him, and a desperate plan leapt into his mind.

Jonquil's abductor twisted away from the course of the fissure and darted into an open landscape of wide shallow slopes, disrupted occasionally by jagged scabs of grey rock. The snowhawk was desperately scanning the terrain below for what Jonquil assumed was a place to hide. The snow looked very deep in the gentle valleys and the banf was just about to consider thrusting up with his sword to force the dragon to release him, when in a desperate attempt to keep its meal to itself the dragon suddenly surged up into a vertical climb and with a tremendous crack of its wings and flexing of its supple spine executed an astonishing mid-air back flip and propelled the banf like a winged missile towards the banks of soft snow.

Jonquil shot through the air like a rock from a catapult and plunged into the shallow slope with an explosion of white powder. The dragon then whipped up a storm of wind with its powerful wings to smooth over the ruptured skin of the snow bank, until it was barely distinguishable from the rest of the sweeping white covering. Then with a sudden burst of speed the snowhawk screamed out of the valley to lure its pursuers far away from its hidden prize.

Whether the dragon was hoping there were sharp rocks just beneath the white surface that would kill its prey, or that Jonquil would simply be knocked unconscious by the impact and lie there immobilised until the creature's return, wasn't certain. In the end the banf was knocked unconscious, and although the soft bank had simply yielded to him like a pillow and left him remarkably unscathed, it had also piled in on top of him leaving Jonquil buried beneath a heavy lid of snow.

The wave of winged pursuers tore through the gentle curve of the valley and continued the chase of the lone snowhawk, whom they would not discover was now devoid of prey for some distance.

Meanwhile another drama was unfolding a little nearer to the dark chasm. A daring lone snowhawk had been planing across the face of the jagged cliffs, trying to upset the brooding mothers of the native species, as their kind was wont to do, when it suddenly spotted an unguarded infant alone on a ledge and swooped in to snatch it. The parent who had turned her back for only an instant immediately raised the alarm and the dominant male of the pride, who had been watching over his harem of nursing females from a prominent sceptre of rock, threw open his awesome wingspan and charged after the robber.

The white dragon would normally have been able to outpace its pursuer with little difficulty, but the handicap of the struggling dragonling suspended from its talons checked its speed considerably and gave it no chance of escape.

The furious male, who ploughed through the air like thunder to exact both rescue and revenge, was a 'kirrock' or 'king-of-the-rock'; his powerful form was a combination of dark ochre scales burnished with gold edges, a deep red underside, and dark wings with pale fingers that filled the air like monstrous flags. The kirrocks were a fierce and proud race of sacrospine dragons, that formed prides or close family groups ruled over by a dominant male and premier female. The family's hatchlings were the most precious beings in the group and were always protected or fought over to the death. Nest robbers were dealt with like vermin. The task of defending the pride fell to the dominant or king male, and the individual which had given chase to the bold snowhawk thief was experienced and battle-scarred, and not a dragon to offend lightly.

The kirrock caught up with the white dragon above a brief rash of snow-kissed evergreens and crashed violently into the flanks of its enemy with its powerful talons. The snowhawk immediately responded by jettisoning the wailing dragonling into the bushy canopy of the trees and then swerved sharply around intending to pounce on the other dragon's back whilst it unwittingly followed the fall of the baby to ensure its safety. Unfortunately for the snowhawk, who clearly was not familiar with kirrocks, the mighty king male did not turn from his attack to give succour to the dragonling, for following closely in its wake were two or three of the other family adults who would tend to the infant.

The king male threw himself, talons and claws to the fore, at the body of the snowhawk, his great crest of spines rampant with fury from the crown of his head to the tip of his long, furious tail.

The two monsters skirmished viciously across the treetops of the evergreens, the noise of their combined roars carrying far beyond the reach of the dark rift. The white dragon tried to push the kirrock away and beat a hasty retreat but the darker dragon only advanced upon it with increased venom, seizing its forearms with his teeth or claws and pulling it back into the fray. At last the snowhawk realised that its only chance was to stay and fight, that it had no choice but to engage in a deadly duel with the 'king-of-the-rock'. The kirrock may have had a slight advantage of weight but the two combatants' size and weaponry were evenly matched; the two adversaries squaring up for a titanic contest.

At first the two dragons only sparred and lunged at each other, both of them

123

testing the strength of their opponent and searching for a weakness. The snowhawk was not accustomed to single combat, he would normally have been joined by a screaming cloud of his fellow predators, who together would have torn their enemy apart; but the greater number of the snowhawk gang had chased after the individual carrying Jonquil and had yet to return to the heights above the chasm. The white robber was alone, and had only his own strength and ferocity to aid him against the wrath of the kirrock.

The indigenous dragons had seen many of their offspring fall victim to the rampaging excesses of the new hostile arrivals. They had suffered enough during Mezereon's reign at Dragonskeep, when the white dragons that marauded their cliffs had borne evil riders, and their babies were stolen for the Dark Sorcerer's experiments. Once Mezereon had been defeated, the native dragons had dared to hope that they might be left in peace, as they had no natural enemies in the wilds of their domain. Then the snowhawks had come, as a deadly white storm howling into the chasm, bringing fear and warfare back to the once peaceful cliffs. The natives had had enough, and the anger that boiled in the veins of the dominant male now doing battle in defence of its young, had been building in his soul since the first white hawk had stolen the first kirrock baby, and now it was time for a reckoning.

The clash of the two dragons shook the rocks and the bellow of their mighty voices bombarded the air. A storm of talons raked furiously at each others armoured bellies, the hooked claws of their forelimbs tearing and scratching to try and penetrate the thick body plates. The awesome crushing jaws of the monsters clashed and mauled, each fearsome gape reaching for the other's throat, whilst the four great canopies of skin thrashed and stabbed at their flailing limbs, causing the pliant heads of the bushy trees below to bend and dance with the resulting squall of gusts.

The long whipping tails of the beasts which were armed with murderous crests of spiny teeth slashed across the other's wings, and then ravelled and writhed as the two monsters were drawn ever closer together.

Finally their fearsome claws and feet locked together in a deadly embrace and the two snarling reptiles surged away from the bed of trees in savage, tempestuous circles, their great stretched spans of skin beating maniacally against the air and each other, their bodies spinning in an hypnotic maelstrom of thrashing wings and tails. Each dragon was trying to fling the other on to the lethal projections of jagged rock rising as spear-like ramparts from the lip of the chasm. It would only have taken one spinning wing bone to connect with the hard teeth of the rocky bastions for the mortal combat to have ended. Yet spin as they might neither combatant seemed able to break through the barrier of claws and gain an advantage.

The twirling death dance would continue until one of the gladiators tired, or the combatants tangled bodies simply lost control of the strenuous updraughts and were dashed against the cliffs.

Suddenly, the snowhawk relaxed its fiercesome concentration for an instant, in an attempt to summon aid from a brace of white dragons it had spotted in the distance. The kirrock immediately took advantage of this fatal lapse and fought his way past the snowhawk's clawing defences to clamp his powerful jaws around the white dragon's slender throat. The white dragon squirmed with panic and with a final effort the king male galvanised his massive strength and heaved the flailing white body into a powerful swing. The snowhawk was hurled savagely towards the cliffs, where it slammed with a mighty crunch into the unforgiving face of the sheer rock. Its body crumpled with the force of the impact and plummeted in a wild death spiral to the scree scattered floor of the narrow chasm.

With a thundering bellow of victory, the triumphant kirrock male trumpeted his warning to the hovering white dragons, his uproarious cry joined by the united, defiant voices of the cliff colonies. The natives were resolved that the snowhawks were free to maraud their families no longer, and they gave unequivocal notice to the sleek white predators to leave their cliffs.

The Deathtreader

Jonquil awoke to a blurred wall of pale shapes, for a few moments his eyes refusing to focus on his surroundings. Then a ceiling of small, twitching faces slowly sharpened into view and the banf started with alarm.

At his cry of surprise the pale creatures retreated until only one remained before him, this individual seemed to be some sort of spokesbeing for the rest. However, to the creature's surprise, its speech of reassurance did nothing to quell the banf's fear and suspicion; and it wasn't until Jonquil spoke back at him that the leader realised they weren't speaking the same language.

Jonquil found himself in a dome of creamy, textured curves that glowed with a strong source of light from beyond. He was lying on a soft bed of mingled moss and silky hair and there was a single gloomy burrow leading away from the tranluscent chamber.

The creature who crouched at his feet had, to the banf, a most bizarre appearance. Almost all of its body was clothed in thick white fur. Its small pink face was reminiscent of a peeper, it also had large eyes, bright blue and inquisitive. Its ears were small and furry and waggled either side of an extraordinary curving beard and quiff which gave these creatures the colloquial name of 'moonfaces', for in profile the heads of the snowy white beings did resemble the youthful moon. The Wizards knew them as snowhoppers, an ancient and loyal race that had dwelled amongst the permanent snow of the north mountains long before Vrorst had proclaimed himself Lord of Winter. Since their homeland had become the realm of snowhawks, icedemons, icetrolls and wolvines, the hoppers had become a secretive and wary people. They rarely made contact with outsiders, although they remained faithful to the peepers, to whom they were closely related. Indeed some of their snow burrows led to the ancient boreholes of the undermountain connecting their mostly 'above ground-below snow' domain to that of the darkness dwellers.

The snowhoppers could move with great agility having strong back legs with which to leap and bound. Unlike the peepers they did not have long luxuriant tails that flowed behind them. Long tails would not be an asset when being chased into a bolthole by a snowhawk or a wolvine, so the hoppers had evolved short plumes of fur that closely followed the curve of their bodies. When out in the snow they rarely strayed far from the mouths of their burrows, even though because of their colouring they were almost invisible, and only detectable if they should move. Indeed, there had been hoppers out on the snow bank when Jonquil had been so violently planted there by the white dragon, and as a consequence of judging the banf to be an enemy of their enemy, he had to be a friend.

The moonfaces had burrowed their way beneath the crust of the white slope to reach the unconscious banf and drag him through their snow tunnels to safety, for they knew the snowhawk would soon return to claim its hidden meal. Carefully filling the holes back in as they moved Jonquil away from the site of his traumatic entry, they effectively removed any evidence of their presence thus not provoking a mad digging frenzy by the dragon as it tried to uncover their concealed runs, most of which lay just beneath the frosted surface.

Jonquil had slept for almost two whole days before his senses had finally returned to him. When he awoke to discover himself a guest of the snowhoppers, after the initial surprise, he managed to convey to them his need for food, inspired by a hole in his belly large enough for a tunnel serpent to crawl through. The hoppers returned to him with a selection of fresh succulent roots, ground nuts and a juicy array of big fat cloud worms . . . a snowhopper delicacy. Jonquil politely declined the latter but feasted with relish on the nuts and roots, the bemused moonfaces having to consume the main course themselves.

When his thoughts were finally his own, the banf discovered that the diminutive furry creature who had remained behind and become his constant companion and guide, was speaking to him in a dialect of the old tongue of the wizards; the hoppers addressed each other in their own version of the peepers' clicking chatter. Jonquil's knowledge of the Wizards' ancient language was thin at best, although eventually, after a good deal of perseverance on both sides, he did manage to decipher the gist of what he was being told. The snowhopper who had befriended him was a female called Cliffspringer, and Jonquil was delighted to hear that she was known and trusted by the Wizards.

When Jonquil wanted to eat, Cliffspringer took him to find food, when he was thirsty she took him to a cool, underground stream. As venturing above the snow was considered too risky for such a visible being, the banf soon began to rely on the beneficence of the friendly hoppers for his very existence.

The banf was amazed by the intricate network of runs and burrows that riddled the footslopes of the low peaks. The softly filtered daylight illuminated almost every tunnel and chamber, and Jonquil soon discovered that although the hoppers had deeper passages and rock chambers to escape to in times of extreme danger, they much preferred to stay close to the surface, playing and exploring through a frozen honeycomb of glimmering caves and corridors.

On hearing from Jonquil that he had previously made the acquaintance of the peepers, as a precaution Cliffspringer sent scouts into the realm of the undermountain to seek out Sollo-Sollo and his clan, and confirm that their good feelings towards the banf were justified. A few days later her answers returned with a bundle of extra news for Jonquil attached to them.

After almost a week of the snowhoppers' beneficial solicitude, the banf began to feel much stronger. His wings were still very stiff and awkward, especially when it came to crawling through some of the cramped burrows, but a lot of the hurt had faded from his wounds. He knew the day for him to leave was drawing near.

Jonquil tried to discover from his new found friends a possible route through the snow-bound mountains to bring him once again to a place where he could continue his quest for Meadolarne and be reunited with his terragon companion, whom the snowhoppers had managed to receive news of via the peepers. The female snowhopper told Jonquil that Rattajack had been secretly observed by Sollo-Sollo and his people and had skilfully wormed his way out of the dark passages and safely into the light, near to the great garrison. These tidings came as a great relief to Jonquil who knew that the terragon would fly straight back to Dragonskeep to summon help. Now it was up to Jonquil to show that he too could bring himself safely out of the wilderness and back on course to find his beautiful banfina.

The snowhoppers offered to guide Jonquil into the rock tunnels and back beneath the mountains to the realm of the peepers, where the friendly tunnel dwellers would then take him to Dragonskeep. As much as the banf longed to speak with Sollo-Sollo and the other peepers again, he declined the hoppers kind offer. If he and Rattajack were to discover news of Meadolarne, somehow Jonquil knew that they would never hear it cooped up inside the dark grey walls of the ancient fortress. He decided to do what the two companions should have done in the first place . . . venture forth on his own. The banf was sure it was the only way he was going to pick up the trail of Meadolarne and the mystery lady.

Cliffspringer and a number of her people accompanied the banf to the secret course of a warm, infant stream; which miraculously didn't melt the snow that concealed it. The snowhoppers guided Jonquil along a meandering burrow which followed the hidden waterway until emerged from the deep snowbank into the bright morning light of a narrow valley.

Before they would let him leave, Cliffspringer and the others tried to convey a strong warning to the banf about the great danger that lay ahead for him. Unfortunately, Jonquil's rudimentary grasp of the language didn't allow him to fully understand the true significance of their words. His memory of Halmarand's maps told Jonquil that if his sense of direction was reliable, he should be heading towards the Morgvale, and beyond that the Doomslang swamp, and hopefully beyond that the settlement of Ischelmynth. The snowhoppers tried valiantly to dissuade him from venturing that way, but at the same time knew that it was the only path open to him. Cliffspringer and the others had tried to heal the worst of the damage to Jonquil's wings, and the banf was able to thank them for easing most of the pain. However, the injuries inflicted by the tunnel serpents and the snowhawk had removed Jonquil's ability to fly, and that they had not succeeded in restoring.

Therefore, whatever path Jonquil was to take from that moment on, it would have to be on foot, and his chances of making it alive across the snowslopes, where the snowhawks, icedemons, icetrolls and wolvines roamed, were none existant; it was the Morgvale or nothing.

Jonquil thanked them for their kindness and their concerns, and for the small matter of saving his life; and then after politely refusing their pleas for him to stay longer with them, turned to face into the dazzling beam of light which beckoned him into the steep valley.

The snow-buried slopes descending from the high wall of mountains guarding Dragongorge eventually plunged into a sharp cleft containing a steaming thread of silver water. The snowhoppers bade Jonquil farewell at the mouth of the small tunnel where the undersnow stream trickled out into the open air.

The banf followed the course of the young stream for some distance warily watching the surrounding ridges for signs of danger but the smooth flanks of snow above him were empty and undisturbed, and betrayed not a single mark or footprint.

After a while the steam from the whispering water which had begun as a hazy, pale curtain curling lazily in the stillness started to rise from the tepid water in billowing plumes. The rock-toothed ridges of the valley had gradually drawn further apart until they were hardly discernible from the milky sky, giving the slopes a more rounded, shallower gradient. The stream grew wider until it was no longer a stream but a convergence of several meandering water channels; the snow began to give way to large tussocks of grass that squelched underfoot and pools of algae-tinged mud that sucked at Jonquil's shoes.

The wide bog of marshy ground was screened by a floating veil of mist which strengthened into an impenetrable blank wall in the far distance. Occasional straggling trees began to appear accompanied by limp fringes of fern, and the cheerful flow of the streams slowed to a thick, lethargic ripple.

Jonquil knew that he was approaching the Morgvale, the wide fog-ridden trench that eventually led to the festering sump that was the Doomslang Swamp.

The banf knew from experience that a great many of the world's most unpleasant and dangerous creatures made their homes in swamps. However, what he was not aware of was that an alternative name for the dark place he was about to enter was 'The Deathtreader' or 'the swamp of certain death'.

If the banf's knowledge of the old tongue of the Wizards had been greater, he could have learned these things from the snowhoppers. As it was he just assumed the moonfaces had been trying to warn him to be careful, which he had every intention of being anyway.

All things considered hardly a great recommendation for continuing along this marshy path, but of course the banf was mindful that he really didn't have any choice. To avoid the swamp altogether would have meant a punishing climb into the snow peaks and exposing himself to the risk of attack by hunting snowhawks, not to mention the host of other terrible foes.

Before long Jonquil was ankle deep in frothy green water enclosed within a tangled forest of trees, creeping vines and broad palms. The constant mist which dwelled in the stillness condensed on the mossy stems and leaves, making it look as if the whole jungle was sweating in the thick, warm air. Flying insects of every size and description emerged at the banf's approach, singing in his ears, hovering about his eyes and biting for his blood. Cascades of waterdroplets rattled through the foliage as Jonquil gradually pushed passed the intrusive growth, and long sodden beards smeared over his face and hair as he climbed between fences of clammy branches.

In places the choked water bubbled or burped with escaping gas, or rose into a throbbing mushroom where a warm spring was vainly attempting to break through the thick scum and add freshness to the putrid ponds. Thick rafts of floating plants carpeted most of the open water, yielding only to suspicious looking logs and stumps; and occasionally the banf would discover worrying channels of clear water, pathways through the slimy soup created by some large, as yet unencountered, creatures.

Large pine trees rose like giant spears from the chaos over the water, their long straight trunks hugged by thick cords of treevine, winding and knitting across the wrinkled, patchwork bark like proud veins on a taught muscle.

The banf had to fight his way through ever thicker vegetation and at times he would swear that some of the wiry shrubs were fighting back. Ugly trees bristling with spikes began to appear, accompanied by thorny bushes with needle-sharp spines as long as his fingers. Jonquil had to gingerly negotiate his way past these vicious obstacles without allowing any of the cruel points to scratch him; he knew from bitter experience that some thorns were poisonous, some even deadly. The banf spotted a burn-elder some way in the distance and was suddenly reminded of his and Rattajack's dreadful abduction by the Swamp Demon and their subsequent capture in Ogrod's rope trap. He wondered if any of the Swamp Demon's relatives inhabited the Doomslang and then quickly assured himself that a place such as this was undoubtedly swarming with creatures far worse.

Jonquil's sensitive ears were alert to the smallest sounds but so far the only noise to hear was that of his own slow progress through the matted undergrowth, now waist deep in black, tepid water. Thick plumes of unseen pondweed stroked his legs, submerged branches snagged and tore his hose and thin wriggling bodies squirmed beneath his feet with almost every step; the water may have seemed unfit to sustain life but in truth it was literally heaving with living creatures.

Jonquil's nerves took a violent jarring when a marshwidger suddenly burst from a rash of palm leaves, growing from an old stump that the banf nonchalantly brushed with his fingertips, its vibrant alarm call shattering the silence of the jungle like a call to arms. The fruit-bat sized dragonet shrieked away from Jonquil with a flurry of agitated wingbeats, finally landing flat against a lichen-coated trunk, wings outstretched, displaying its brightly coloured intimidation patches; it then proceeded to scold him loudly and flash furious golden eyes.

The piercing distress calls of the widgers, of whatever type, could be the explorer's best friend if it was an enemy's silent approach that alarmed them, but when it was your own secret progress at stake they were the last creatures in the world you wanted to disturb. Jonquil's sentiments were akin to the latter, especially as this particular individual was creating an inordinate amount of noise even by their loud standards.

Jonquil had visions of every evil monster within slinking, creeping or slithering distance lifting their ears and then nostrils to the air, attracted by this unignorable furore and perhaps thinking; "here comes supper!"

The tiny dragon's tail flicked angrily as it fluttered from tree to tree, strangely reluctant to depart, its violent widgering not yielding a single decibel. Suddenly a notion struck Jonquil, he had an idea he knew why the insistent creature kept circling him through the surrounding foliage, watching the banf intently, flashing its warning colours and sometimes even feigning injury to try and attract his attention. Jonquil climbed on to the nearby horizontal trunk of a large fallen tree, carefully straddling an impressive armoury of long spikes that rose from its gnarled bark; he leaned towards the mess of palm leaves from which the small reptile had fled and gently parted them to look inside. As Jonquil did so the marshwidger's cries of anguish increased and its activity became even more frantic. It flapped and jumped through the surrounding branches desperately trying to draw the banf's attention away from the palm cluster.

What Jonquil expected to see when he peered into the tall leaves was a neat little nest of woven reed pipes or sedge and a clutch of five or six sparkling blue eggs lying within. All the banf actually saw was the thick mat of fibrous roots at the base of the palm fronds, no nest in sight.

An uneasy feeling suddenly gripped the back of Jonquil's neck and he could almost feel the absent Rattajack quivering with alarm at his side. The banf quickly glanced at the phrenetic marshwidger, the reptile's wild eyes almost pleading with Jonquil to follow it into the jungle; in the very next moment the fallen trunk beneath the banf's feet started to move.

Jonquil flung his arms wide to balance himself as the long, horizontal 'tree' began to glide across the surface of the water, leaving a broad canal through the crust of floating plants in its wake. Whatever it was the banf had used as a ladder to reach the palms, it certainly hadn't been a dead tree. It was impossible to see what manner of beast the banf had stepped on to because of the dense hedges of shrub and thicket that hung over the water, obscuring all of its distinguishing features.

As he was being carried along, Jonquil dared to throw a glance behind him and saw an endless spiked tail snaking through the still water in wide effortless sweeps barely causing a ripple. Were there legs beneath him? Powerful, clawed talons sprinting through the weed? The water, when it was uncovered, was so black and thick with manes of algae Jonquil couldn't tell. The front end just kept on weaving between the feet of submerged trees, ploughing through the low vegetation and carrying the banf deeper and deeper into the steaming swamp.

The marshwidger having tried its best to warn the banf of the imminent danger, now lost interest in his plight, and after idly preening itself for a few moments, chattered its way into the distant trees, quickly melting into the mingled wall of leaves.

Up ahead, across Jonquil's path, draped with a long, ragged fringe of beard and bound with a tight-gripping net of furry vines, the low lying limb of a marsh oak reached out over the water like a long shaggy arm. The creature moved swiftly beneath it, the high column of spines rising from its back teasing the lowest of the wispy beards as they passed underneath. The banf was being propelled towards the low lying branch with disquieting speed, his arms flapping wildly to keep from tipping into the unfriendly water. As the stout, hairy limb approached, the creature seemed to accelerate so that Jonquil was brought to it even faster. He leapt up to grab hold of the vines and was slammed hard in the chest as he made contact with the bough.

When he recovered some of the wind that had been knocked out of him, the banf found himself dangling precariously over the black depths, the tips of his shoes dipping into the green scum on the water as the remainder of the monstrous tail slid past.

Apart from the soft vines the bark of the branch was coated with a thick sheath of drenched moss, which together with the delsidian shirt helped to cushion the blow of the sudden impact. The slippery green fur oozed moisture as Jonquil struggled to improve his grip but steadily with the aid of the sturdy vines he was able to swing his legs upwards and around the limb; and with a little more effort he was able to climb to his feet and 'tightrope' walk across to the main trunk.

With a sudden, deafening roar and a mountain of green, leaf-strewn water the monster began to rise into the trees. Jonquil flattened himself against the lichen-patterned bark of the trunk and stared in horror as the creature's dark silhouette reared up out of a great lake of slime. The ridge of spikes that ran the length of its broad, muscular body had torn long strips of weed and algae from the water which together with snarled saplings and wrenched grass tussocks hung as a dripping crest of vegetation along its back. Lily pads and floating plants were stuck to the rippled, warty skin of its flanks creating a bright spotted pattern over the folds of dark green scales.

Through the intermittent screen of foliage Jonquil saw the long arched body twist as the creature turned back towards the marsh oak and suddenly the terrifying slime-streaked head of a furious swamp dragon entered the bower of branches close to Jonquil, hunting for his scent.

Tails of dripping slime hung from the two curved horns rising from the rear of its head and fringed its large pointed ears which flicked with excitement; bright red eyes, glaring with venom and narrowed with rage bore down on the banf from beneath two fiercely slanted, spiny brows. Curling lips drew back to reveal a gleaming armoury of blood stained teeth; strong walls of backward facing daggers divided and fronted by long scimitars of discoloured ivory that closed over one another to form a petrifying, deadly grin.

As the huge head slid further into the tree and closer to Jonquil, a powerful, webbed fore-limb armed with the cruelest set of hooks slowly grasped the outstretched branch which held the banf and eased the dragon forward until the scales beneath its long neck began to rasp on the bark as it followed the line of the bough which led to its prey.

Jonquil knew he had to move, the dragon's drooling jaws were barely six paces from him and although the banf's head and body were ready to go, his feet were rooted to the spot. Those dreadful burning eyes were pinning him to the bark, devouring his energy, sucking the strength from his limbs, willing him to surrender. As the dragon drew nearer the banf felt gradually weaker until he finally slumped on to his haunches and waited for the fangs to strike.

Suddenly a high-pitched voice screamed inside his head, every bit as sharp and clear as a marshwidger's cry;

"No! No!" It shrieked. "Run, you fool, run!"

The shrill voice coincided with a terrifying hiss from the dragon as its glistening teeth flew through the air to seize him.

Jonquil threw himself from the bough just as the dragon's barbed jaws thudded into his shadow on the spongy bark; two more of the banf's few remaining, precious flight feathers were lost to the monster's powerful bite but that was all of Jonquil the dragon was to have on this encounter, for the banf was now leaping with astounding dexterity, borne of blind terror, from limb to limb making good his escape.

Jonquil's crippled wings may have been useless for flight but he had noticed during his precarious tip-toe across the low lying limb of the marsh oak, that they could be a positive aid to balance. Squirrel-like the banf scurried and leapt along a network of overlapping branches, flinging himself into the air with almost mindless abandon. There was no time for caution or faint-heartedness, Jonquil had to keep on the move; for the murderous beast crashing through the undercover of matted bushes and root-growths just a breath below him, could strike out and snatch him from the horizontal limbs if he should falter for even a moment.

Despite the noise of his violent pursuer, roaring and thrashing below him, Jonquil tried to focus all of his attention on the boughs beneath his feet; never daring to look down or take a moment to rest; the dragon was there, thundering between the trunks and snorting like a storm, always within murdering distance and that was all the banf needed to know. He just kept on pounding along the rugged beams, grabbing various upright branches along the way to propel himself forward even faster and never allowing his eyes to wander from the next bough.

Gradually the banf found himself climbing higher into the trees until he was practically beyond the swamp dragon's reach; and after Jonquil safely negotiated his sixth tree the chasing monster abruptly halted itself, creating a huge stagnant wave that rolled angrily into the crowded bushes dousing them with fizzing, green foam. It decided Jonquil was not worth the effort of charging and clawing through the obstinate vegetation. The swamp dragon shook some of the coat of weed and branches it had acquired during the chase from its great bulk, and after growling a few curses at Jonquil, slunk sulkily away into the curdling murk to find an easier meal.

Jonquil allowed himself a brief moment for self congratulation, he was quite impressed with his nimble, arboreal balancing act. He decided he liked himself as a squirrel and wanted to see how much further he could travel through that dreadful place without having to touch the ground, or what passed for ground down below. Walking in the trees was not only safer than struggling through waist deep, slimy water, unyielding plantlife and over-affectionate mud, it was also quicker and infinitely more pleasant. Jonquil could almost have been tempted to describe his elevated journey through the trees as blissful compared to the aforementioned alternative accompanied by half of the known insect world.

Jonquil continued his progress over the seething water for some distance until he was stopped by a familiar sound, a marshwidger in distress. As the banf had slowly come across the mournful cry he knew that he could not be the cause of the poor creature's alarm. Was it the same widger? Jonquil gingerly ventured forward through the foliage to find out. Using the grating noise as a guide, Jonquil eventually came upon a network of long branchless boughs, smothered with thick moss and lichen beards, rising up into the canopy and down into the unfathomable sea of green jungle in sweeping graceful arcs. For a few moments the banf's attention was drawn away from the widger's cry by the sight of an astonishing collection of large, bizarre blooms growing on the wet green velvet.

They were porropods or dragon poppies; gaping flowers consisting of two hinged flaps or petals, patterned with a kaleidoscopic marbling of bright colours, lying open around a succulent, turgid pistil reeking with the promise of sweet nectar. Unfortunately this was a plant that failed to keep its promises, for each fleshy petal was one half of a cruel trap, edged with a fence of sharp thorns and waiting in tense anticipation for some unsuspecting creature to be attracted to its trigger; the bright purple honey flask temptingly offered from the flower's centre was not only its prize but its deadly bait. Jonquil and Rattajack had encountered these vicious parasites before and had passed many an exciting hour daring each other to try and snatch the honey pots from the blooms before their powerful spring-loaded jaws snapped shut; for the honey from the porropods, if it could be attained, was sweeter than any manufactured by an insect and ideal for making porropod mead, a rare delicacy and a banf speciality.

The unfortunate creature that was lured to these carnivorous flowers, if it was small enough, was swiftly imprisoned by the trap and doomed to slow digestion by the plant. Creatures that were too big to fit inside the jaws were either killed by the thorns, which in some species were venomous, or at the very least deprived of a limb in the struggle to escape. With some relief the banf observed that these porropods were a slightly smaller, non-venomous variety, about three spans in diameter but still armed with curved fangs the size of his little finger.

Jonquil looked about him for signs of the marshwidger which was still calling out into the trees for all it was worth. As the banf had expected the wretched creature was imprisoned inside one of the deadly blooms, its cramped body wriggling with terror against the closed leaves of the trap. A pathetic panic-stricken little face peered out from behind the interlocked teeth, its tiny fingers vainly trying to prize the muscular jaws open. The marshwidger was obviously a young one, firstly because of its small size and secondly, a widger who had lived to enjoy maturity would have long grown wise to such inviting dangers.

Jonquil surveyed the scene of the crime; the offending porropod was situated on an adjacent moss-infested bough which reached down from above, bent to the horizontal a little way before eventually plummeting into the green void below. A few unoccupied flowers bloomed around the one containing the widger, presenting a hazardous climb if he was to rescue the poor creature; Jonquil knew of more than one banf at home who had lost a finger to the lightning jaws of a dragon poppy. Nevertheless, Rattajack could not have continued on his way without helping the little creature and neither could Jonquil.

With the urgent widgering still emanating from within the sprung floral trap, Jonquil easily made the short gap from his bough to the other. His ravaged wings swept open instinctively as the banf leapt through the air but they did little more than steady his passage and aid his balance on landing; Jonquil realised with a heavy heart that it would be a long time before he was flying like a bird again, his wings needed serious rest and healing; he couldn't help thinking that the swamp would have been an infinitely more bearable experience if he had come to it with the power of flight.

Once he had steadied himself on the new branch, careful not to slip on the treacherous wet moss, Jonquil regarded the almost vertical climb before him. The wriggling, closed trap of the porropod was just beyond arms reach, and the banf saw that to enable a strong hold on the snapped jaws, he would have to climb about half of his own height up the ascending ragged limb.

Despite the relatively short height Jonquil found it very difficult to rise even the smallest distance up the bough. The thick coat of moss simply refused to bear his weight and his feet continuously slipped from their holds and slid back down again. Jonquil saw with some uneasiness that the only way he was going to ascend the slippery slope and reach the trapped marshwidger was to use the deadly porropod blooms growing in between as a ladder.

Praying that the ferocious parasitic flowers had strong roots, Jonquil very gingerly eased his foot behind the spiked petals, being extra careful not to catch the sensitive pistil as he lifted his leg, and slowly raised himself upwards. To his surprise and delight the plant held him, and Jonquil then looked for his next foothold. Gradually the banf rose to the desired height and manoeuvred himself into a position to get to grips with the closed porropod; to free his hands he had to try and grip the slimy bark with his knees, careful to aviod the lusting gapes of the open porropods which surrounded him.

The marshwidger intensified its rasping cry when it saw Jonquil approach and actually drew blood from one of the banf's fingers as he tried to force them between the plant's strong jaws. The surprise of the bite nearly caused Jonquil to lose his grip on the tree and topple backwards but luckily the grasp he had on the lips of the flower saved him and he was able to steady himself once more. Jonquil told the terrified creature in his softest voice that he was trying to rescue it not hurt it but it wasn't until the banf succeeded in parting the plant's jaws slightly that the widger was distracted from its aggression towards him and began to contemplate the prospect of freedom.

All went well for a while; despite incredible resistance from the porropod Jonquil applied every ounce of strength his arms could muster and managed to prise its sharp teeth further and further apart. As soon as a reasonable gap appeared for the marshwidger it eased its way between the fences of cruel thorns and emerged into the light once more. Then to Jonquil's horror and fury instead of spreading its wings and flying away to safety, the cheeky little dragon turned around, perched on the quivering jaws that the banf was straining to keep open and proceeded to finish gorging itself on the delicious honey pouring from several bite marks in the purple pistil, the very act that had got it into trouble in the first place. Jonquil pleaded with the widger to fly away, furious at its impudence and also because the smell of the glorious honey it was selfishly enjoying was lifting into his face making his stomach grumble with longing.

Distracted by the foolhardy opportunism of the marshwidger, Jonquil failed to notice the dangling tatters of his ripped sleeve tickling the glistening, sticky head of another purple honey flask on a neighbouring porropod. With a muffled pop the second flower sprang shut snaring Jonquil's sleeve, pinching his flesh in the tightly pulled material. The force of the bite caused a scream of shock to burst from Jonquil's throat and wrenched his hand from the near-side lip of the flower, tipping him dangerously off balance; the banf just managed to flick the fingers on his other hand out of the way before the two spiked jaws slammed shut again. Jonquil's sudden cry had been enough to put fright to the young dragonet and as the banf's feet slipped from their moorings and he swung out into open space suspended from the second porropod by his sleeve, the marshwidger shrieked in protest into the neighbouring trees.

It was a question of which was going to give out first; the dragon poppy or the material of Jonquil's sleeve. For a few dreadful moments the banf just hung there, holding his breath with dread, trying not to hear the creaking of the bark behind the flower trap and the slow tearing of his suit. Below him was a flimsy screen of leaves and below that, who could tell?

"Knowing my luck," Jonquil thought to himself, "the waiting jaws of the swamp dragon!"

Finally, a loud, conclusive rip literally ended the banf's suspense; warm air breathed into a growing hole at his armpit and in the very next instant Jonquil was crashing through the leaf bowers on a rapid descent.

A wail of desperation abruptly changed to a shocking falsetto as a stout mossy limb rammed him between the legs. Every last ounce of breath was squeezed out of Jonquil's chest with the rude impact of his straddled arrest but this was only the beginning. The momentum of his landing started Jonquil skidding along the straight bough on his behind as if it was a greased pole; the downward sweeping limb eventually dived into the lower canopies and Jonquil slid along the course of its steep arc, wailing like a marshwidger, wringing a spraying surf of treedew from the thick moss as he went.

After swooping low the long curving beam suddenly curled up at its end. Jonquil careered down the long green shoot gathering great speed and then hit the upturned end and was launched into space tumbling like a storm-blown leaf.

The world spun around the banf in a short lived kaleidoscope of blurry images; as he plummeted towards the water, he caught fleeting glimpses of palm leaves, shaggy trunks, the misty sky on a black pool, mounds of green-skinned muscle and then warm darkness as he finally splatted into a large steaming heap of rotting weed.

Jonquil sat up quickly and wiped the gunge from his eyes; his face was now painted with a slimy green mask and the rest of his body smeared with similar stains. He knew that he ought to be grateful for the softness of his landing and for being saved the terror of the deep, scum-crusted water, but the strong feeling of foreboding and the brief pictures that had registered during his fall suggested a phrase including the words 'frying pan' and 'fire'. Jonquil's vision was still spinning wildly when he first opened his eyes but when it finally cleared, the sight that greeted him caused a lump the size of a fist to rise in his throat.

Jonquil had landed smack in the middle of a ring of six burly swamp trolls.

The large green monsters seemed almost as shocked by the banf's unexpected arrival as he was; their fat, ugly faces staring back at him in angry bewilderment. The six giants were standing waist deep in a small clearing of murky water around the island of piled litter, each of them frozen in the act of whatever they were doing before Jonquil so rudely interrupted them. They were all holding the broken remains of large, glistening vessels in their clawed hands; one troll caught with his black tongue mopping up the inside of a shiny fragment, another pouring a sticky, glutinous stream into his cavernous mouth, which now just dribbled aimlessly down his chin and dropped into the water in a thin, elastic string, as his attention was claimed by Jonquil. The rest had paused in other poses; finger licking, sucking, biting, scooping; employing a variety of simple methods to extract the liquid contents of these curious objects.

Swamp trolls were formidable creatures; the most feral and beast-like of their kind. The male of the species was as large if not larger than an ice troll; and like their Winter relatives active by day and night and possessed of a foul disposition. The female of the species, the great she-trolls, which mercifully were very rare, usually no more than one to an entire swamp, were three times the size of their male counterparts; suffering no company or trespass, these awesome giants stalked alone through the vaporous forests they ruled, their massive heads scraping the canopies.

The six hefty male specimens surrounding Jonquil were easily the biggest he had ever seen; they had necks and shoulders like mountain ranges, arms and legs like knotted tree trunks, great bulging chests hanging above a ladder of deeply rolled abdominal muscles; their heads were long and bulbous, textured with a network of proud, wriggling veins; a thin central crest of lank, slime-matted hair flopped on to their grimy green skin in oily tails, eventually bushing out and falling into the deep valley of their backs as a dense, shaggy mane. Their eyes were a cold, piercing yellow, fenced in between deep overhanging brows and high protruding cheekbones. Two large pointed ears, a broad flattened nose and a wide, tooth-filled chasm of a mouth, armed with four long, ochre stained fangs, completed their savage faces.

Unlike all the other trolls, swamp trolls wore no clothing, from the waist down they were covered only in their own thick shaggy fur which was invaluable for repelling the dampness and saving their skin from the worst of the vindictive jungle undergrowth. Indeed, on the upper halves of their bodies which were mostly smooth, all of the trolls boasted a varied collection of duelling scars; deep scratches or wounds that might have been the work of savage thorns, but were more likely to have been inflicted by each other, for trolls of all colours were notoriously quarrelsome.

For a few dumb-struck moments Jonquil and the trolls just stared at each other but then one individual with a thin fringe of long green hair snaking down between his eyes, pointed a thick, yellow clawed finger at the banf and said in a thunderous burst of bass;

"Whassat?"

A chorus of deep growls and mutterings erupted from the rest of the troll ring and sensing the need for immediate action, Jonquil leapt to his feet and prepared to make a dash for it. As he did so, the banf suddenly noticed more violated pearlescent vessels strewn across a deep, raked out depression in the centre of the warm mound. A clammy chill slowly crept over the banf and he realised just what it was he had fallen onto; the steaming pile of matter was a huge nest and this angry ring of trolls were in the process of raiding it. Although Jonquil had never seen eggs the size of those currently being desolated by the swamp trolls before, the texture and iridescent colour of the shell was reminiscent of those laid by widgers and other members of the dragon family.

"It's too big for a goblin, Hogbat. What say you, Numbat?"

"Too puny for a goblin," growled Numbat, a slightly stouter troll with boulder-like shoulders and bald but for one long plume of hair spouting high on his ridged forehead.

"'Sides, they don't have wings," he continued.

"I can't see no wings!" snapped Toombat, the troll who had previously spoken.

"Whas 'em then, pupfish?" boomed Hogbat, the giant with the long straggly fringe; and he pointed again at Jonquil, this time indicating the two plundered arcs of muddy, green-smeared feathers which hung in shame either side of the banf's soiled figure.

"Bah! He's one o' Sheylag's mob!" protested Shrewbat, a slightly shorter troll with a wild bush of hair erupting from the centre of his oval scalp and a deep diagonal scar weaving across a blind, white eye and halving his face.

"You wouldn't know a goblin if you had one stuck in your teef! You sapsucker!" roared Hogbat.

"Neever would you! You lousy seedsnipe!" bellowed Shrewbat.

"Wanna try it, mudslug?" screamed Hogbat. "Want me to blind your other eye for ya?"

Jonquil could only cower between these two furious monsters as they continued to hurl violent insults and occasional handfuls of soggy weed at each other. The thundering row eventually degenerated into an alternate duet of "Oh, yeh!" Culminating in both trolls balling their fists, fiercely clenching every fibre in their powerful bodies and roaring like demented dragons at each other. Great balls of rippled flesh expanded beneath their green skin and proud veins stood out from the tensed ribbons of muscle like tangled knots of thick rope.

Amazingly, the other trolls hardly batted an eyelid at this ferocious but clearly not unusual display, and nonchalantly ignored the fracas; some of them picking over the remnants of the nest to see if there were any unbroken eggs they had missed; one idly extracting tiny squirming creatures from about his person and tossing them with relish into his mouth; and another trying to prise a shiny black leech the size of Jonquil's arm from the back of one of his fellows, finally resorting to using his sharp teeth on the offending bloodsucker and carelessly wrenching a strip of the other troll's skin away with it. This of course developed into a second fight, these two trolls, Ragbat and Moonrat, adding their own murderous threats to the already incensed voices of Hogbat and Shrewbat.

"Come on then, Hogbat!" bawled Shrewbat, oblivious to the advent of another scrap. "Or are you just a lousy bagflapper?" And with that the one-eyed troll screamed his attack and launched himself towards the other.

Hogbat did the same and the two titans smashed into each other over Jonquil's head with a ground-shaking grunt. The banf just managed to fling himself out of the way before Hogbat, already having achieved a swift arm-lock around his opponent's neck, twisted Shrewbat off his feet and felled him with considerable force, the one-eyed swamp troll's substantial weight and momentum bringing him crashing down on to the leaf-litter mound with a resounding splat. Hogbat then dragged Shrewbat by his hair until his head and shoulders were hanging over the side, rammed the broad span of his hand into the other's face and with a triumphant roar viciously drove Shrewbat's head beneath the frothy skin of the water.

The one-eyed troll's howling insults became a defiant fountain of bubbling scum as his face was quickly submerged, his clawed fingers immediately flew at Hogbat's face, hunting for his eyes, they found his fat jowels and raked deep parallel grooves into his soft flesh before Hogbat could beat them off with his free fist. Hogbat threw back his head to let fly his scream of agony but before he could make a sound, a new roar burst into the air of a different quality, the sheer volume and fury of which extinguished all other sounds.

The swamp trolls instantly forgot their quarrels and stared up into the trees like surprised rabbits to face the source of the great voice that shook the air like a volcanic explosion.

Jonquil followed the terror-struck gaze of the trolls and his fearful eyes ascended a quivering mountain of dark green scales, a shaggy coat of weed and plants hanging from its reared form. Its mighty roar emanated from a huge gape of gleaming death daggers, and its murderous red eyes flashed with fury and outrage. The monstrous reptile towered over them like an avenging executioner surveying the scene of violation, its terrible eyes condemning them all for the desecration of its nest. Its ivory talons slashed the air in anticipation and its powerful, spiked tail thrashed the wall of trees and bushes behind it ripping great clouds of debris into the air.

"Jaggarang!" screamed Hogbat, and then turned and fled into the jungle, hands held aloft in panic.

The other trolls, including the half-drowned Shrewbat, let forth their own wails of terror and started after him, flinging aside the shiny fragments of incriminating evidence as they ran. The swamp dragon arched its massive back, tensing its retracted neck and body, and then lashed out in a green blur, its head striking like an arrow into the fleeing group of trolls. The dragon's heavy front limbs plunged into the black water either side of the nest mound as it crashed down on to all fours, the writhing body of Toombat sandwiched between its savage jaws. The unfortunate troll was held high like a trophy, and his blood fell like black rain on to the upturned face of Jonquil, who suddenly realised that he was still squatting on the rotting heap of vegetation, watching the drama unfold around him as if in a dream.

Before the mighty Jaggarang could shake the last ounce of life from the ill-fated Toombat and cast his limp body to the dark water, Jonquil had caught up with the rest of the fleeing swamp trolls. The banf wasn't really sure why he had run after the muscular monsters as they frantically scrambled through the snarling shrubs and creepers to escape the wrath of the female dragon; the trolls were just as likely to kill him as she was. However, the five fleeing giants certainly knew the lie of the jungle better than the banf, and Jonquil had to gamble that they would all be too preoccupied with saving themselves to bother

with him, and that during the course of their flight they might unwittingly unearth some safe hiding place for him.

The furious dragon launched herself into the tangled forest, her thickly-muscled limbs kicking up angry sheets of filthy water as they powered her great weaving mass through the knotted walls of obstructive growth. Screens of creeper-twined branches were torn down by the formidable spines on her massive bulk; thin, strangled trees were bent aside or ripped up by their roots as she irresistibly wrenched her way along the egg robbers' path. Jaggarang scythed a broad trench through the close vegetation with violent sweeps of her powerful head, her snorting nostrils hunting for the trolls' scent and the path of their flight; everytime the dragon found a trace of her prey she blasted the jungle with her ear-splitting voice, her wrath and thirst for vengeance freezing the blood of every living creature that quaked before her mighty advance.

Jonquil had thrown his lot in with Hogbat, who he had decided was the strongest of the five remaining trolls, and the one most likely to survive this deadly episode. He doggedly followed the powerful green-skinned creature who cleared a path through the fierce undergrowth by swinging his huge fists in wild arcs; unlike most of his fellows, who had chosen the less obstructed routes to escape the dragon, Hogbat seemed deliberately to have sought out the areas of densest vegetation; which, although resulted in slower progress, clearly afforded the best shelter.

Despite being driven by the crashing noise of the dragon's furious pursuit perilously close behind, his limbs electrified by panic, there was still room for Jonquil's dread of wading waist-deep through the opaque swamp water; he could not get the image of the huge black leech clamped on to Moonrat's back out of his mind. Every broken branch or palm stem that floated back to him from Hogbat's destructive work up ahead made him flinch, and he was forever beating submerged roots or leaves away from his legs convinced that they were the investigating advance of some foul bloodsucker. To make matters worse, Jonquil frequently saw huge specimens of the real thing; hanging from broad leaves overhead like gobs of dark jelly just about to drop, or sliding over tree trunks and thick roots, their fluidly metamorphic heads hungrily probing for prey. To the banf's further discomfort he soon discovered that the monster attached to Moonrat's muscular back had only been a baby.

Jonquil's heart thumped against his chest like a fist every time the dragon's roars shook the forest and the pounding of her great, taloned feet sent shock waves across the skin of the stagnant water around him. The frenzied activity of the troll up ahead never slackened and he refused to waste even a moment's industry by looking back. Jonquil, however, could not resist throwing the occasional glance into the jungle behind him, as he frantically dragged his legs through the clinging liquid to try and keep up with Hogbat; and it may have been his feverish imagination but the banf fancied he caught occasional glimpses of a vast dark shadow swaying behind the thick screen of foliage, a towering, horned silhouette searching for its next victim.

Whilst the banf was struggling along in Hogbat's wake he spied an ancient marsh oak a little way off to the right. The tree was squat with a wide girth, its time-ravaged bark harassed by festoons of long haired creepers and reticulating vines. Like many oaks, some of its roots squirmed above ground, or in this case above water, forming an intricate cage and providing an easy climb into its lower branches. Jonquil was torn between diverting to the oak or remaining in Hogbat's shadow, suddenly heavy footfalls thumped into the water behind him, and without thinking the banf dived into a nearby bank of sedge to hide.

When he secretly parted the tall stems to observe who or what was noisily approaching from behind, Jonquil saw the broad bulk of Numbat thunder past, showering the banf with his resultant wash. The other swamp troll had clearly decided, like Jonquil, that Hogbat was the best bet against the dragon, and had left the other three swamp trolls led by Shrewbat to their fate. When Numbat finally splashed his way up to his fellow monster, he was greeted by a hushed growl of insults and curses, but then grudgingly Hogbat allowed the other to battle along side him against the high wall of the jungle, in a joint quest for sanctuary.

The scream of the dragon ripped through the misty air yet again and she sounded unnervingly close. Would she follow the scent of Shrewbat's group through the clearer water, or hunt the impenetrable brakes for Hogbat? Jonquil decided not to wait around to find out, he pushed his way to the back of the rash of sedge and began to scramble towards the roots of the old tree.

Suddenly there was a loud crack and a young evergreen slapped into the green water like a whiplash, when Jonquil instinctively turned to investigate the sound, his eyes fell upon a giant clawed foot bearing down on the snapped trunk. Then a rush of hot air washed over him from above and the banf looked up just in time to see a deep cave of glistening, ivory spears reaching for him out of the roof of foliage. Jonquil ducked down into the water and then with a terrific surge of energy flung himself forward into an incredible frog-like dive to evade the grasping jaws of the dragon. The furrowed snarl of the great head swung after him as the banf scrambled to his feet and staggered on towards the marsh oak. Jaggarang's terrible grin widened as she urged her powerful bulk after the flailing form of the banf, but Jonquil didn't wait for his stumbling legs to carry him to the rootcage of the oak, he simply threw his arms forward, bowed his head and leapt once more from the water. The crushing, dagger-lined jaws of the dragon rammed the entwined walls of the rootcage just as the banf's body fell inside, the tips of Jonquil's feet scraping on the edge of the monster's upper wall of teeth.

The dragon bellowed her fury through the twisted bars of the cage, the force of her cry causing a rash of trembling peaks to rise on the water about the banf. The horrendous sound reverberated inside the confined hollows beneath the tree with such intensity that the banf was forced to clamp his hands over his ears to save them from the damaging effect of such a deafening assault; as it was his ears would be ringing for hours on end, that is if he managed to survive to hear them. Jaggarang then set to work on the roots themselves, grasping them with her jagged bite to tear them bodily from the tree to get at her quarry; but oak trees of all breeds are notoriously tough and sinewy, even for powerful dragons; and try as she might Jaggarang could bend the thick arms of wood a little, but could not break them. The dragon attempted to drive her wide snout between the roots to reach Jonquil and although she succeeded in penetrating the cage a little way, she was completely unable to open her jaws, and all she could do was snort blasts of angry air into the banf's face. A heavy foot slammed hard into the stout body of the tree, shaking its every fibre, then the dragon's muscular shoulder was laid against it and Jaggarang tried to topple the oak using the full force of her formidable strength and weight. She charged the oak, ramming her armoured skull against the shaggy bark, scratched at it with her claws, thrashed it with her tail, bit it, gouged it; she even tried to gnaw her way through its thick girth with her awesome teeth such was her rage and frustration but although the marsh oak trembled, groaned or squealed with every attack, it did not surrender.

Jonquil was almost sick with fear, this murderous dragon seemed determined to have him no matter how long it took. He wriggled even further into the heart of the root hollow until only his head was visible above water, and that so dirty and slime streaked as to be hardly recognisable as a living thing. Jonquil loathed having to sit so deeply in the black slime, he hardly dared imagine what slithering horrors might have made their homes within the nest of knitted stems beneath the tree, and were now reaching out with interest towards his quivering form; nevertheless, even if the largest leech ever to draw blood decided to dine on him, he had no intention of moving a muscle; for his fear of the dragon's teeth was far greater than that of the bloodsucker's bite.

Jaggarang raked the wall of knotted roots with her hooked talons and then tried to force one of her front claws through the tangled barricade to try and tease the banf out that way, but the span of her foot was too wide, and Jonquil now too difficult to see in the shadows, that the dragon had to keep withdrawing her claw to locate her target.

It soon became clear to the mighty dragon that her rabbit had gone to ground for good, and it was beyond her capabilities to flush him out; perhaps if she hadn't had other prey to catch she might have sat it out and waited for sheer starvation to drive the banf from his hole, for dragons can be possessed of immeasurable patience – as it was, there were the other five trolls to reckon with and whilst she was wasting valuable time fighting with the tough old marsh oak they were making good their escape. Reluctantly and with a final frenzied assault on the rootcage, Jaggarang turned from the oak and sidled off into the jungle, snorting at the bases of trunks and bushes to pick up the swamp trolls' trail. Jonquil watched her weave her way into the green backdrop and then with probably the hugest sigh of relief in his life, gingerly crawled out from within the rootcave and set off through the greenery himself, but naturally in the opposite direction.

The Flight of the Fugitives

The grim face of Dragonskeep frowned as a swooping line of snowdragons flew into the startled mouths of its dragonports. The returning flight bore important 'passengers' and they were ushered without delay to the austere chambers of Halmarand's command headquarters.

Hawkhood, Tuatara's lieutenant, led the stern procession through the maze of winding corridors and up the relentless flights of stairs. By the time the dragonriders had reached the High Keep, their prisoners, who had already been exhausted when they apprehended them, were fit to collapse.

The two fugitives staggered into the wide room which contained all the great charts and plans, and were pushed on to a wooden bench next to the great roaring fire which belched its heat into the spacious chamber.

The two miserable fugitives sat next to each other, their faces stained with an orange glow, their eyes wide and fearful. They were both mindful of Halmarand's formidable reputation, and they waited with a growing sense of apprehension and panic for the great general to appear.

Suddenly from along a lengthy sweep of hollow corridors, the loud strike of heavy footfalls was heard striding confidently and purposefully towards the firelit room. As the sound grew and carried towards the two prisoners with a menacing echo, they glanced at each other nervously, fear and foreboding burning in their eyes.

When Halmarand finally made his entrance the two cringing figures were hoisted swiftly to their feet in salute, and then on his silent command pushed back down again on to the wooden bench. If the two fugitives had thought Halmarand's reputation to be impressive, then his appearance as he strode before them, bathed in the flickering adoration of the fire, must have drained the very last vestiges of composure from their withering bodies.

Halmarand was clad in his finest ceremonial flying dress. He was encased from head to foot in gleaming plates of embossed golden armour. His polished breastplate bore the insignia of the Golden Alliance; a magnificent flying dragon pictured against the fanned beams of a rising sun; in the wavering light of the fire, the dragon's wings seemed almost to be beating, the beams of the sun radiating waves of gold into the rest of his glittering armour. His arm and leg plates spiralled and swirled with finely engraved patterns, dragons coiled along his shins and forearms, every last ounce of detail brought alive by the reflected glory of the rising wall of flame.

The gleaming splayed wings of a second golden dragon swept down either side of the general's peaked helmet, an extravagant, towering fountain of white plumes soaring from his crown and falling in a feathery cascade upon the bright drape of a scarlet cloak.

Halmarand's face was grim and oppressive, his eyes coldly appraising the pathetic forms of his two prisoners. Slowly his fists rose to his hips and his masterful voice broke the tense silence.

"Well?" he growled at last. "Tell me what you know?"

The wretched faces of Wargren and Vakari turned briefly to each other to exchange mournful glances. Then the two former captains of Winter began their long stories for the general and his gathering in the High Keep. Halmarand remained deathly silent, standing in the same imperious manner throughout both the fugitives long accounts of their seven years exile; his rigid stance both threatening and commanding. When they had finished, the imposing figure of the general turned without a word and marched out of the chamber, his advisors close at his heels. Hawkhood and his company were left behind to attend to the prisoners.

Some time later, the great general was in close conference with Carobus, High Wizard of Summer; the illustrious sorcerer's visit to Dragonskeep the reason for Halmarand's personal show of ostentation and ceremony; the summer wizard was suitably impressed.

The man and the sorcerer were not only fellow high servants of the Wizards, they were also good friends, and their councils were always relaxed and good natured.

Carobus had only arrived by dragonflight from the Canvas City an hour before but was eager for news, and Halmarand had a wealth of tidings to share with him; for since his stern audience with Wargren and Vakari earlier in the day a succession of messengers had flown in from the north with more and more news and rumours of Mezereon and Hexerne.

Halmarand sank back into his chair and lit his pipe, Carobus did likewise, and the two illustrious beings sat facing each other across the wide glow of the roaring fire, delicate rings of blue-grey smoke rising from each chair into the gloom of the ceiling.

"Well?" Carobus prompted gently. "Pray don't keep me in suspense any longer. You said you had news of our rabbit?"

Halmarand slowly emptied his throat of pipe smoke and nodded thoughtfully, rising a little in his chair before responding to the wizard.

"A good deal of it, my friend," he answered. "A good deal."

The general tilted his head slightly to stare into the golden heart of the fire, as if he needed the wall of flames as a backdrop on which to paint his tidings.

"As you know, my friend, Wargren and Vakari are now our 'guests' here at Dragonskeep. They told us a pretty tale of their long years in hiding. Most of it irrelevant, but some of it not. Most of it known to us, but some of it not. There were a few surprises."

Carobus nodded knowingly.

"I'm sure there were," the wizard said.

"Of course the facts that we were most interested in were those concerning Mezereon . . . "

"And the Orb!" interrupted Carobus.

"And the Orb," Halmarand concurred.

"What did they say about him?" the wizard asked, his eyes thoughtful and slightly concerned.

Halmarand then relayed the details of the two Winter captains' encounter with the Dark Sorcerer, exactly as the general had heard it from their own lips. He told Carobus about how they had pleaded with Mezereon to adopt the Orb of Winter as his own and wield it against their enemies; and how the Dark Sorcerer had stubbornly refused to accept Vrorst's legacy.

"It's hard to believe," Carobus said afterwards, shaking his head. "It's hard to believe that he kept it all those years and resisted its temptation."

Halmarand nodded, "Indeed!" He said. "What's more, they also spoke of the girl, Hexerne."

"Hexerne?" Carobus responded with a note of alarm.

"She's with him," the general told the wizard. "They're travelling together."

Carobus betrayed an inner turmoil in his eyes which Halmarand quickly noted.

"Does that trouble you?" He asked the wizard.

The sorcerer did not answer for a moment but fixed the rolling flames with a long stare, his brow slightly furrowed and his mouth drawn; he was deep in consideration.

"Yes," he said at last. "Yes, it does. But I'm not sure why." Eventually the shadows cleared from the wizard's countenance and he sucked on his pipe and seemed to relax once more. "But please," he coaxed Halmarand. "Please go on with your news."

The general proceeded to inform the wizard about the goatherd's shack that had provided a brief respite for Mezereon, and that Halmarand had since despatched a dragonflight to the remote site to thoroughly inspect it.

"Of course I didn't expect to find our fugitives still in residence," the general explained. "But there was always the chance, however slight, that they may have decided to abandon the Orb there."

"Very sensible," added Carobus.

"I didn't relish the thought of leaving it there for gormless rock trolls to get their hands on it!" Halmarand continued. Carobus gave a mock shiver and blew a fat smoke ring into the fire. Halmarand pursued it with one of his own and then continued with his epic briefing.

It had been almost a month since Wargren and Vakari had left Mezereon and the girl at the remote shack in the mountains. They had spent their time since then slinking around isolated towns and villages, trying to stay anonymous and unremarkable; but eventually they had tried to solicit aid from one of Vrorst's old allies and had been noted by one of Halmarand's resident spies. Hawkhood had been despatched and the first of Vrorst's fugitive high servants captured by the Alliance.

"After I had heard from the two renegades," Halmarand told Carobus. "I received word of Mezereon and Hexerne from the Kingdom of Anconeus."

"Anconeus?" Remarked the wizard with surprise.

"Yes. They tried to convince King Hadros to help them. I think he would have done had it not been for his advisor, some semi-sorcerer sort of character."

Carobus nodded.

"Yes, Juvula. I know him. Not the most principled of beings it must be said. A somewhat shady character."

Halmarand continued his tale.

"Well, whatever his shortcomings, one thing is certain. He knows on which side of the mountain the sun is shining! Hadros was afraid to refuse Mezereon and would have helped him, but it was this . . . Juvula person, who alerted our garrison at Glostomorg."

Carobus's eyes suddenly blazed with anticipation.

"And were they apprehended?" He asked hurriedly.

The general sighed heavily.

"No. Our forces arrived there at dawn, to discover the birds had already flown."

The wizard's shoulders sagged with disappointment, and his eyes returned wanly to the fire.

"They had escaped in the night," Halmarand continued with a tone of bitterness. "I just wish I knew how. The palace of Anconeus was built, in happier times, by one of my countrymen; a Fforlian architect. It is a fortress of formidable proportions. Not the easiest of places to escape from; believe me, I know, I was its prisoner myself once."

Carobus smiled thoughtfully.

"I remember," he said.

The general leaned towards him with an urgent expression, his arm outstretched entreatingly.

"Carobus, my friend. Are you sure Mezereon hasn't used the Orb? I can't think of any other way he could escape that place!"

The wizard shook his head adamantly.

"The Three Lords would know," he replied firmly. "You must remember, Halmarand, the four Fire Orbs were originally cut from the same slab of crystal. They have a unique empathy with each other. That was how Vrorst was able to use the Orb of Winter to cloud and confuse the other three globes, when he was all powerful. It would be impossible for Mezereon to draw upon the enchantment of Vrorst's Orb without the other Fire Orbs sensing it; and I tell you that the Three Lords have felt nothing. The Winter Orb has cloaked itself with a shroud of darkness, that even the great Wizards themselves cannot penetrate."

Halmarand nodded with a wry smile and lowered his chin to his fist.

"There was one other item of news reported to me," said the general. "I thought it unrelated at the time. Silfaladil was seen in the city."

Carobus stared at Halmarand with genuine surprise.

"The Prince of the Northern Elves?" he said incredulously. "In Anconeus?"

Halmarand nodded in agreement.

"Yes. I thought it was something of a strange coincidence myself. But I can't believe the two are connected. The northern elves wouldn't do anything to help Mezereon. He's their sworn enemy . . . "

Carobus stopped him with his raised hand.

"They do have enchanted powers," he told Halmarand.

The general tried to interrupt.

"Well, yes . . . I know . . . but . . . "

"And they do practise a fierce code of justice, independent of the Common Law," the wizard continued.

Halmarand was gripped by silent contemplation for a long moment and then his eyes suddenly brightened.

"Are you suggesting that . . . ?" The general began to say.

Carobus only smiled.

"Hah! It's extraordinary!" Halmarand gasped in wonder. "You really think that . . . ?"

The wizard released another chain of floating rings into the air and then calmly responded to the general.

"You said yourself, the two of them would never have escaped from Hadros's palace without the aid of enchantment."

Halmarand continued, his voice gaining a harder edge.

"Then Silfaladil wasn't helping Mezereon and the girl to escape. He was stealing them from us!"

The wizard nodded.

"Just as one fox steals a rabbit from another."

Halmarand buried his gaze in the fire and pondered the plot for a while, humming to himself thoughtfully. Eventually he turned back to Carobus.

"At least the rabbit has been caught, my friend," the general said at last. " It might work to our advantage?"

The wizard considered.

"It might," he said. "And then again it might only serve to confuse our quest. The elves are only interested in exacting retribution upon Mezereon. But what of the Orb? What will they do to the Orb?"

The wizard became transfixed by perilous thoughts, his eyes rigidly focused upon an image far beyond the dark walls of the firelit room. For the first time he seemed genuinely troubled.

"The one consistent and emphatic command from the Three Lords is that the Orb of Winter must not be destroyed," Carobus spoke gravely to the general. "And the further north it travels the more vehemently must that rule be observed." The wizard paused as a dark thought entered his mind. "If they should try to smash it . . . !"

Halmarand snatched the pipe from his lips and rose purposefully to his feet.

"Then we shall have to make sure they don't get the chance!" He growled. "Let us fly to the elf kingdoms at once!"

Carobus once more halted the wizard with a calmly raised hand. He spoke carefully and in earnest.

"Let us not act too hastily," he began. "A dragonflight should be sent to Ckristinial, to warn the elf king of the approaching danger, in that you are right. But we must not simply assume that Silfaladil's success in deceiving the two fugitives is assured. He is no doubt masquerading as their guide to the far north; but Mezereon is no fool, and he'll be wary. Also we should not underestimate the influence of the Orb. If it should suspect treachery, then Silfaladil's own life might be in danger.

"But to reach the far north they must first pass through the wall of the northern forests," Halmarand remarked. "And Silfaladil's people will be waiting for them. He's luring them into a trap."

"I agree," Carobus responded. "But we must not take it for granted that all will be caught. They may take Mezereon, but I fear the power of the Orb, and I do not believe the elves are strong enough to restrain it."

The wizard rose sharply from his chair and paced restlessly across the broad pool of amber light thrown out by the fire.

"It is the girl that worries me now," Carobus continued, his voice stained with foreboding. "She is an unknown quantity. And who can say what part she might yet play in this grave adventure."

Halmarand's brow was furrowed by a frown but his eyes were strong and confident.

"What is your counsel, Carobus?" He said quietly.

The wizard turned to face into the full glow of the fire, his golden robes shimmering with a majestic radiance.

"I think we should assume the worst, and try and get to the Spire ahead of them." The wizard told the general. Halmarand's face lit up in wonder and Carobus answered his unspoken question. "Yes, my friend, Vrorst's sanctuary does exist; the Three Lords have no doubt."

The general's expression suddenly darkened.

"But the roof of the world is shrouded in dense, treacherous mists. Not even the most skilful snowdragon could penetrate them."

Carobus gave a knowing smile.

"One might. If its rider knew the way."

Halmarand looked perplexed. The wizard continued.

"There is one amongst us who might be able to find a way into the great chasm of ice."

The general's eyes grew bright again as he recognised the being to whom the wizard was referring.

"Ah, yes!" He cried. "Yes, of course. I'll send for her immediately!"

Halmarand issued the necessary orders to his subordinates and then he and the wizard returned to the fireside to discuss further the weighty developments that had come to light.

'The great rabbit hunt', the alternative title the general had flippantly dubbed the quest for Mezereon and the Orb, seemed to be drawing near to its conclusion.

The fugitives had managed to get much further north than Halmarand had expected, but they now had enemies before and behind them; the last corner of the net was about to be drawn in.

Jacquarondi

After a while, Jonquil reached a wide, open expanse of lily-encrusted water, the floor of which sloped down dramatically the further Jonquil waded out from the shade of the trees. Before the water rose too far up his body, he halted to survey the still, green lake.

If this dull stretch of water had been lying anywhere but in the poisoned basin of the Doomslang, the carpet of lily plants would have been graced with clusters of delicate star-shaped blooms, attended by merry nectar-seekers and haunted by jewel-like dragonflies; but instead the clefted discs were pale and ragged, stained with yellow and brown patches. Occasional buds had braved the foul water but had wilted unopened, rotten and flyblown, their precious, pale rosettes secreted within doomed to perish without ever embracing the heavy, warm air.

If the water about Jonquil had not been so thick and opaque, he might have seen a large, dark shape, gliding towards him beneath the floating lid of flat leaves. The banf was idly tracing a weaving line between the lily pads with one of his index fingers when suddenly a long, green blur burst through the ragged crust like an explosion, five hooked digits flying up towards him. Jonquil instinctively threw himself backwards but to no avail, the large hand clamped around his waist and thrust him into the air. At the same time a monstrous form rose from the water, a mantle of lily pads clinging to its head and massive shoulders; slimy rivulets ran from its muscular bulk like heavy rain, splattering on to the crust of round leaves as the remainder of its broad bulging body lifted from the lake.

Jonquil stared breathlessly into two bright yellow eyes glaring from beneath deep, arched brows. Drenched lengths of dark hair snaked down the furrowed contours of its bulbous features, its wide lips drew back to expose its glistening ochre spikes and a terrible sneer suddenly grew and squashed its already ugly expression.

The swamp troll held the banf close to his fearsome face, the tiny black slits in his gleaming yellow irises widening as his hooded eyes narrowed.

"You belong ta me, ya little mudslug!"

Hogbat's giant hand was clamped so tightly about Jonquil's waist that the banf could hardly draw breath.

"Let's pull his arms and legs off one by one!" giggled another gravelly voice, and Jonquil noticed for the first time that a second troll had risen from the water and was now standing shoulder to shoulder with the first. It was Numbat, and the second troll made a grab for one of Jonquil's ankles as if to begin the gruesome game, but Hogbat quickly jerked his prize away from Numbat and punched the other troll violently in the chest with his free fist.

"Get your 'ands off 'im, sapsucker! He's mine!" Hogbat roared. The first troll then turned his attention once again to the struggling banf; who by now was turning an unhealthy shade of blue beneath his streaky green mask.

" 'Cause of you, ya snivellin' little pupfish, four of our mates is dead!" Hogbat bellowed into Jonquil's trembling face.
"You woke 'er up! You brought 'er to us!"

It appeared that the great she-dragon, having picked up Shrewbat's easier scent trail, finally caught up with the three trolls on a different stretch of the very same wide clearing of lily-covered water. They had just stumbled through the line of trees that bordered the green lake when the huge reptile fell upon them, pinning two of the trolls beneath her cruel claws and seizing the third in her terrible, dagger-studded jaws. The last thing Shrewbat saw with his one good eye was the dark tunnel of Jaggarang's throat, and then he and his two fellows knew nothing more.

Luckily, Jaggarang had been satisfied, for that day, with her bloody retribution, and sloped back into the jungle to grieve for her unborn babies. However, from that day forward the other two trolls and Jonquil were marked, and they would all pay with their miserable lives if they ever came within striking distance of her again; she knew their scent now and like all dragons would never forget.

This was all grossly unfair to Jonquil, of course, who was completely innocent of any crime against the dragon or her embryonic offspring, but as the dragon only believed the evidence of her eyes, Jonquil was condemned by association.

"Bite 'is 'ead off!" Numbat urged, who was now peering angrily over one of Hogbat's broad shoulders, his hateful eyes betraying both impatience and jealousy; he wanted to have a play with the lanky, winged goblin himself.

"Na!" Hogbat snarled. "I'm gonna crush 'im slowly in me 'and, til 'is guts spew out 'is mouf!"

"Yeh! Yeh!" Numbat enthusiastically agreed. "And bagsy me 'as first lick!"

Jonquil struggled against the tightening ring of Hogbat's fingers and was just on the brink of passing out as a result of the slow asphyxiation inflicted by the green monster's slow squeeze, when suddenly something incredible began to happen. The banf's rolling eyes were shocked into focus and then widened with disbelief as the swamp troll's hand started to grow about Jonquil's midriff; the stout fingers swelling, enlarging, swallowing his body with an expanding wall of rough green flesh. Hogbat's open grip gradually closed as it grew, the banf steadily disappearing inside a mountain of giant digits. Then Jonquil was in the dark, a prisoner of the swamp troll's enclosed fist, the sharp stench of Hogbat's sweaty palms thick in the banf's nostrils.

Was this real? Was Jonquil's whole person really being held inside the giant's clenched grip! Or was this a dream of the unconscious?

Hogbat's hand grew so large that his sticky skin began to pull away from the banf, yielding its hold on him and Jonquil felt himself starting to be squeezed through the narrow shaft of the swamp troll's fist, until he dropped through the last of Hogbat's curled fingers and fell into daylight again.

The world that Jonquil returned to, however, was very different to that he had just left. He was surrounded by giants; giant trolls, giant trees and giant lily pads, one of which provided a soft, spongy cushion for him when his downward journey finally came to an end.

The banf leapt to his feet and marvelled at his strange new environment; the jungle, which before Hogbat had grabbed him had been so close, now seemed so far away and ten times taller. Jonquil saw a pathway of vast overlapping circular leaves lying across the skin of the water, leading to the huge twirling roots of the nearest tree; and then the truth hit him, the world hadn't exploded – he had shrunk! Shrunk to the size of a fly!

Hogbat was staring in total bewilderment at his empty palm, his wonder-struck expression perfectly mirrored by Numbat's whose mouth had dropped open in shock. Then the two monsters frantically began to search the lake about them; Numbat wading further into the water to fish beneath the lily plants, in case the banf had inexplicably drowned; Hogbat feeling along the underside of his arm and down his side and finally raking angrily through the long fleece of shaggy fur that covered him waist down, to see if the shrunken banf had somehow fallen into a dark crevice or got entangled on some part of the troll's body.

Jonquil, being the true opportunist he undoubtedly was, decided not to waste valuable escaping time by trying to work out what had happened to him, but took to his heels and fled over the raft of gently yielding pads, making for the darkness of the exposed root cages.

It was Numbat, stooped low over the still water, who saw the now tiny banf leaping across the last few lily pads leading into the base of a nearby tree and was just about to roar his discovery to Hogbat, when a long, narrow shape suddenly stabbed up through the green crust of vegetation below him, sharp fang-filled jaws at its head, streaking through the air and seizing the troll beneath the chin, killing the cry in his throat.

The force of the creature's attack knocked the swamp troll off his feet and he crashed back into the water with a gurgled scream.

Hogbat heard the commotion and turned to see his companion wrestling in the shallows with a deadly pondstriker mauling his neck, the strong serpent-like creature swiftly winding thick coils of its long, scaled length about Numbat's wildly thrashing limbs.

Hogbat rushed over to his stricken fellow and tried get a grip on the slimy, writhing trunk of the grievous animal. Its squirming body slipped through Hogbat's grasping fingers denying him the purchase he required to prise the monster away from Numbat, even the crest of fins that rose along its back refusing to be gripped. The strong coils that had wound themselves tightly about Numbat's torso began to constrict and when the unfortunate troll finally managed to wrench the vicious head of the reptile from his throat, his desperate cries of agony and terror burst from his mouth to assail the misty air.

Jonquil peered out from behind the stout, twisting body of a shaggy root stem, regarding the savage act being played out before him with abject horror. Hogbat had now grabbed the savage jaws of the striker and was attempting to twist its head and snap its neck, but the foul creature was too strong and the troll was being thrown from side to side and even off his feet as the powerful reptile weaved and shook in resistance. The rings around Numbat drew ever tighter, his strong muscular arms being gradually crushed into his ribs, his pitiful groans of agony growing fainter.

Jonquil decided to wait no longer, both trolls were more than occupied with the great snake beast, now was the best time to make his escape. He turned and fled along a hairy, horizontal arm of root leading away from the open water, almost running headlong into a fat toad squatting motionless in the dark shadows. The warty, corpulent beast eyed Jonquil with stoical interest and the banf became suddenly, painfully aware that he was now the same size as a large, juicy fly; just right to be deemed a tasty morsel. To make matters worse he had wings as well, albeit rather sorry ones, and a hungry toad might not care to identify him properly before opening its wide mouth and snatching him with its long sticky projectile. The banf tentatively edged along the mossy root, resisting the strong urge to bolt in case he should provoke a sticky response from the quiescent animal. The nearest of the two, large amber eyes poised high on the dark amphibian's head watched him closely every step of the way, but in the end the warty beast moved not a single muscle, and Jonquil was able to complete his slow journey along the root stem without incident.

The toad, unbeknown to the banf, had recently gorged itself on swamp flies and so wasn't the least bit interested in him anyway, and after Jonquil had surreptitiously crept out of sight, nonchalantly carried on with its quiet rest within the shadows unperturbed and unmoved.

No sooner had Jonquil emerged from the skirt of tangled roots spreading from the foot of the tree than the world around him began to shrink; he felt himself rising once more into the air to regain his former stature.

Hogbat suddenly turned from his labours and saw the newly restored Jonquil silently creeping away into the thick wall of growth that began the steaming jungle. The swamp troll roared his fury after the banf and was just about to abandon his mate to give chase to Jonquil when the pondstriker pulled its deadly jaws free of Hogbat's hold and sank its rows of needle sharp teeth into the muscular, green flesh of his forearm and yanked the troll back into the fray.

The banf decided flight was his best option and darted into the tangled curtain of creepers, with never a backward glance, determined to put as much distance between himself and the trolls, and that fearsome crushing serpent, as was banfly possible.

When he was satisfied that he had travelled a safe distance into the jungle, Jonquil took a moment to reflect on the amazing phenomenon that had recently taken place; his incredible shrinking episode!

Leaning back against the soft bark of a wide marsh pine, he found his thoughts returning to the grand council at the court of King Merlion, and more specifically to something that Orolan, Lord of Summer had spoken of. Jonquil remembered the Summer Wizard's words concerning the fairies; he had mentioned that the enchanted folk could make themselves as small as flies to sneak past the eyes of the enemy, or words to that effect. Then Jonquil recalled Queen Trinia's words when she had presented him with his fabulous delsidian coat, which despite all of his severe trials and tribulations was still in pristine condition, which was more than could be said for the rest of his attire. Trinia had told him that a delsidian coat was the most wondrous and precious of things, a rare gift that would reveal its unique and extroadinary qualities at the most unexpected moments.

So it was his beautiful shirt of fairy mail that had caused him to shrink to the size of a fly; each exquisite leaf of carved delsidian alive with enchantment, and ready to respond to the threat of danger. Jonquil was reminded of the fallon leaves that he once had worn on his leggings, they too responded to danger, by turning the wearer invisible, but they had been lost during the Battle of the Green Oak, and until he was able to return to the secret part of the Green Sky where the fallon trees grew, he would not be able to replace them.

"Imagine," Jonquil thought to himself. "How useful it could be in times of danger to be both tiny and invisible!"

Suddenly a splash of water charged his heightened senses with fear, and his attention was immediately drawn to a thick brake of bushy shrubs in the near distance. At first his eyes could distinguish little through the diaphonous screen of floating vapour other than the pattern of the dense foliage, but then he gradually focused on a small figure, barely two thirds of his own height, standing motionless as a statue in front of the shrubs, staring back at him.

The small creature seemed to be some sort of goblin, it had all of the usual characteristics; short, stocky legs; disproportionately long, sinewy arms; a squashed, primitive face with cold, glaring eyes and protruding lower fangs. There was something unusual about it though; its size. All of the goblins that Jonquil had encountered up to yet had been at least as tall as himself, this diminutive individual was nowhere near that height. It could have been a juvenile, of course, Jonquil proposed to himself, but there was something about the ruggedness and gravity of its expression that suggested maturity.

As Jonquil continued to appraise this small, goblinesque figure, he noticed that it had struck a rather curious pose, with both of its hands delicately holding a thin pipe to its wide lips; almost as if it was about to play a tune. Suddenly its cheeks swelled with air and then a hollow, spitting sound was heard and a missile, which travelled through the air like a bright moth, flew swiftly towards the banf as straight as an arrow.

Jonquil, who knew no reason to be alarmed by this intriguing, colourful projectile, casually watched it sweep past his cheek and thud into the soft bark of the tree behind him. It wasn't until the banf made a closer inspection and discovered the object to be a needle-sharp dart flighted with colourful feathers, that he realised his danger. Jonquil turned back to the small goblin and saw it standing in the same place busily inserting a second dart into the mouthpiece of its pipe, which the banf now knew was definitely not a flute.

Jonquil took to his heels and charged into the undergrowth, the swamp goblin completing his task of reloading before giving chase. As he thrashed his way through the clinging forest the banf sensed that more of the small goblins had joined the hunt, a volley of darts singing past his ears like giant mosquitos and clattering into the layers of leaves about him confirmed his fears.

He was fleeing without any sense of direction, relying on sheer instinct and luck to guide his pounding feet. Whoops and screams rang out from amongst the trees and bushes behind him, as the green-skinned pygmies shouted encouragements to each other, no doubt urging their best marksmen to stick the banf with their deadly pins.

Jonquil rounded a huge column of shaggy growth that was a lichen populated iron beech and ran headlong into a gruesome curtain of suspended skulls. The hollow craniums danced and clattered about the banf, scores of dark, empty eye-sockets glaring at him angrily for disturbing their rest. The skulls were all suspended on beaded thongs, hanging at varying heights from a low branch. Some of the heads had been decorated with feathers, fragments of hair that still stuck to the exposed bone had been threaded with beads, freshwater pearls and shells. This fearsome exhibition was intended to either scare, impress or boast, and that was all very well but so far he had encountered Jaggarang; the mighty swamp dragon, the carnivorous porropods, the swamp trolls, the pondstriker and now a murderous tribe of swamp goblins, so Jonquil was hardly likely to be thrown into panic by a mere display of severed heads!

Another swarm of darts peppered the air around him and Jonquil ducked into the bushy brakes once more, an angry mob of pipe wielding goblins scrambling noisily after him.

The chase continued for some time; Jonquil crashing through the scabby water, dashing between a slalom of hairy trunks and at the same time dodging the constant bombardment of multi-coloured missiles. He tottered along the mossy cladding of fallen trunks, swung across threatening pools on creaking ropes of vine; crawled, sprinted, climbed, jumped; his every movement accompanied by a chorus of staccato spitting sounds.

Despite the goblin gang's superior knowledge of the swamp's topography, the banf's longer legs and superb balance kept him one step ahead. However, after a time it began to look as though Jonquil was carrying more than his generous share of banf luck, for without fail every new direction he took proved to be the best for him and the worst for his band of attackers. He had no idea whatsoever of where he was going, but at every junction a clear, decisive voice inside his head cried "left" or "right". The banf naturally assumed it was his own determined thoughts, given volume and clarity by a torrent of adrenalin burning in his veins; but at the same time there seemed to be a different tone, almost another voice, matching if not manipulating his own inner decisions. Nevertheless, the green pygmies were strangers to defeat and no matter what manner of obstacle rose in their path they doggedly pursued Jonquil like tireless hounds after a stag.

After a while the banf found himself hurrying through a part of the swamp that was haunted by thicker mists. There were fewer trees and bushes, and instead of a constant thigh depth of slimy water to wade through, the going underfoot became heavier, muddier, with balls of hot air in languid pools belching pockets of steam into the already drenched atmosphere.

Cushions of tough grass grew like emerald stepping stones across the bubbling bogs and if ever one of the banf's feet slipped into the active gunge, the mud would suck with all its might to try and drag his whole body down into its consuming embrace. Jonquil didn't rate his chances at all if he should suddenly lose his balance and fall into one of the gurgling ponds; but with the veils of mist growing ever thicker, it was becoming increasingly difficult to be sure of his steps.

Traversing this dangerous terrain became an inevitably slow affair thus giving his band of green attackers ample opportunity to catch up.

To Jonquil's surprise, however, the angry swamp goblins seemed reluctant to venture across the mud, instead they waved their blowpipes in annoyance and shouted expletives at him in their own guttural tongue. Jonquil suddenly had a strange notion; if the tribe of swamp goblins hadn't just chased him halfway across the swamp baying for his blood, he fancied they might just have been trying to warn him; but they were a bizarre bunch of creatures and their manner was wholly foreign to him, he could very easily have been misinterpreting their frantic body language.

The banf wasn't sure whether to be pleased or perturbed by the goblins' attitude towards the steamy mud pools. They seemed determined not to pursue him into that dreadful place, but was it the quagmire they feared or something worse? Jonquil couldn't be sure but he fancied he saw movement in the wobbling sludge other than the lethargic rise of fat air bubbles. He thought he saw squirming limbs, tentacles perhaps, horrible searching feelers groping for an unsuspecting ankle to seize. The hot ponds suddenly seemed alive with a seething mass of wriggling, slithering, elongated bodies, twisting and coiling like a lake of vipers. Jonquil's head began to swim, his hitherto impeccably safe feet to tremble, the heat from the pools conspiring with the thickness of the air to make him swoon. Then the banf felt a sharp biting pain just below his right wrist, the sudden stab wrenching his attention from the mud and swiftly focusing his swirling senses. When he looked down at his hand Jonquil found a long, slender spine decorated with bright yellow and blue feathers protruding from his flesh. A cheer of triumph went up from the goblin sharpshooter responsible and the rest of the group hushed their clamour and fell into an expectant communal murmur, watching the banf intensely through the milky air for some awaited reaction.

Then a spark of light deep inside the wall of fog ahead caught Jonquil's attention, the goblins saw it too and shied away from its steady advance. Gradually a pale figure materialised before the banf; it was a white-whiskered old man. He was dressed in full length robes also of white, that despite the inherent paleness of the air, gleamed like hazy moonlight in the gloom. In his right hand he carried a long staff crowned with a magnificent, sculpted crystal, and it was from this fabulous earth-bound star that the sharp light emanated.

The old man, who had a kindly, beneficent appearance, spoke to Jonquil, but his words, rather than distant and dampened by the mist, sounded clear and precise inside the banf's head; and Jonquil immediately thought he recognised the sharp, insistent voice.

"Come!" The old man urged. "Follow me closely!"

The group of swamp goblins were very animated now, some of them screaming like petrified marshwidgers at the banf. Then Jonquil remembered the dart in his wrist and he swiftly plucked it from his skin; if that was the manner of reception he could expect from the green-skinned warriors, then he was determined not to move in their direction.

"Quickly!" The old man spoke again. "We must not linger here. There is great danger in the pools!"

Then the white robed ancient threw a significant glance at the mud, and as if to prove his words, a long paddle shaped limb rose from the slimy soup, making waving, serpentine progress through the air. Suddenly it struck like an arrow at Jonquil's feet, wrapping itself irresistibly around his right ankle. The banf could feel immense strength in the pull of the attacking limb as if it was but a small part of a much greater being; lying patiently beneath the mud, waiting for Jonquil, or any other poor victim, to be presented to its ever hungry jaws.

Jonquil let out a cry of terror as the strong limb began to drag him from his grassy island and in the very next moment a streak of white lightning flew from the crystal on the old man's staff and smote the taught assailant, burning a grievous wound into its slime-wrapped hide. The soft ground beneath the banf shook violently as if a huge unheard roar had just emanated from deep within the pools and in an instant the long tentacle had removed itself from Jonquil's leg and retreated smartly beneath the bubbling lid of the mud.

The old man spoke again to Jonquil, this time with a harder note of command in his voice.

"We must hurry!" He said. "That will only hold them for a short while. Follow me now!"

"Them!" Jonquil thought to himself. The prospect of one such creature dwelling beneath the slime filled him with horror, but the thought of an actual population vying for his flesh with snatching tentacles, put a hot burst of energy into his legs that carried him quickly to the strong light of the old man's staff.

Despite his close proximity, the features of the old man were still shrouded by the floating veil. Two dark wells were all the banf could see of his eyes and before Jonquil could peer any closer, the ancient turned from him and strode purposefully out into the blankness, the crystal lantern waving on ahead, a beacon in the pallid void.

"Stay close to me," the old man urged. "Tread only where I tread. We have a good distance to travel before we are safe."

Jonquil, having being offered no other alternative and realising that this was clearly not the place for explanations or assurances, decided to trust in this elderly stranger, who was undoubtedly a wizard of some measure, and dutifully followed along.

The journey across the wide expanse of the quaking bog was fraught with peril, without the old wizard to guide their precarious steps along the thin pathway of grass banks, the deadly marsh would certainly have claimed Jonquil. Such was the complexity and deviousness of their meandering route that the banf couldn't imagine anyone succeeding in traversing that terrible place without the old man's expert knowledge. He knew which grass tussocks were solid and which would maliciously subside and deliver the unsuspecting traveller to the vacuous mud; he knew which decaying fallen logs were safe as bridges and which would roll or sink beneath their weight; and always the fog remained, thick and consistent, obscuring all of the world except the small fragment beneath their feet.

Just as the banf thought he would faint from exhaustion, the wizard brought them to a wide wall of grass which led them up and out of the cloying quagmire and finally provided them with firm ground to tread upon. The high bank turned out to be the shore of a small island and as they proceeded an incredible vision slowly loomed out of the mist. Jonquil's jaw fell in astonishment.

Rising from the island was a sceptre of gleaming white rock, soaring into the pallid, misty air with a single tower at its pinnacle. Jonquil's body began to sway as he gazed up at the gleaming white vision, his eyes struggling to remain in focus. His head felt very heavy and was beginning to pound, his legs felt increasingly weak; it was almost as if the intensity of the pale spear of rock was sapping his strength.

The banf turned to look at the old wizard whose kindly face was gently bathed in the reflected glory of the tower. The old man raised an arm towards the white rapier stabbing the fog and cried;

"Behold, Jacquarondi, the Secret Tower!"

Jonquil smiled weakly at the wizard and then his eyelids slammed shut, his legs folded and he dropped like a stone at the old man's feet.

When the banf's eyes finally prised themselves open, he found himself to be lying on a small cot inside the lofty white tower.

The main chamber of the pinnacle was round with a partly domed ceiling, the highest point of which disappeared into a narrow hole leading to an ornate spire of crystal. The white stone walls and ceiling were modestly decorated with relief pattern and carvings but the high room could not have been described as ostentatious; more, pleasantly rudimentary. The tower was illuminated by a ring of tall arched windows, which allowed narrow slithers of soft light and swamp mist to drift in and out of the open chamber.

The only object of note that the banf could see from where he was lying was a large polished crystal globe, held by an elaborate tall cradle of delicately forged iron filigree.

A door closed from somewhere behind Jonquil and the swish of a robed body entered the room. The very next moment a white bearded face leaned over his bed and cheerfully bade him good morning. After Jonquil had raised himself and discovered a painful headache waiting for him, he asked the wizard where he was.

The white-clad sorcerer smiled and told the banf that he had announced the name of the tower to Jonquil two days earlier, when they had first arrived, but as he had fainted in the very next moment, the wizard wasn't too surprised that the banf could not remember.

"Two days ago?" Jonquil asked incredulously.

"Yes," the wizard replied. "It was the goblin's dart I'm afraid. Those pesky little blighters will use the most potent drugs for their blowpipes!"

The wizard then glanced wryly in the direction of the door, and there, dwarfed by the arched portal was the stocky green body of a swamp goblin. Jonquil cried out in alarm.

"It's all right, my friend," the wizard soothed. "There's no need to be afraid. This is a friend. The goblins don't mean to be unfriendly, it's just their way."

Jonquil couldn't believe his ears.

"Just their way?" He cried. "That tribe out there chased me halfway across the swamp and tried to kill me!"

The goblin at the door snorted with laughter and then strolled arrogantly into the room.

"Nah!" he croaked, in a deep, gravelly voice. "That's just our way of saying hello."

The goblin had an impudent, thick set body; muscular but distinctly lacking in height. A long, ragged loin cloth hung from his trim waist and his profile had the slightly ape-like characteristics of the goblin kind, but was not too unfortunate. His eyes were bright yellow with surprisingly oval black pupils, not cruel slits, set beneath a low knitted brow. A tufty beard trailed from his chin and a thin crest of black hair rose on the dome of his scalp and fell as a tangled shower over his back. His ears were overly large and pointed with big dangling lobes that had been pierced and stretched into a series of gaping holes, some

164

of which contained little boxes and bundles of flighted darts. He wore necklaces made from what Jonquil could only assume was hair, his or someone elses the banf didn't care to ask. Suspended on these woven cords were teeth, shells or shards of flint, and held by a thin band which tightly gripped the ball of muscle on his strong left arm, was a short slender blowpipe.

In his right arm he brandished a large, decorated jawbone, reinforced with an array of spikes and barbs.

The green-skinned figure who had a not unattractive impish grin was introduced to the banf as Sheylag, Chief of the Swamp Goblins. A great warrior and leader of his people, and a good friend to the wizard. It appeared that swamp goblins may have shared a superficial resemblance to their mountainous cousins but that was where the similarity ended. Although 'Sheylag's mob', as the ill-fated Shrewbat had referred to them, could never be described as noble, they were, on the whole, fierce rather than evil.

The white robed wizard then introduced himself as Gembranosus or Swamp Star, as the goblins affectionately knew him, because of his habit of guiding lost adventurers through the mires with his shining staff.

"I was placed here by the Wizards, donkey's years ago," he told Jonquil, "as a ray of hope for those noble hearts foolish enough to enter the dreaded Doomslang."

"Did you come here for the treasure?" Sheylag's deep voice boomed out.

"What treasure?" Jonquil asked.

"Why, the treasure in the caves!" Gembranosus exclaimed.

Jonquil looked blankly from the goblin to the wizard.

"What caves?"

Gembranosus smiled warmly and drew Jonquil towards the large crystal globe on the wrought iron stand.

"I know you didn't come to the swamp for the treasure, my friend, but that's usually the reason most adventurers like yourself do. The hidden caves of the Doomslang are reputed to be bursting with gold and gems, although no-one has ever lived long enough in this fearsome swamp to remove any."

Jonquil stared into the glassy depths of the orb and regarded his own distorted reflection staring back.

"This is my window on the world," Gembranosus explained. "This is how I know all about you, Jonquil. I've been following your every move ever since you left the Banf Kingdom."

"You have?" The banf said with wonder.

"Yes, indeed." Gembranosus replied. "Of course it's only a seeing globe. Only high wizards have listening and speaking globes, and I haven't reached those lofty heights yet."

Jonquil suddenly became very animated and he gripped the wizard's pale sleeve.

"Would it show pictures to me?" he implored.

"Why of course, my friend." The wizard assured him. "Ask away."

Jonquil took a deep breath, not really sure if he wanted to know the answers to his questions, but knowing that he had to ask them. Then he bade the globe show him Meadolarne, wherever she was. The orb clouded over just like his own smaller version, and the image of his beautiful banfina slowly grew before him. Jonquil's heart burned when he saw the sadness in her distant eyes and he desperately wanted to plunge his hands into the shimmering glass and hold her.

The banf then asked the globe to reveal her location and when the picture of soaring towers and high battlements drifted into view, Gembranosus took a keen interest.

"I know that place," he announced.

"You do?" Jonquil urged.

"Yes. That's the palace at Anconeus! King Hadros's residence. Then another picture slowly replaced the castle, it was a male figure dressed in long elegant robes of black and red. He carried a staff capped with a crystal and a curious headdress rose from his arrogant brow. The image of the figure did not seem to suggest a pleasant disposition, and the eyes of the high being were cruel and shiftless.

Gembranosus hissed when he recognised the character.

"Who is it?" Jonquil asked.

"A very unsavoury character, believe me," the wizard told him. "His name is Juvula. Not a personage you'd want to cross, my friend! Or trust very far for that matter. He's ambitious, cruel and ruthless, well, just look at those eyes!"

As the wizard raised his finger to the globe the image faded.

"Thank goodness for that!" Gembranosus sighed.

Jonquil was a little confused.

"But why did the globe show him," he asked the wizard. "when I didn't ask to see him?"

Gembranosus pondered this question for a few long moments and finally threw up his arms and shrugged. He clearly had no idea. Jonquil wondered if the noble orb had been trying to give them a warning about this shady Juvula character, and the banf certainly didn't like the idea of Meadolarne being alone in a palace with such an unsavoury individual loose to stalk the dark corridors. However, at least the banfina was alive and looked well cared for, there was much to be glad about.

Now for Rattajack. Jonquil summoned forth the image of his faithful friend and was astounded to find him seated behind the graceful fur-clad form of none other than Tuatara herself. Flying above the world on her magnificent snowcharger, Starblade. Jonquil laughed out loud when he saw the expression of sheer agony haunting the petrified terragon's features; Rattajack never had got used to heights.

The two passengers were part of a small dragonflight searching the vast spread of the northern mountainscape for signs of Jonquil.

"But how do they know I'm not still in the tunnels?" the banf wondered.

Gembranosus explained.

"Because, Jonquil, when Rattajack found his way out of the undermountain, he straight away returned to Dragonskeep, to raise a search party. And of course, being the highly intelligent being that he is, the first thing your terragon friend did was to go to your seeing orb given to you by the Lord Orolan, to find out what had become of you."

"Oh, yes!" Jonquil cried. "I left the orb in our room by mistake."

The white wizard smiled.

"That was no mistake, Jonquil, that was providence! You certainly have a guardian angel watching over you. I've seen the evidence of that here in the Doomslang. Of course, I threw you the odd line of encouragement now and then, but you really didn't need it!"

Sheylag tutted, and he and Jonquil exchanged ironic glances.

"So how do I tell them that I'm here?" the banf said at last.

Gembranosus's smiles suddenly faded, and he then sadly informed Jonquil that because of the vast fog which permanently entombed the whole crater containing the Doomslang, it was impossible for anything to penetrate the gloom.

"Then they'll be flying around up there for ages looking for me!" Jonquil sighed.

The wizard could only agree.

"They might never find you!" Sheylag offered cheeringly.

In despair and frustration the banf glanced helplessly about the chamber, his eyes finally resting on the hole in the ceiling directly above the globe that led up into the crystal spire. Jonquil suddenly had an idea and he reached into the pouch of his ripped tunic that was now laid across his cot and brought out the fragment of Sunfire.

Both Gembranosus and Sheylag gasped with wonder at the sparkling golden gemstone. Jonquil had no idea if it would work or not but ever the optimist, he placed the shard of precious crystal on the top of the seeing globe, and then all three figures cautiously took a step backwards.

At first nothing, but then instead of clouding over white, the orb was transformed into a burning ball of fire. Suddenly the iron stand beneath the globe began to shake with a building force, like the rocks around an imminent geyser will tremble before a fountain of boiling water spouts from the ground. Then with a scream of searing enchantment, a jet of golden fire burst from the blazing orb, soared into the crystal spire and was projected as a thin, fog-piercing lance of gold into the pale blanket draping the Morgvale.

Rattajack's sharp eyes spotted the signal and he instinctively knew that it was from Jonquil. With a cry of joy that alerted all of the other snowdragons in their flight. Tuatara and Rattajack dived into the lake of mist to find the source of the golden light.

The adventure continues . . . . . .

OLD FROZEN PALACE
VRORST'S KINGDOM
MOUNTAINS of MENACE (DARK MOUNTAINS)
DOOMSLANG
FFORL
GATES of FROZEN KINGDOM
DRAGONGORGE
THRONE CITADEL
THE FOREST RIVER
POWER WATER
THE CANVAS CITY